One

Jane Blythe

Bear Spots Publications
Melbourne Australia

bearspotspublications@gmail.com

Paperback
ISBN: 0992418070
ISBN-13: 978-0992418076

Cover designed by QDesigns

I'd like to thank everyone who played a part in bringing this story to life. Particularly my mom who is always there to share her thoughts and opinions with me. My awesome cover designer, Amy, who whips up covers so quickly and who patiently makes every single change I ask for! And my lovely editor Mitzi Carroll and proofreader Marisa Nichols, for all their encouragement and for all the hard work they put in to polishing my work.

MAY 4TH

12:23 A.M.

He felt so tightly on edge he was a little surprised he didn't crack.

Every nerve was aquiver; every part of his body tense and primed, ready to spring into action.

Above him the sky was so clear and so black that the stars and the moon seemed as bright as the sun. The millions of tiny white diamonds, that as a child he had believed were the lights from the homes of the angels who lived in the sky, cast such a pretty glow that it was hard to reconcile it with his reason for being here.

He could have looked up at the beautiful sky forever, but he had a job to do.

It wasn't every night that he stood in someone else's front yard, ready to enter a quiet, peaceful home.

Still, he was here for a reason and he wasn't leaving until it was all taken care of.

He crept quietly toward the front door, over a lawn that was in bad need of a mow and past flower beds that were in bad need of a trim; clearly, the people who lived here were not keen gardeners. He slipped in between two cars, another two were visible in the open garage, indicating that multiple drivers resided here.

Reaching a hand out to the doorknob, he was frustrated to note that it trembled more than it should have considering the number of times he had done this. Focusing, he stilled the tremors and got himself in the zone.

Easing open the door, he was met by the tranquil silence of a home at midnight. Taking note of his surroundings before

1

proceeding, he was standing in a small entry hall with only a coat rack and a small table, atop which sat several sets of keys. From his position he could see into a cramped lounge and dining room, throughout which were scattered stacks of magazines, a pile of what he guessed was clean laundry, and a number of children's toys. To his right was a study, which was impeccably tidy and organized, indicating at least one member of the family was a neat freak.

Nothing and no one stirred within the dark shadows. It was hot inside, perhaps indicating a lack of air conditioner—or maybe a broken one. The carpet had once been nice but was now quite worn, same with the furniture and the wallpaper.

Stepping inside, he felt his edginess intensify a hundredfold.

Heading straight for the back of the house, he eased through another door and found himself in a messy kitchen—plates covered with food dotted the countertops, and someone's attempt at homemade cookies still littered the space around the oven. The kitchen opened onto a family room, and if the lounge and dining room had been untidy then this room looked like a bomb of clothes, toys, papers, shoes, books, magazines, and junk food wrappers had exploded inside it.

Still there was not a sound or a movement.

He climbed the stairs slowly—not knowing if one might creak—and sidestepped a pile of neatly folded clothing and some more toys. Reaching the top, he found himself at the end of a long hall. There were six doors—three on each side, all of which were closed—and unsurprisingly, the narrow space was cluttered with junk.

Picking the first room on his right, he cautiously eased the door open and entered quietly. He found himself in a young woman's bedroom where everything appeared to be in its place, and he wondered if this was the resident neat freak.

As he took a step closer to the bed a sheath of moonlight spilled through the open window, illuminating an arm that hung over the edge of the bed. The skin on the arm was so pale it was almost translucent, and he could actually see the long thin blue veins snaking their way from wrist to elbow.

Moving closer still, in the half-light he caught sight of something that made his own veins turn to ice. With a hand that still shook more than he'd have liked, he reached it slowly down toward the slender neck of the young woman lying tangled in the bedclothes.

Realizing with a start that he was holding his breath, he forced himself to resume a normal breathing pattern, but couldn't help letting out a strangled squawk when the woman's lids popped open and he found himself looking into astounding white eyes.

"Kate, call an ambulance," Detective Xavier Montague screamed over his shoulder, one hand pressed to the young woman's neck, the other to the heavily bleeding wound at her shoulder. "This one's alive."

* * * * *

6:35 A.M.

Detective Xavier Montague couldn't get those white eyes out of his head.

They weren't really white, of course, just such a pale shade of blue that they appeared almost colorless.

"Xavier," his partner, Kate Hannah, flicked him in the arm.

"What?" he blinked and realized he'd been daydreaming.

Rolling her dark blue eyes, she asked, "What are you daydreaming about?"

Embarrassed, he didn't want to tell his partner he'd been thinking about the young woman that had been rushed to the hospital. Sidestepping her question, he stepped back through the front door through which they'd crept just six hours ago. "Come on, let's go back in."

Flicking her long blonde hair over her shoulder, Kate eyed him with delighted suspicion. "Did you meet someone? A *girl* someone?" she added.

"No, I didn't." Xavier couldn't quite help cringing at the thought of falling for someone new; he'd sort of sworn off women the last few years.

"Xavier," Kate groaned, "when are you going to move on? It's been three years since Julia."

Xavier was well aware that it had been three years since everything had blown up with Julia. In fact, to be exact it had been three years, one month, eleven days and four hours since everything had blown up with Julia. He had messed up badly with her, and it had left him shaken.

"I don't want to have that conversation with you again," he told his partner sternly. Kate had been his partner for almost seven years and she had been right by his side when things fell apart. She had supported him, sat for hours listening to him while he tried to sort out his tangled web of emotions, but she believed that now he needed to move on and try to find happiness again.

With a frustrated sigh, Kate let the topic drop and followed him back inside the Englewood house. "Did she say anything to you?"

"No." Once more, his thoughts dipped to Annabelle Englewood's eerie white eyes. "She looked at me for just a moment and then she was gone." Xavier didn't think Annabelle had been conscious for more than about five seconds before she had slipped away again. "It doesn't look like anything's been disturbed down here," he commented, taking in the messy downstairs rooms, looking even untidier in the light than they had in the dark.

"Yeah, it looks like all the action was upstairs," Kate agreed, beelining for the stairs.

He followed her up the stairs, the coppery smell of blood growing stronger with each step, until it almost seemed to take on a life of its own as it invaded his nose and mouth.

At the top, Diane Jolly, both his and Kate's favorite crime scene tech, met them. To look at, Diane seemed nothing exceptional—fifty-years old, medium length gray hair, brown eyes, average height and build, dedicated to her job and her adopted family. But Diane Jolly had a wild side. She was a skydiving fanatic. She was always trying to convince people to go with her, but so far, she was yet to convince him. Xavier didn't see how jumping out of a plane and plummeting towards earth could be considered fun.

Today, Diane's normally placid face was lined with shock. "It's like a slaughterhouse up here."

Xavier hadn't seen inside the other rooms yet, hadn't seen the horror hidden behind the closed doors. Annabelle's room had been the first he'd entered, and after he had realized she was alive he had remained by her side, ripping off his shirt to press to her shoulder in an attempt to stem the flow of blood.

When the EMTs arrived, he'd helped them load her onto the stretcher, maneuver her down the stairs and into the waiting ambulance. By the time it had departed, the crime scene unit had shown up and started their painstakingly careful once-over of the crime scene.

He and Kate had passed the time, until they were allowed back inside, by speaking with the neighbors who had lined the streets to see what all the hubbub was about. Garnering nothing useful, they had been debating going to the hospital to see if Annabelle was awake when Diane had called to say they could come in.

"Did the girl say anything?" Diane asked.

"No," he explained again, "she just looked at me and then passed out."

"So we still don't know why all of this," Diane waved her hand at the hall, "happened."

He shook his head. "Where did it start?"

"Parents' room," Diane replied. "End of the hall."

Traipsing down the corridor past the other bedrooms whose doors remained closed, Xavier steeled himself for what was to come. Even though he'd thought he was prepared, as Diane swung the door open he couldn't quite contain a small moan of dismay at the scene before them.

Working with the easy stuff first, he surveyed the room. It was like someone had drawn a line down the middle, one half was impeccably tidy with not a thing out of place and the other was strewn with clothes, shoes, handbags and makeup.

Finally, unable to put it off any longer, Xavier let his eyes fall on the bed, where John and Kathy Englewood's lifeless bodies lay. Deep gashes crossed their necks, nearly separating their heads from their bodies. Blood drenched the sheets and puddled around the bed. There were black holes where their eyes used to be. Inside their gaping mouths, they were missing most of their tongues. Their hands had been removed and were now resting on top of their owners' stomachs, each cradling an eyeball, the tongues resting in between each pair.

Xavier made himself look beyond the macabre sight for any details that might help explain what exactly had happened here. The covers didn't appear to be mussed, and it didn't look like either John or Kathy had struggled. It seemed as though they had been killed in their sleep. But how had whichever of them was killed second not awakened during the first murder?

"Why did . . .?" he started to ask.

"The other not wake up?" Diane finished. "I'm thinking they were drugged."

"There was food still on the bench in the kitchen," Xavier remembered from their earlier trek through the house.

"Already collected," Diane nodded.

"You think it started in here?" Kate asked.

"Looks like it," Diane confirmed. "Bloody footprints lead out of this room but not into it."

"Who was next?" he asked.

"Oldest son would be my guess," Diane headed for the door.

Following the trail of smudgy footprints out the door of John and Kathy's room, the three walked into the one next door where a similar scene met them. Twenty-year-old Paul Englewood, the spitting image of his father, lay in his bed, killed just as his parents had been by a slice across his throat. Once again the eyes, tongue, and hands had been removed and left arranged in the same way.

The young man looked in top physical condition, but once again, there were no signs of a struggle, so Xavier decided it was a safe assumption for the moment that the family had been drugged. This added a definite aspect of planning and forethought.

"The footprints lead to Julian's room," Diane spoke softly.

Not really wanting to see another copy of this room, Xavier reluctantly followed the bloody trail once again, feeling like he was trapped in a sinister version of The Wizard of Oz's follow the yellow brick road. The room across the hall belonged to seventeen-year-old Julian and, as expected, was where the boy had met the same grim fate.

Barring Annabelle's room and the bathroom, that left just one other.

One that Xavier couldn't bear to ask about. For the last room belonged to a little girl aged just seven years old.

Meeting his eye, Kate gave a single nod. They'd worked together long enough to read each other, and right now his partner's face confirmed that the little girl had been murdered and mutilated just like the rest of her family.

On autopilot, his feet began walking toward the last closed door. Almost against his will, his hand found the handle and turned, leading them all into a world of pink. The walls were bright pink, stenciled with pictures of ballerinas. The curtains, too, were pink, although a paler shade this time and one that matched the carpet. A white desk contained a Barbie laptop, and a stack of books whose covers were graced by ballerinas and princesses.

Toys spilled out all over the room. The toy box was open, and the shelves were crammed almost to the point of overflowing. The closet had been left wide open, showcasing a range of little girl outfits.

On the bed by the window rested the tiny body. Her hair was still in braids, and in her open, tongueless, mouth he could see that her two front teeth were missing. Her small hands were clutching the eyeballs.

The sight literally brought tears to his eyes to think that anybody could do this to an innocent, defenseless, little child.

Absently, he turned away from Katherine Englewood and headed out of her bedroom door and into the room opposite. Annabelle's room. The twenty-three year-old was the only survivor of this carnage.

"What would possess her to do this?" Xavier asked at last to no one in particular. "What would possess someone to slaughter their entire family in such a horrible way and then attempt to take their own life?"

* * * * *

4:41 P.M.

"Well, it looks like a pretty open-and-shut case," Xavier told his boss, Lieutenant Robert Hollow. "There was no evidence of a break in."

"No broken windows, nothing to show the locks had been picked, and the door was locked from the inside," Kate elaborated, pulling her blonde locks into a neat ponytail.

"Right," he shot a small frown his partner's way; he hated it when she interrupted him. "At the moment, all the evidence points to Annabelle Englewood slaughtering her family and then attempting suicide." The picture in his head of Annabelle's white eyes had been replaced by one of her little sister's empty black holes, and he felt a white hot rage bubble up inside him.

"So how did Annabelle Englewood manage to slaughter her whole family without any of them waking?" Rob's bushy eyebrows were wagging madly.

"We think that she drugged them," he explained. "We're just waiting for Diane to confirm whether the leftovers from the kitchen contain traces of drugs."

"So, they eat dinner," Rob mused aloud as he walked himself through the most likely scenario. "Everyone feels tired, so they all head to bed. You don't think they would have thought that odd? That all of them were suddenly tired after eating?"

"Kid in the house," Xavier suggested, his sisters and brothers all had houses full of kids and various colds and bugs were always working their way through the family. "They're like magnets for colds and flus. They probably assumed Katherine had picked up a virus and passed it on to the rest of them."

"Okay," Rob nodded, "so they all head off to bed assuming they're coming down with the flu. Then, when they're all asleep, Annabelle grabs a knife from the kitchen and heads from room to room slitting her parents' and siblings' necks, cutting off their hands, gouging out their eyes, and slicing off their tongues."

Picturing the bloody bedrooms once more, Annabelle must be one messed up young woman to commit such vicious murders. Again, an image of her white eyes formed in his head, and determinedly he pushed it away.

"Bloody footprints all over the place, leading from one room to the other," Kate was saying. "Did you see blood on her feet, Xavier?"

"I'm not . . ." he trailed off, about to say he hadn't been sure but then a flicker of memory spurted into his mind. As he'd held his shirt pressed to Annabelle's shoulder the wait for the ambulance had seemed like an eternity. He hadn't moved her from the bed, not wanting to risk causing any more damage, but as he'd been helping the EMT's shift her to the stretcher, he had seen blood smeared on her feet.

"Xavier?" Rob was narrowing his gray eyes, impatiently waiting for an answer. "Did she have blood on her feet?"

"Yeah, she did," he nodded confidently.

"Great," Rob gave a grim smile, "so no break in and blood on Annabelle Englewood's feet; now if we can just get a confession, we can move on."

It sounded as though Rob was being harsh and cold; however, Xavier understood that his boss was not dismissing the trauma and horror of the Englewood murders. But they had dozens of other open cases, ones where the perpetrator was still out there somewhere; and as awful as her crimes had been, Annabelle was safely tucked away at the hospital under police guard. The quicker they got this wrapped up, the quicker they could concentrate their energies on the rest of their cases.

"At least we can be thankful for small favors," medical examiner, Billy Newton, announced as he entered the room, plonking down into a seat and looking every bit as exhausted as you'd expect an overworked, underpaid, father of seven to look.

"What's that then?" Rob asked, trying not to look annoyed as Billy propped his feet up on the table.

"The Englewoods were all dead when their bodies were mutilated," Billy explained. "That girl was lucky to survive; you think whoever it was got spooked when you two showed up?" When no one responded, Billy's dark eyes grew wide, "You think she's the killer? Murder/suicide? Or at least murder, attempted suicide. Why? What possible reason could this young woman have for killing her family? And the way she did it," Billy shuddered. "She must be one angry girl."

Xavier couldn't disagree with that. Or maybe instead of anger, it was insanity that filled Annabelle Englewood's mind.

Billy's wrinkled brow wrinkled further in confusion, "So she killed her family, calls nine-one-one, then tries to kill herself?"

"Actually, the nine-one-one call came from the house next

door," Kate explained. "Apparently the neighbor couldn't sleep and was sitting reading outside in his yard when he thought he saw someone with a knife in one of the upstairs bedrooms. He went back inside, found his telescope and looked through into the parents' bedroom, saw the blood, and called nine-one-one."

"The one time it's helpful to have a nosy neighbor," Billy mused.

"It would have been more helpful if he'd noticed earlier," Xavier grumbled, still thinking the neighbor sounded more creepy than helpful. Who kept a telescope in their house? And what did he usually look at through it? They were yet to talk with the Englewoods' neighbor, a Ricky Preston, because he'd been out at a doctor's appointment all day; he'd apparently been injured at work recently.

"We're still waiting on toxicology results," Billy informed them. "I heard you guys were thinking that maybe the family had been drugged before they were killed."

"When will you have them?" Kate asked.

"Soon, I hope," Billy assured them.

The phone on Rob's desk chirped, and while their boss answered it, Billy shot them all another perplexed frown. "I still can't understand what kind of person would do something like this."

"You never really know what's going on inside someone's head," Kate commented. "All the neighbors Xavier and I talked to had nothing but nice things to say about the entire Englewood family."

"Maybe they argued over a guy she liked but the family didn't approve of," Billy suggested.

"She was twenty-three," Xavier reminded him. "I don't see why she would have had to do what her parents wanted."

"Maybe she had some sort of psychotic breakdown," Billy tried again, obviously desperate to gain some sort of understanding as to why he should have to perform autopsies on five people killed and mutilated by a family member.

"Well, hopefully, you're about to get your answers." Rob hung up his phone and included all of them in his grim smile. "Annabelle Englewood is conscious."

* * * * *

7:12 P.M.

Annabelle was getting frustrated.

No, that wasn't quite true; she was way past frustrated. She was now bordering on full-blown panic. Her stomach was churning with that all-too-familiar sense of dread and foreboding. Instead of carrying oxygen around her body, her blood felt like it was carrying little tiny drops of stress.

She was in the hospital, her left shoulder ached so she surmised that was the reason she was there, but she couldn't remember a thing that had happened after she and her family had eaten dinner last night. At least she was assuming it was last night, but who knows how long she had been lying here in the hospital?

No one would tell her anything. They wouldn't tell her what had happened to her. They wouldn't tell her where her family was. And they kept giving her strange looks.

What Annabelle really wanted to know, though, was why her wrist was handcuffed to the side of the hospital bed. Did the police think she had done something bad? Was that why no one would talk to her? But what had she done? She couldn't remember doing anything, but then again she couldn't remember much of anything since dinner.

Closing her eyes, she forced herself to focus her swirling mind, trying to push it into recalling the events that had landed her in the hospital. Annabelle was just starting to get her brain to reach back tentacles to the last thing she remembered when she heard the door to her hospital room open and footsteps march across the floor, stopping beside her bed.

Not in the mood to face another doctor or nurse whose face was painted with the same mix of pity and revulsion, she kept her eyes firmly closed.

After a long wait, an impatient voice spoke, "Miss Englewood?"

Steadfastly, Annabelle ignored it. She was good at ignoring things, had spent most of her life doing it.

With an irritated sigh the voice spoke again, "My name is Detective Montague. I'm here with my partner, Detective Hannah. We need to talk to you about what happened."

Grabbing at anger, not an emotion Annabelle was particularly good at, she was much more equipped at being a doormat than at letting others know when they'd hurt her. "I don't know what happened," she snapped.

"What do you mean?" a female voice demanded.

"I mean, I don't remember anything after eating dinner," she shot back, her resolve to stick with fury wavering; she turned to jelly the second anyone raised their voice at her. "Why am I handcuffed to the bed?"

"Would you please open your eyes?" Detective Montague pleaded tiredly.

Reluctantly complying, when she opened her eyes, she realized the face that looked down at her was one she'd seen before. Surprised, her brow creased in concentration, "You were there," she mumbled. The light brown hair, the hazel eyes, the sharp features, this man was somehow linked to whatever had happened to her.

For a second his hazel eyes softened before growing hard once more. "Yeah, I was."

"Well then, you can tell me what happened," she pounced on that delightedly. "You can tell me how I ended up here."

"That's what we're here to find out." Detective Hannah pulled a chair up beside the bed and sat, her blue eyes probing.

"You don't know?" she demanded. "Where are my parents?" Annabelle couldn't understand why they weren't here by her side. Whatever John and Kathy Englewoods' faults, they would be by their oldest child's side if she were in the hospital. A thought occurred to her, "Are they hurt, too? Is that why they don't come? Are they here in the hospital, too?"

The two detectives exchanged glances above her head. "You really don't remember anything?" Detective Hannah asked.

"No," she shrugged helplessly, ignoring the burning that produced in her shoulder. Annabelle was finding herself dangerously close to tears, and right now tears were not going to get her the answers that she needed.

"What is the last thing you remember?" Detective Montague asked.

He spoke calmly, but Annabelle could see something lurking in his eyes, something she was still a little too groggy to make out. "The last thing I remember was eating dinner last night. At least, I think it was last night, but I'm not sure how long I've been here . . ." She looked to the detectives for confirmation.

"It was last night," Detective Hannah confirmed, fiddling with the ends of her blonde ponytail.

"Who cooked dinner last night?" Detective Montague asked.

"I did. Why?" She wondered what possible bearing that could have on anything. She was wrong, though, because once again the detectives exchanged glances. "That's important...why?"

"Did anyone help you?" Detective Montague pushed.

She was unsettled by the way he kept staring at her with such deep intensity. "No." Annabelle was still confused about why this was important. "I cooked dinner on my own, but earlier in the day Katherine and I made cookies." Another exchange of looks, and this time when they looked at her, their eyes showed nothing but icy coldness and Annabelle felt herself shiver. She needed to know what was going on. "Why am I handcuffed to the bed?" she asked, pleased that her voice came out with more strength than she had anticipated. "Did I do something wrong?"

"You could say that," Detective Montague said harshly. "Your family is dead."

A black hole seemed to start growing inside her head. Growing quickly, bigger and bigger, swamping every part of her. Her surroundings began to fade until they joined the blackness in her brain. Annabelle started to feel light, like she was floating, flying through the dark night sky.

"Xavier, maybe we should call the doctor."

Detective Hannah's voice floated by her. Annabelle could actually see each word in the dark, glowing like musical notes.

"Just give it a second." Detective Montague lightly tapped at her cheeks. "Miss Englewood. Annabelle."

As quickly as the blackness had come, it swept away, leaving her shaking and empty. "They're really dead?" she asked in a small voice. "All of them? My mom and dad? The boys? Katherine?"

"All of them," Detective Montague nodded, holding her in a forceful stare.

"How?" She wondered if someone had broken into their home and killed her family, trying to kill her, too, only somehow she had survived.

"You killed them."

She expected the blackness to come creeping back, but instead, Annabelle realized that all she felt was anger. How dare this man suggest that she would kill her parents and siblings. Sure, it wasn't like they got along all the time; they had their problems just like all families did—but she would never in a million years hurt them, let alone murder them. "How dare you!" she spat out, surprised at the venom in her voice. "How dare you say that!"

If Detective Montague was surprised by her outburst, he didn't show it. "You had their blood on your feet, your bloody footprints were all over the house, and there was no sign of a break in. You did it. I don't know why you did it, but you did. I don't know if you really blocked it out and can't remember or if you're setting up some sort of insanity defense or if you really had some sort of psychotic breakdown, but it doesn't change the facts."

He was staring at her so coldly that it made her wonder what had happened to him that made him see the world in such a way that he could believe someone like her could kill their family in cold blood.

And then she realized what was happening.

This was simply a dream. A horrible nightmare. That was the only explanation. If she could just wake up, then everything would be back to normal. Raising her right hand, she began to smash it into her injured shoulder, a little shocked when it caused arrows of pain to shoot up and down her arm.

Startled, Detective Montague snapped a hand around her wrist. "What are you doing?"

"Trying to make myself wake up," she answered simply.

Pocketing her phone, Detective Hannah stood. "We need to leave, Xavier. Now," she added when he raised an eyebrow at her. Then she leaned over and whispered something in his ear, something that made his eyes grow wide.

"We'll be back later," Detective Montague turned his attention away from his partner and back to her.

"This is really happening, isn't it?" Annabelle whimpered.

He watched her warily now, as though not sure what to make of her. "It really is." Seemingly realizing he was still holding her arm, he set it down gently against the stiff mattress, pulled out a key and removed the handcuff, and then he was gone.

Alone, Annabelle did the only thing she could think of that would help her. She pressed her buzzer to summon a doctor and requested something to make her sleep.

* * * * *

9:03 P.M.

"Annabelle Englewood absolutely, positively, one hundred percent did not kill her family."

"How can you possibly know that?" Xavier demanded.

"Take a seat and I'll explain everything." Diane sat at her desk and gestured to the two other chairs in the room.

In the middle of their interview with Annabelle they'd received a call from Diane telling them to stop what they were doing and get to her office immediately because Annabelle was not the killer. When Kate had first whispered that in his ear, he hadn't known what to think. He had to admit that Annabelle didn't look like someone who would slaughter her family in their sleep, but then again, he knew very well that looks could be deceiving. Although at the time he hadn't wanted to see it, now Xavier had to admit that the shock and grief in her eyes when they'd told her what they thought she'd done was genuine.

"First of all, the family was drugged and the samples of food contained traces of sleeping pills. He probably crushed some up and added it to the pasta sauce . . ."

"Annabelle said she was the one who cooked dinner for her family last night," Kate informed Diane.

"There was a bottle of pasta sauce in the fridge," Diane explained. "When I found out they'd been drugged, I sent someone back to collect it. The sauce had the drugs in it too, so it doesn't matter *who* cooked the meal. And Annabelle was drugged as well."

"That doesn't discount her," Kate protested warily. "She could have been the one to add the sleeping pill powder to the jar, and she could have drugged herself to throw suspicion off herself. Or maybe it was the only way she could attempt to kill herself."

"What else have you got?" Xavier asked, more prepared than his partner obviously was to give Annabelle the benefit of the doubt.

"She didn't have any of her family's blood on her," Diane told them. "We tested all over her pajamas; no blood but her own."

"Maybe she showered," Kate suggested, pulling her hair free from its ponytail and shaking it out, his partner hated wearing her hair up. "And washed her clothes before putting on her pajamas."

"No blood in any of the showers," Diane countered. "And no clothes in the washer or dryer. Maybe she waited while the clothes went through both then folded them up and put them away before stabbing herself, but I'm thinking probably not."

"Okay," Xavier nodded, completely agreeing with Diane's logic. "What about the blood on her feet?"

"Painted on."

"What?" he exclaimed.

"Someone painted it on her feet, she never walked through her family's blood. In the footprints, we found a couple of hairs from a paintbrush. There were some in her bed too. And the footprints were all wrong. She wasn't walking on her own; someone was walking her around. I spoke with her doctor and he said the angle of the wound indicated it was someone standing above her. It wasn't self-inflicted."

Xavier drew in a shaky breath as he realized they were no longer dealing with a murder/suicide but an unknown killer who hated the Englewood family so much that they would set all of this up and murder them in such a horrible way. That also meant that there was someone out there who hated Annabelle so much that they would frame her for her parents' and siblings' murders. Once again, the young woman's white eyes flashed into his head.

"Plus," Diane continued, "we never found the knife. Searched the whole house from top to bottom, the yard, too, but we couldn't find it. So unless Annabelle Englewood painted her own feet with blood, or possesses the ability to make objects vanish, and to clean herself without an ounce of water, then there is no way that she committed those murders."

"Okay," Kate admitted reluctantly, "maybe she didn't actually commit the murders, but that doesn't preclude her being involved somehow."

"Like how?" Diane demanded.

"Maybe she was in on the plan to kill her family and hired someone to do it, only that person tried to take her out, too."

Diane arched a skeptical brow. "So your theory is that Annabelle Englewood hired a hit man who then tried to kill her, too?" Xavier asked, knowing that Kate was still clinging to the idea that Annabelle was involved, because it made their job so much easier.

"Or maybe she and a boyfriend were in on it together. He kills the family, then the two of them are supposed to ride off into the sunset together—only he realizes he's just not that into her and tries to kill her, too," Kate put forward.

"I buy that a little more than your first notion," he acknowledged, still thinking it was more likely that Annabelle was, in fact, an innocent victim in all of this. "Di, was there any evidence of someone else being there?"

"No fingerprints other than family members on the door handles, but there are hundreds of fingerprints, fibers and hairs in the rooms, which is not unusual. The kids have girlfriends, boyfriends, friends, all of whom I'm sure spend time in their rooms. So far, nothing suspicious. We'll keep plodding through what we have, but I don't think it's going to lead to anything useful. And I for one like the idea that a stranger, or at least someone with a grudge against the family, committed those murders rather than that girl slaughtering her own family in such a vicious way," Diane stated firmly.

Xavier had to admit that he definitely did, too. "Well, tomorrow morning we have an appointment with the next-door neighbor who called it in; hopefully, he'll be able to give us something to go on. Then we'll talk with every relative, family friend, and co-worker we can find and try to get a picture of the family and who, if anyone, might hate them enough to kill them. And then…" He paused for a moment, wondering how they were going to face Annabelle after they'd accused her of murder and whether she'd be willing to help them, "...then we'll go see Annabelle."

With shocked dismay, Xavier realized that the thought that Annabelle Englewood—a woman he'd met less than twenty-four hours ago, bleeding to death in her home, spoken maybe a hundred words to, and had believed to be a killer—might not forgive him actually made his stomach clench in a way it hadn't in a really long time.

* * * * *

11:17 P.M.

He was giggling like a schoolgirl.

He'd watched every glorious second.

From the time the first unit had responded, he had watched with eager anticipation as the male and female detectives edged their way through the front yard and into the house. He'd watched as more police cars and an ambulance had barreled down upon the house. He'd clapped with glee as the paramedics and the male detective had carried Annabelle Englewood out into the waiting ambulance. He'd been pretty sure that the girl would survive the wound he'd inflicted on her. He'd been very careful not to plunge the knife too deep; he didn't want to sever anything vital or cause the girl to bleed to death before she arrived at a hospital.

When the place had begun to swarm with crime scene techs and the two detectives had begun talking to people in the crowd, he had taken it as his cue to—reluctantly—disappear.

Arriving home, he had quickly switched on the news and spent the day glued to his television. He'd been pleased when he heard them reporting the story as a murder/suicide where the murderer had somehow managed to survive, and he wondered how long it would take the police to discover that Annabelle had been framed.

It was nothing personal against the girl, nor had it been necessary, but sometimes in life a little fun *was* necessary, and the idea of framing one of his victims had appealed to him so he had run with it.

Of course, he had been careful not to frame her too well, he didn't actually want the police to shut the case down because they believed that they already had their killer in custody. So he had painted the blood on her feet, and then walked her limp body from room to room. He'd made sure to leave the front door locked behind him when he had slipped out one of the windows.

Lacing the pasta sauce with sleeping pills had been easy. The Englewood family were fairly predictable, especially Annabelle, and it hadn't taken him long to learn their patterns. Each night of the week had its own specific dinner, always cooked by Annabelle, and when he'd snuck into their house the other day, the pasta sauce had seemed a good option since he could stir in the powder until it was invisible.

Drugging them hadn't really been necessary; he could have handled things without having to resort to that. However, if he wanted the police to think that Annabelle had done it, then he had decided they might be suspicious about how a five foot five, hundred and twenty-pound woman could overpower her much larger father and brothers.

Now it was exactly twenty-four hours since he had crept inside the silent home. The sight of the sleeping bodies lying so helplessly beneath him had been incredibly intoxicating. As the knife had slid so smoothly through the thin flesh of his victims' throats, he had found himself mesmerized by the gushing blood. It had looked so beautiful in the moonlight, shimmering like a sparkling river. He'd been unable to resist putting his hand in it and letting the thick liquid dance through his fingers.

Before that moment, he'd never realized how beautiful blood was. It had been a disappointment when he'd cut off the hands that there had been comparatively so little of it, but still there had been plenty to enjoy.

In the end, it had been very hard to tear himself away from the glorious sight, but once all the bodies were dead and Annabelle had been injured, it had been time to slip silently away. Now that he was home, he realized he was yearning to be back there. That blood was so intoxicating.

Stretching out on his bed, he tried to recreate the scene in his mind. He pictured the rooms and the bodies, the warm air, the smell of copper; but it just wasn't the same, it was missing the most important ingredient.

Rooting around under his bed, he pulled out the knife that had been used to slay the Englewood family. For a moment he was captivated by the glinting metal, the way the thin light of his lamp bounced off it, making it seem as though the knife were swaying to a song only *it* could hear.

Bringing the tip of the blade to his arm, without a second's hesitation, he made a light split in the skin. Watching with great awe as a trickle of blood oozed out, the fingers of his other hand dipping into it. Lifting his hand, he was enthralled once more by the beautiful sight of the blood that clung there.

Picturing perfectly the scene in the Englewood house, he curled up in bed and willed sleep to come so he could relive every delightful second in his dreams.

MAY 5TH

2:09 A.M.

Vanessa Adams was on cloud nine.

Every couple of seconds she kept glancing at the clock. Only twenty-one minutes to go until he'd be here.

Her parents didn't approve of him, but she was seventeen now, and as far as she was concerned they had no input into whom she dated. Besides, Vincent Abrams was so dreamy, more than any girl could hope for. He was a college sophomore, he rode a motorbike, he had amazing blue eyes that Vanessa could stare into for hours, and thick reddish brown hair that felt amazing running through her hands.

There was no doubt about it. She was in love. Head over heels in love.

Vanessa couldn't think of anything more wonderful than to be lying in Vince's strong arms, nestled against his hard, muscled chest, his hands roaming her body.

Tonight was the night.

The night where they planned on taking their relationship to the next level.

She had been dreaming about this for months. Ever since she had seen him at her cousin's football game, it had been love at first sight. And Vanessa was positive that Vince was the man she was going to spend the rest of her life with.

She was so tired of her parents telling her she was too young to have a serious relationship, that she didn't know what she wanted, and that she would soon lose interest in Vince or he in her.

They didn't know what they were talking about.

She was seventeen, not seven, and she knew how she felt about Vince. The way her heart squeezed whenever he was nearby, the way her stomach turned somersaults, the way her brain turned to goo and she lost all track of time. Vanessa knew that Vince was her other half and she was ready to give herself to him.

Glancing at the clock, now it was only eleven minutes to go.

She decided that another quick check of the house was in order. She certainly didn't want anyone barging in on her right in the middle of things, and just because it was the middle of the night didn't mean that no one was lurking.

Five months ago her dad had lost his job, and then not long after that they'd lost their house and been forced to move in with her grandparents. Now it seemed like she was never alone. With her dad home most of the time, he had made it his business to get all up in her life. He insisted on driving her to and from school each day, hovering over her while she completed her homework, and inserting himself into every aspect of her life. Vanessa hated it. She was a big girl. Her parents had never before been interested in what she'd been up to; she wasn't used to that level of attention.

As if her dad losing his job wasn't bad enough, her little brother seemed to have gotten a million times more annoying since they'd moved here. Justin was thirteen and a horror movie nut. He had a whole case full of them, insisted on spending all his time watching them, and when he wasn't doing that, he was spouting out useless horror movie trivia. Last night at dinner he'd been rabbiting on about how any young girl who gave up her virginity in a horror movie was destined to be brutally murdered.

That sent tremors of excitement tingling through her. Not the horror movie part, but the part about losing her virginity.

Another glance at the clock, only four minutes to go.

Unable to keep still, Vanessa climbed out of bed, fiddling with the sexy lingerie she'd bought for tonight and wishing that her parents and grandparents would let her put a lock on her door. Apparently a lock didn't say happy family, so when she'd asked, she had been given a resounding no by all four adults.

Grabbing her desk chair, she carried it over and propped it up under the door handle. Even though her check of the house had found everything quiet and dark it didn't mean things would stay that way, so if anyone should be up and about and hear something, then at least the chair would slow them down a little.

Next, she lit the scented candles that were dotted about her room, and smoothed out the satin sheets she'd been hiding in the back of her closet in preparation for this night. She stood at the open window where she anxiously waited for her prince charming to arrive.

One minute to go.

Wanting to look just perfect when Vince arrived, she stretched out on the bed and tried to assume a sexy, womanly pose. Vanessa had to admit she was a little nervous. She was only seventeen and still a virgin. Vince was nineteen, and with his gorgeous looks, he was sure to have been with any number of beautiful and experienced women. She didn't want to look stupid or inexperienced; she wanted everything to be perfect.

When Vince had first broached the topic of sex with her, she hadn't been sure, but then he'd said that he understood and that he loved her and that if she was sure that she loved him then nothing should stop them from joining their bodies together. Even though she was excited, she was also plenty anxious, she really hoped she wasn't about to make a fool out of herself…

"Hey, pretty girl."

Jumping, Vanessa realized she'd dozed off for a minute there and now Vince was standing above her. He looked amazing, and Vanessa wondered once again why someone like him would even give someone like her the time of day. She wasn't ugly exactly, Vanessa supposed; she was just plain, with ash blonde hair and brown eyes, a little too tall for a girl her age, and a little too chubby. Still, the way Vince was looking at her right now made her feel like the most beautiful woman in the whole world.

"Hey, yourself," she gave him a dopey, lovesick smile.

"Are you sure you're ready?"

Enjoying his silky voice, Vanessa hardly heard what he said, already her body had begun beating with desire. "I'm ready," she gushed.

She watched with delight as his hands began to fumble with his buttons, and within seconds his shirt lay discarded on the floor beside her bed. It didn't take long for his shorts to join them, and as he slid off his boxers she couldn't help a thrilled gurgle escaping her lips as she took in the sight of him.

Still, an anxious fluttering took up residence in her stomach as his hands reached for her clothes, but she made no move to stop him and before she knew it she was lying naked before him. For one horrible second, Vanessa was sure that Vince was going to be repulsed by her, but then she saw his hungry eyes and all her doubts flew away.

Ever so slowly he stretched out on top of her, his lips finding hers, his hands exploring her body and Vanessa readied herself for the most amazing night of her life until all hell broke loose…

* * * * *

8:41 A.M.

"Sorry I wasn't able to be available for you yesterday."

Ricky Preston apologized for at least the twentieth time since they'd arrived here to speak with him approximately one and a half minutes ago.

"We understand," Xavier assured him, although it was quite annoying that they'd been unable to speak with the man who had made the 911 call, but by the time they'd arrived at his house, he'd already left for his doctor's appointment. Still, if they'd known then what they knew now, that Annabelle had not slaughtered the rest of the Englewood family, then they would have tracked down the neighbor and insisted on speaking with him immediately.

"It's just, you know what doctors are like," Ricky continued as he led them into a den. "I didn't want to lose my appointment; I'm pretty anxious to get back to work." He held up his arm, encased in a bulky cast.

"How did you break your arm?" Xavier asked, trying to get comfortable on what had to be the world's worst sofa. As he tried to arrange himself in such a way that didn't make it feel like a brick was pressing into his back, he took in the rest of the room. It seemed as though Ricky was quite the art collector. The walls were filled with what looked like expensive pieces of artwork, several sculptures were dotted around, and there were even a couple of ancient looking masks in a cabinet in the far corner.

"Work," Ricky smiled ruefully. "I'm a carpenter. I was up on a ladder working to finish the top of a cabinet, fell off and broke my arm. Pretty bad, too; had to have a pin put in it. I'm just itching to get this cast off and get back to work." He narrowed his eyes, "I heard that you think Annabelle killed her family."

"What exactly did you see?" Kate asked, wiggling uncomfortably.

"Annabelle would never hurt anyone," Ricky persisted.

"Why don't you explain to us exactly what you saw that night?" Kate suggested patiently.

"Annabelle is the sweetest girl I've ever met," Ricky insisted. "She wouldn't hurt a fly, takes good care of her family." Catching their frustrated glares, he sighed, "Fine. I've been having trouble sleeping since I broke my arm. Sometimes I just toss and turn in bed, but sometimes I get up, watch some TV or read, and sometimes, especially when its warm, I like to go and sit outside in the yard. I was out there, just kind of gazing at the stars, when something caught my eye. I looked and I thought it was someone holding a knife, it was glinting in the moonlight. I thought it might just be my overactive imagination, so I came inside and got out my telescope. My spare bedroom looks out onto John and Kathy's room. There was no one in there with a knife, but I saw blood—lots of blood—so I called nine-one-one."

"Did you get a look at the person holding the knife?" Kate asked.

"No, I just saw a shadowy figure standing, holding something that I thought looked like a knife," Ricky replied.

"So you couldn't tell if they were male or female, old or young, tall or short?" Kate peppered.

"No, just a black figure," Ricky repeated.

"And you only saw one figure?" Xavier asked, thinking of his partner's theory that Annabelle and a boyfriend may have committed the crimes.

"Yes, just one." He eyed them shrewdly. "Why? You can't honestly think that Annabelle did this."

"What can you tell us about the Englewood family?" Xavier asked, instead of answering.

Clearly annoyed by their refusal to answer his questions, Ricky Preston sighed once more but answered, "They're a really lovely family. Been living next to them for going on four years now and never had a single problem. John and I both like football, he'd come over, we'd watch together pretty regularly. Kathy, she was a really nice lady, even brought me over some chicken soup when I had the flu last winter. The boys were great kids, and that little Katherine was an absolute doll, sweetest little girl I've ever had the pleasure of meeting."

"What about Annabelle?" Xavier asked, waiting with baited breath for the answer. He couldn't seem to shake a sense of intrigue where Annabelle was concerned.

"She is an amazing young woman," Ricky gushed. "She's sweet and caring and thoughtful. She'd spend most of her free time taking care of little Katherine when she wasn't cooking or cleaning or doing the grocery shopping."

"Was there something going on between you and Annabelle?" he demanded, a little more intensely than was necessary.

"What? No!" Ricky looked genuinely shocked at the suggestion. "Annabelle's just a girl and I'm old enough to be her father."

"Annabelle is twenty-three, right?" Kate queried.

"Right," Ricky appeared to be trying to figure out where they were heading.

"Is there any reason that she still lives at home with her parents? Not that I'm saying there's anything wrong with that; it just seems like it's a little odd for someone her age," Kate added with a smile.

"You'd have to ask Annabelle about that," Ricky smiled back.

"Annabelle's a teacher, right?" he asked.

"Right, kindergarten."

"That must be pretty tiring," he mused. Xavier always felt more wiped out after an afternoon with his nieces and nephews than when he'd been up for a couple of days straight without sleep.

"I'd imagine so," Ricky agreed warily.

"And then she comes home and babysits her little sister, and then cooks dinner and does the cleaning, as well. Any reason why her mom or dad didn't help out with the chores?"

"Again, you'd have to ask Annabelle about that," Ricky's blue eyes danced merrily.

For a man who had to be in his mid-forties, Ricky Preston was in great shape. His muscles bulged beneath his white t-shirt, and his tanned face was smooth and wrinkle free. His honey-colored hair was combed neatly in place, and Xavier wondered whether perhaps there actually was something going on between Annabelle and her neighbor. "What was Annabelle's relationship like with her parents?"

"Annabelle gets along with everybody. I told you, she's a really sweet girl. So before you ask, yes, she also got along with her brothers and Katherine, and everyone else on the street." Ricky's face clouded over with sternness. "Look, I don't know what you want to get out of me, but Annabelle is a great person and there is absolutely no way that she would hurt—much less kill—anyone. So if you're waiting for me to say something incriminating about her, then you're wasting your time. Annabelle Englewood is *not* a murderer," he finished off with a challenging stare.

"We no longer believe that Annabelle committed the murders," Kate informed him calmly.

He uttered a deep sigh of relief, "Good, because being accused of murder is the last thing that girl needs at the moment."

Xavier was frustrated with himself when a wave of guilt washed over him for adding to Annabelle's trauma over finding out her family had been brutally murdered by accusing her of being the killer. "Forensics have indicated that Annabelle was not responsible for what happened, which means someone else is."

"What did Annabelle say?" Ricky asked. "Did she see who attacked her?"

"We haven't spoken with her yet," Kate answered vaguely.

"You mean you haven't spoken with her since you decided she's not a killer," Ricky corrected.

"Is there anyone you can think of who might have some sort of grudge against the Englewood family?" Kate asked.

"No, I already told you they were a nice family."

"We'll count Katherine out since she's only seven, but there's no one you can think of who might want one or all of the Englewoods dead?" Xavier pushed; they needed something, no matter how small.

"No arguments with any of the neighbors or friends, no jilted girlfriends or boyfriends of the kids, no jealous exes of anyone Julian or Paul were currently dating?" Kate suggested.

"No, nothing. I've met Julian's girlfriend once or twice. She's nice, and as far as I know, Paul was focusing on his studies right now."

"Okay, then what about any suspicious people hanging around the street?" Xavier tried.

"Maybe," Ricky bobbed his head thoughtfully. "A couple of days ago, or maybe a week, I thought there was a car that seemed to be always hanging around, parked right outside my house."

Xavier perked up, "Did you get a license plate number?" he asked eagerly.

"No, I'm sorry; I only looked at it through the window," Ricky answered sorrowfully.

"What about a make and model?" he tried.

"No, sorry."

"Color?" he asked halfheartedly.

"Red," Ricky offered a little smile. "I'm sorry, I noticed it a couple of times during the day, but by the time I realized it had been hanging around for too long and decided to go and get a license plate number, the car had gone."

"You didn't get a look at whoever was inside?" Xavier clung to the hope that a breakthrough could be right around the corner.

"Some guy—I didn't really look."

"And there's really nothing else you can give us that might be helpful?" he demanded, frustrated that they were getting nowhere and antsy about their next stop—Annabelle's hospital room.

"No, once again, I'm sorry. Perhaps you'll have better luck with Annabelle," Ricky proposed.

"All right, call us if you do think of something," Kate passed Ricky a card.

They were just stepping through the door when Ricky stopped them. "Don't stress about Annabelle. She may be understandably mad that you accused her of murder, but she'll get over it eventually and she'll do whatever she can to help you find the person that took her family from her."

As they walked to the car, Xavier wondered whether Ricky Preston had just read his mind or whether he was really that transparent.

* * * * *

10:36 A.M.

"You don't have to feel guilty, Xavier," Kate announced as they walked through the hospital corridors. After working together for seven years, she could read her partner like a book.

"About what?" Xavier scowled back at her.

"About Annabelle," she replied, even though she knew he knew what she'd been talking about. "We didn't do anything wrong. At the time, it looked like Annabelle was the killer. Now we have all the facts and we know that she didn't do it, there's nothing for you to feel guilty about."

"I don't feel guilty," Xavier snapped. "We were just doing our job."

She rolled her eyes. "Fine," she agreed.

Since Julia, Xavier had changed a lot from the guy she had first met seven years ago. She'd been twenty-nine and lonely; he'd been twenty-five and gorgeous, and for a while the two of them had kind of danced around the mutual attraction. Then one night after a particularly horrific murder scene they had fallen into bed together. In the morning they had both regretted it, decided they were better as friends and partners than lovers and moved on.

Back then, Xavier had been fun and energetic—a golf and hiking fanatic. He'd been a night owl, preferring to work through the night rather than waste time in sleep. Now, however, Xavier had lost his spark—lost it when he lost Julia—and although Kate had done everything she could think of to help him get it back, including attempting to set him up with an endless parade of fantastic women, so far nothing had worked.

Not that Kate thought a woman was the answer to all of Xavier's problems, but she also knew that until he gave himself permission to move on, he was never going to go back to the man he had been before.

"Am I really that transparent?" Xavier asked, losing the annoyed look and replacing it with a worried one.

"I think it's just that I know you too well." She gave him a reassuring smile. "Xavier, you're not developing a crush on her, are you?" As much as she wanted her partner to move on, she didn't want him to do it like this, in a way that was doomed to end in disaster before it even began.

"It's her eyes," Xavier said distractedly, "the way they looked at me when she regained consciousness—their color, I can't stop thinking about them."

"Thinking is fine, it's the acting on it that I'm worried about," she mused. "Aside from the fact that Annabelle is a victim in a case we're working, I don't think you're in any place to be helping someone deal with trauma."

"Kate," Xavier whined, "it's been three years. I am not still dealing with trauma."

"Okay," she singsonged, knowing full well that wasn't true, but experience had taught her that arguing with Xavier only pushed him into being more obstinate. However, when they reached Annabelle's door, she couldn't help but inquire, "You sure you're up to this?"

"Kate..." Xavier's whine was still in place.

"Okay, okay, okay," she surrendered, deciding she'd press him again later; now was not the time. "Let's go in." Kate wasn't much further behind Xavier in dreading facing the young woman who had just lost her family in such a horrendous way, almost lost her own life, and then been accused by the police of being a coldhearted killer.

When they went inside, they found Annabelle lying on her bed, her eyes were open but staring sightlessly at the ceiling. She didn't indicate that she was aware that they were there, but Kate guessed the girl was pretty used to doctors and nurses coming and going. "Miss Englewood?" Kate placed a hand on the young woman's shoulder.

Slowly, the girl's blank face came to life. As recognition flickered in her eyes, she grew stony. "What are *you* doing here?"

"We need to talk to you about what happened," Kate told her. She had to agree with Xavier, Annabelle's eyes were extremely unusual; she'd never met anyone with eyes so pale a blue they appeared white.

"Well, I don't want to talk to you." Annabelle closed her eyes to shut them out.

"We don't think that you killed your family," Xavier explained.

"Congratulations," Annabelle snapped. "I already told you that, but it's so nice for you to finally believe it."

"That means," Xavier continued, "that whoever *did* kill your mom and dad and brothers and sister is still out there. The person who hurt you is still out there, and we need your help to find them."

Annabelle remained steadfastly silent, alone in her pain and anger.

"Annabelle, please," Xavier half begged. "Please open your eyes and talk to us. We're sorry that we thought that you had hurt your family, but you have to understand that we were just doing our jobs..."

"I don't have to understand anything," Annabelle fired, her eyes popping open to shoot arrows at them. "You called me a murderer. You had me handcuffed to a hospital bed. You let me lie here on my own not knowing what had happened to me, not knowing where my family was, and then you came in here and you just announced that my family was dead and that I had done it. My family was murdered and you accused me of doing it," she broke off as she choked on a sob.

"Then help us make it right," Xavier spoke softly. "Help us make it up to you by finding the person who did this."

With eyes that brimmed with tears, Annabelle studied Xavier, then sunk back against the pillows. "I already told you: I don't remember anything," she said sullenly.

"That's okay," Kate assured her, "we can start with something else. Why don't you just tell us a bit about your family. Your neighbor, Mr. Preston, didn't really want to disclose much about your personal life."

"Yeah, he's a sweet guy," a ghost of a smile lighting her pale lips.

"Are you involved with him?" Xavier asked calmly, but Kate could see the tremble in his eyebrow, a sure sign he was annoyed but trying to cover it.

She huffed out a snort. "No, but we *are* friends, we just talk."

"About what?" she asked.

"I don't know." Annabelle shifted uncomfortably, "About stuff."

"Can you be more specific?" Xavier pushed.

"Just stuff." Annabelle shut down once more.

"You're a kindergarten teacher, right?" Kate decided a change in topic was needed.

"Right," Annabelle nodded unenthusiastically.

"That must be fun," she smiled encouragingly.

"I guess."

"Mr. Preston said that you usually look after Katherine when you get home. Any reason why you do that instead of your parents?"

"They both usually work late and I don't mind."

"Do you get along with your parents?"

"I guess," Annabelle shrugged but Kate detected a slight hesitation.

"What about your brothers?"

"They're my little brothers," Annabelle said as though that explained everything.

Kate didn't have any little brothers but she *was* a younger sister, and she knew how much she had loved annoying her big sister when they were kids, so she could quite easily surmise how frustrating Annabelle's two little brothers had been. "Annabelle, is there anyone you can think of who might want to hurt you or your family?"

"No, why would there be? There's nothing special about us."

"Well, someone thinks differently," Xavier reminded her gently. "There're no ex-boyfriends or girlfriends, or no jealous exes of one of your brother's girlfriends, no work colleagues or old friends with a grudge, no problems with anyone in your neighborhood?"

"No." Annabelle was becoming frustrated and was again close to tears. "We don't have any problems with anyone."

"Have you noticed anyone hanging around you at work or at your home?" Kate asked, thinking of the car Ricky Preston had mentioned.

"I can't think of anything. I'm not sure; I don't remember." Annabelle was crying now. "I don't pay attention. Do you think that whoever did this just picked us at random? Why would they do that? Why would someone do this?"

"Annabelle," both she and Xavier said simultaneously, each reaching out a hand to comfort the girl.

"Don't. Don't touch me," Annabelle shrunk away from them.

"We'll find the person who did this," Xavier assured her, his hands hovering helplessly between himself and Annabelle.

"I don't care." Annabelle was sobbing now. "I don't care who did it. It's not going to change anything; my family is still dead. Oh my gosh...they're really dead." Her eyes grew wide and panicked, as if truly registering this for the first time. Her sobs took on a more hysterical tone and she struggled to suck in air.

"Try to calm down." Xavier took hold of Annabelle's shoulders; this time she didn't fight him.

"I think I should get the doctor," Kate announced.

Before she could make it even a step toward the door, it swung open and one of the doctors came running in, quickly surveying the situation.

"I think that's enough for today." Dr. Daniels produced a syringe full of sedatives. "Annabelle," he approached the sobbing girl slowly, "I'm going to give you something to help you sleep, okay?" Annabelle didn't respond, nor did she seem to notice as the doctor lifted her arm and injected the sedative.

It began to take effect almost immediately. Annabelle's sobs began to fade and her eyes started to flutter closed. Before she drifted away, Xavier took her hand. "I promise you, I am going to find who did this."

As Annabelle drifted off, Kate wondered exactly how they were going to keep Xavier's promise since they had no leads, no suspects, and no idea where to go next.

* * * * *

11:06 P.M.

Restlessly, he paced the rooms of his house. Heading out to the backyard, he began to jog in a circuit around the perimeter, dodging the fruit trees that Julia had planted when they'd first moved in here. He needed to rest, but he didn't want to sleep.

Xavier hated dreaming.

It was like being stuck between a rock and a hard place. If his dreams were good, it only served to remind him when he awakened that things were not good anymore. And if his dreams were bad, then it was just another reminder of what a failure he was.

The dream that had just roused him from sleep, with his heart beating so hard it had felt like it could have hammered its way out of his chest, and sweating so profusely he could have filled a swimming pool, had been a good one.

At least it had started out that way.

He and Julia had been out at the lake where they had spent their summers together. They'd been laughing and fooling around and having fun when suddenly Annabelle had appeared, dressed in the pajamas she'd been wearing when he found her and dripping blood. Immediately he had rushed to her aid, but when he'd turned back to Julia he saw her curled up in a little ball sobbing and screaming how could he not notice something was wrong with her.

That was really what had been eating him alive these last three years. He hadn't noticed that anything was wrong with his wife until it had been too late. He'd been so wrapped up in his work and hanging out with his friends that he hadn't noticed that Julia was changing.

Exhausted, he flopped down on the grass, panting as he tried to catch his breath. Xavier wasn't pleased that Annabelle Englewood was now creeping into his dreams. Apparently it wasn't sufficient that she was quickly becoming a permanent fixture in his brain; now, she was also infiltrating his subconscious.

Recalling his conversation with Kate at the hospital earlier, he wondered if he really was developing a crush on Annabelle. As much as he felt guilty about accusing her of being a killer and as stuck as he was on her unusual white eyes, Xavier didn't believe in love at first sight.

When he had first met Julia, he had been entranced, sure, but not in love. He'd thought she was sweet and funny and pretty and he'd known that he wanted to get to know her better, a *lot* better, but he had not been in love. Over the course of the month or so that he and Julia had dated before eloping to Las Vegas, he had quickly fallen head over heels in love with the beautiful Julia, and he had been sure that they were destined to be together forever.

Maybe they would have been if things hadn't fallen apart the way they had. He had truly loved her, but he had let himself get so consumed with work that, in the end, he had never even noticed that something was wrong with her.

Kate thought that he had changed since Julia had left his life in such a dramatic fashion, but it was more that he now focused his energies in another direction. He hadn't been hiking or golfing since Julia had gone. He didn't hang out till the wee hours of the morning partying with his friends. He wasn't as loud and energetic as he used to be. But he was still the same person. Now he just took all the energy he used to spend on fun and focused it onto work and just a few close friends.

Like Kate and her husband, David. He had almost ruined things with Kate. His partner was pretty with long blonde hair, which she usually wore down, dark blue eyes framed by long dark lashes. She was around five foot eight, slim and delicate looking, but deceptively strong, and Xavier had been enamored with her from the first time they'd met.

Despite the fact that he knew they were partners and nothing should ever happen between them, he had flirted with her relentlessly. In the end, after visiting a particularly horrific crime scene involving a seventeen-year-old boy who had slit the throat of his thirteen-year-old sister and her six friends before beating them until the girls were unrecognizable, he and Kate had fallen into bed together.

In the morning he had realized what a mistake it had been. He hadn't wanted to lose Kate as a partner or as a friend and they had both vowed it would never happen again. And it hadn't. Within a few weeks of his tryst with Kate, he had met Julia and she had met David.

Rousing himself, he headed back inside. Xavier knew he needed at least a couple of hours sleep if he was going to be able to function tomorrow.

His thoughts drifted to Annabelle, all alone in her hospital room, scared and grieving. And he thought of the promise he had stupidly made to her just before the sedative had taken affect. He had promised her that he would find who had done this to her.

It was a ridiculous promise.

Right now they didn't have any leads, they didn't have any

clues, they didn't even know if this was personal against the Englewood family or if it was a random act.

Xavier knew he shouldn't have promised Annabelle that they would find the person who had destroyed her life when he knew he might not be able to deliver, yet he wasn't sorry that he had done it. He had wanted to ease her suffering, if only for a moment.

He wondered whether it was possible that he *was* falling for her. It had been so long since he had been on a date, or even been interested in a woman. Sometimes Kate tried to set him up, but usually he bailed before the actual date. His track record with women was disastrous; he didn't want to end up causing Annabelle to lose more than she already had.

And yet, he couldn't get her out of his mind.

As he tucked himself back into bed, he knew that he was going to dream about Annabelle again and the thought actually made him smile.

* * * * *

11:58 P.M.

"Eenie, meenie, miney moe, catch a tiger by the toe, if he hollers let him go, eenie, meenie, miney moe," he sang softly, his finger coming to rest on one of the faces in the photo he clutched.

Standing in the quiet living room of the next family on his list, he was even more excited than he had been last time. The Englewood family had been his first. He'd been excited but also a little apprehensive. He hadn't been entirely sure how things would go. He'd known it would bring satisfaction, but he hadn't been anticipating the rush he'd got seeing the blood.

This time he knew what to expect and that had him wound up all the tighter.

He couldn't wait. He was almost squirming as he set the photograph back down on top of the cabinet. He'd chosen which family member was going to survive. With the Englewoods, it had been easy, he'd always known it would be Annabelle. But this time he didn't really care, hence the game of 'eenie, meenie, miney moe.'

As he slipped down the hall to where the bedrooms were located at the back of the house, he wondered whether the family member left behind was the lucky one because they got to live, or the unlucky one because they didn't get to die with the rest of their family.

This time he had decided to go without the drugs, make things a little more interesting. And since it was the wife and mother who was to survive, it was also going to be fun killing the husband without her seeing anything important.

There were four members of the family: twelve-year-old Callie, fourteen-year-old Timothy, and parents, Henry and Nicole. He should be able to take out the kids easily enough—they were, after all, a lot smaller than him—and their rooms were a little away from their mom and dad's in order to give the parents some privacy.

Arriving at the door to the first room he opened it and took in the smells, the sights, the sounds—savoring every single second. He knew it would be all over way too soon.

Without hesitation, he crossed to the bed and before the boy even knew what was happening, he'd slit his throat.

That now familiar rush tingled through him as he watched the blood spill everywhere. This time he couldn't resist putting his hands in it, letting it slide all over him, enjoying the feel and the smell and the way it dribbled down his fingers like little red rivers. It was so beautiful.

However, he knew it was not the time to get distracted; there was more work to do.

With a few deft strokes of his knife, he removed the tongue

and the eyes. Mildly annoyed at the sawing it took to sever the hands, when it was done he set each eyeball in a hand and the tongue in between. When he was satisfied that the scene was perfect and that none of the other residents of the house were aware of his presence, he moved on to room number two.

The girl's room was next, just across the hall, her name spelled out in bright green letters across her door. Inside, the green theme continued—green walls, curtains, cover on the bed, and he couldn't help but feel a little queasy. Green did that to him sometimes, reminded him of something he'd much rather forget. Still the room wouldn't be green for long; soon it would be a bright, shining red.

Bending over the sleeping girl, his every nerve was aquiver with the expectation of what would soon happen. Lifting his knife, still glittering with the blood of young Timothy, he was about to bring it to little Callie's neck when the girl's eyes suddenly popped open, growing wide with horror when she saw him and even wider when she spotted the knife.

Suppressing a chuckle, he brought his finger to his lips to quiet the girl. Then before she could utter a sound or make an attempt at escape, he brought the knife to her neck, her blood mixing with her brother's as he slit her throat.

In the split second when she realized her life was gone, the shock and surprise that lit her eyes intrigued him. He hadn't seen it in the Englewoods because they had all been drugged, hadn't known what had happened to them, but that look was almost as intoxicating as the blood.

He'd have to bear that in mind next time. It was too late for this family. In order to kill the husband before alerting the wife, he'd have to do it quickly. But next time he just might have to alter his plan a little.

Finishing off the girl, he left the room and headed to finish off the job. Entering the parents' bedroom he drew a deep breath wanting to memorize every delicious second so he could replay it over and over again.

Then in the interest of making sure nothing went awry, he moved quickly to the bed, slicing the husband's throat before he had a chance to realize anything and thrash about.

Pleased when the wife remained asleep, he pulled the roll of duct tape from his pocket, cutting off a strip, he crossed to the other side of the bed. Excited about how this would work out, he slapped the tape down across Nicole's eyes. A fraction of a second later, the woman sprung awake, squawking in terror, her hands clawing, her legs kicking.

Without a word, he brought the blade of the knife to her neck. When she felt the cold, slick metal pressed against her flesh, she went instantly still. Since he planned on letting the woman live, he decided it was better not to speak. Instead, he plunged the knife into Nicole's shoulder, careful just as he had been with Annabelle not to hit anything vital.

The woman shrieked in pain, so he cut off another piece of tape to cover her mouth, smothering her howls so they were nothing more than muted whimpers. He looked on, enthralled as her chest rose unevenly with each gasped breath, as her pulse thumped in the hollow of her neck, as tears tried to force their way through the tape to wind down her cheeks.

As fun as it was to watch the woman's terror, he had to keep moving. So he proceeded to remove her husband's eyes, tongue and hands, positioning them in his special arrangement.

However, as he painted the blood on Nicole's feet, he felt himself losing control.

All he could see, all he could think about, was the beautiful thick liquid. He knew as surely as he knew he was here in this room that he had to be a part of it. He had to make it a part of him.

Before he even registered what he was doing, he had stripped off all his clothes and was scooping up handfuls of blood, rubbing it all over himself until he was pretty much covered from head to toe. Dancing and springing across the carpet, he ripped open the curtains so the moonlight streamed through, illuminating him and the glorious blood.

At last, as all good things did, he knew it had to come to an end. Checking to make sure Nicole was unconscious, he ripped off the tape from her eyes and mouth, threw his clothes back on over the top of the blood, then headed back downstairs.

Pausing at the phone, he dialed 911, then set it down on the table. The unanswered phone would eventually bring the police running. Then he walked back outside, climbed into his car, and drove away immensely satisfied.

One step closer to finishing his goal.

MAY 6TH

3:16 A.M.

"This one is worse," Diane cautioned them as they arrived at the Jenner crime scene. "A lot worse."

"How are we so sure that this is related to the Englewood murders?" Xavier asked. Images from his dream about Annabelle still lingered in his mind. For the first time in three years, he had been disappointed about being roused from sleep; his dream about Annabelle had been simple and fun and nice. Being woken by a phone call from his partner informing him that the man who killed the Englewood family had struck again had certainly put a damper on his peaceful mood, yet he couldn't help but feel pleased that they had another reason to visit Annabelle again.

"You'll see once we get inside," Diane replied glumly.

"So, we just wasted an entire day trying to track down someone with a grudge against the Englewood family," he sighed. After visiting Annabelle, they had spoken with every colleague, friend and family member they could find, but had come up empty—obviously this was why. It seemed like they had a serial killer at work.

"Only two days in between kills," Kate mused thoughtfully. "It feels like he's on a mission."

"We can always hope that he only had two families on his list," Xavier suggested halfheartedly. They all knew that this killer would never stop after only two kills. Probably would never stop until he was dead.

"Four members in the family?" Kate asked as they followed Diane inside.

"Uh huh," Diane confirmed. "Thirty-six-year-old Henry, thirty-four-year-old Nicole, twelve-year-old Callie, and fourteen-year-old Timothy."

"Who got left behind this time?" Xavier asked, noting that once again it looked like the only action was going to be in the bedrooms. The rest of the house looked undisturbed.

"The wife. She's pretty shaken up."

"Any sign of a break in?" he asked.

"Yeah, the glass panel on the back door was cut, so he probably came in that way. First responders said the front door was left wide open, so it looks like when he was done he walked straight out the door," Diane summarized.

"That kinda seems like working backwards," Kate frowned in puzzlement. "You'd think he would have broken in, and then worked up to stealing a key."

"Maybe he just found the Englewoods' Hide-A-Key," he suggested. "We can ask Annabelle when we see her next." Ignoring Kate's raised eyebrow at the mention of Annabelle, he continued. "*He* called it in this time," Xavier thought aloud. "He wanted us to find them immediately, wanted us to know what he'd been up to."

"Maybe he was planning on calling in the last one, only the neighbor beat him to it," Kate suggested.

"Bedrooms are down the back." Diane led them through the living room, dining room, kitchen, games room, and a den to where the bedrooms were situated. "Looks like he started with the boy." She led them into a room that could easily have been one of the ones from Annabelle's house.

The scene had been replicated perfectly.

Once again, there were no signs of a struggle. Both the bed and the boy were drenched in blood from the slit to his throat. The post-mortem mutilation was identical. "He drug them again, Diane?"

"No leftovers in the kitchen, but we've taken everything from the fridge and Billy will do a tox screen." Diane couldn't take her eyes off the boy's face.

"Where'd he go next?" Xavier asked gently.

Rousing herself with a shake, Diane crossed the hall. "Daughter's room." She opened a door across which green letters spelled out the name Callie. "She was only twelve, her brother only fourteen." Diane shook her head in disbelief. "I have three teenagers; what kind of person does this to kids?"

"The kind who's going to slip up eventually," he replied, hoping that was true.

Nodding somewhat halfheartedly, they all knew that the killer would likely kill a lot more people before he was caught or killed himself. Diane refocused herself. "Covers on Callie's bed are a little mussed. Maybe she woke up before he killed her. Might suggest that he didn't use drugs this time, or..." she sighed deeply, "...or maybe the girl was just a restless sleeper."

"So he takes out the kids first," Kate began thoughtfully, "instead of taking out the dad, the biggest physical threat. He leaves him till last and does the children first—pretty gutsy."

"Pretty stupid," Diane muttered under her breath.

"But it gives us a good insight into what makes him tick," Xavier added. "You said this scene was a lot worse than the Englewood murders. So far, everything looks identical."

"You haven't seen the parents' room yet." With a last look at Callie's lifeless body, Diane headed for the door. Passing through a small living room, which seemed to be used exclusively as a retreat for Henry and Nicole, then past a sparkly white bathroom complete with spa and double shower, a huge walk-in closet filled with enough clothing to clothe a small city, and finally entering the master bedroom.

Immediately, he saw what Diane had been talking about.

The room was literally covered in blood.

It was all over the walls and the carpet, there were drips of it spattering the curtains, the window and most of the furniture. It looked as though someone had smeared blood all over themselves and then danced around the room.

"He didn't do this last time," Xavier observed.

"Maybe he didn't realize how much he liked the blood until he'd seen it," Kate proposed.

"But he had to have killed before," he added. "He couldn't have just started with the Englewoods; he had to have worked up to it."

"Agreed," Kate nodded. "Maybe he hasn't killed with a knife before. Didn't know how much he'd like the sight of the blood, but I'd say now that he's tried it he's definitely enamored. Anything else different this time, other than all the blood?"

"Everything else appears to be the same. Nicole Jenner was already on her way to the hospital by the time I got here, but the first responders said she had a stab wound to her shoulder, just like Annabelle Englewood. They also said she was semi-conscious. They asked her if she saw who attacked her but all she could say was 'blood,'" Diane explained.

"Greetings," a voice spoke behind them.

They all turned to see a very haggard looking Billy standing in the open doorway. "Hey, Billy," Xavier greeted the medical examiner. "You look terrible."

"Oh, and you look like a meadow," Billy snapped, then softened. "Sorry it's been a long day and an even longer night. Why do hot days always mean more crime, and almost summer, a broken arm?"

"One of your kids break an arm?" Kate asked.

"Yes. Bike riding. Apparently Felicity thought it would be a great idea to try and jump her bike over her little sister, suffice it to say all did not end well. So…" His gaze flitted to Henry Jenner's body and the blood that dressed the room. "I guess it's safe to say this conclusively counts Annabelle out as a suspect. She was safely tucked away at the hospital, and she would have no reason to have the Jenner family killed." He raised a challenging eyebrow.

"I'm convinced," Diane joined in with Billy's challenge.

"Me too." Xavier was positive that Annabelle was not involved. They all turned their attention to Kate.

"Hey, I'm not the enemy. I agree. I don't think that Annabelle is involved in any way other than as a victim," Kate surrendered.

"Which means we are definitely hunting a serial killer."

* * * * *

8:00 A.M.

"Right on time," Robert smiled at them all; their boss had a thing for punctuality.

She yawned so widely it felt like it split her face in two, she was exhausted already and it was only eight in the morning. "Billy, you get anything yet?" Kate knew there wasn't enough time for Billy to have done full autopsies, but she also knew that he would have done something, and right now they needed anything to point them in a direction. Any direction would be good at this point.

"No drugs in their systems," Billy looked even more tired than he had earlier.

"Any drugs in the food?" Xavier asked Diane.

"No, food was clean this time," the CSU tech replied.

"Maybe he was nervous the first time," Xavier suggested. "It was his first, and he might have been worried about someone waking up and ruining things. The Englewood murders went smoothly, so he gained confidence and decided he didn't need to bother with the drugs this time."

"What else was different this time?" Rob queried.

"He called it in himself," Kate explained. "Well, at least he dialed nine-one-one on his way out, and when the operator got no response but the line remained open, they sent a car over."

"Prints on the phone?" Rob directed his question to Diane.

She nodded. "Yes, but so far no luck matching them with anyone in AFIS. In fact, there are prints and fibers all over the place. Most of them are probably not related to the case, but we're matching everything we have with what we collected from the Englewood house. It doesn't seem like this guy is afraid of being caught."

Kate nodded in agreement; she was getting the exact same feeling about their killer. "It feels like he's on some kind of mission."

"You think we have a spree killer?" Xavier asked.

"I think that we have a killer who has a particular goal in mind and isn't going to stop until he's accomplished it," she replied, trying to best articulate what she was feeling.

"You don't think he chose these families at random?" Rob asked.

"No, I think he chose them for a specific purpose. We just have to figure out what that purpose is." They all knew that was going to be easier said than done.

"It's hard to get a read on this guy," Xavier tapped his pen as he spoke. "On the one hand, he seems to be organized; he brings his own weapons, he kills methodically replicating the scene over and over, he gets into and out of the houses unseen, and although he seems to leave fingerprints and stuff behind, he seems to know it won't lead us to him. Yet, on the other hand, he seems to lose control whenever he sees blood, so much so that he smeared himself in it and danced around the Jenner master bedroom."

"You think these murders are the guy's first and that's why he's not in the system?" Diane asked.

"It seems hard to believe he could go from nothing to murder overnight," Billy looked doubtful.

"I think he knows we're not going to catch him through forensics," Xavier replied.

"I think when we find out why he's doing this, we'll find him," Kate proposed. "He's not killing for profit; nothing was stolen from either the Englewood or the Jenner house. I don't think he's killing for the thrill of it. He seems to not even want his victims to know they're about to die, killing them in their sleep. Maybe he's killing for control, which could be why he always leaves one family member alive. Or maybe," she paused and cast her partner an anxious glance, "his motives are sexual."

Xavier tensed instantly and went completely still, the others joined her in watching him warily. "Were any of the victims raped?" he asked tightly.

"Katherine and Kathy Englewood weren't and neither was Callie Jenner," Billy assured him.

"Hospital said Nicole Jenner wasn't either," Diane added.

"What about Annabelle?" Xavier demanded fiercely.

Too fiercely, Kate thought, and worried once again that her partner was falling for Annabelle Englewood. She did not want to see history repeat itself. It was nothing personal against Annabelle; she was sure the girl was a lovely person, as every single friend and colleague they had interviewed had attested. But Xavier was not in a position to be helping anyone deal with trauma right now, and Annabelle was going to need a lot of help to get through her family's murders. Plus, from Annabelle's point of view, she was pretty sure that Xavier would be about the last person in the world she would want to help her come to terms with all that had happened, since he had accused her of murder.

"I don't know," Diane replied, then continued quickly, "when she was admitted to the hospital, they thought she had just slaughtered her family then attempted suicide. Under those circumstances, there was no need for a rape kit."

Xavier swallowed audibly. "We'll ask her when we speak with her again, but if Nicole Jenner wasn't raped, then chances are Annabelle wasn't either." Xavier sounded like he was trying to convince himself.

"All right," Rob began to summarize so he had things straight in his head, "so method of murder was the same, same post-mortem mutilation…"

"He used a hacksaw to cut off the hands, but probably just an everyday carving knife to slit their throats and remove the tongue and eyeballs," Billy inserted. "It was pretty crudely done; this guy didn't have any medical training."

Rob nodded, taking this in, then resumed, "…and he left one family member alive both times. He painted the feet again, Diane?"

"Yes, paintbrush hairs in the bed and blood pools, same as there were with Annabelle."

"Okay," Rob continued, "but this time he breaks in, he calls it in himself, and he goes crazy and dances in the blood."

"And he used tape to cover Nicole's eyes and mouth," Diane added. "The hospital said there was irritation in the skin around the mouth, and her eyelashes had been pulled out. He didn't do that last time; I guess since he didn't use drugs, she woke up while he was killing the husband."

"So far our best bet at finding this guy are Annabelle and Nicole," Rob stood. "Kate, Xavier—talk to them, try and get them to remember something. Then re-interview friends and family of the Englewoods and interview friends and family of the Jenners, see if anyone matches up. There has to be a link there somewhere."

* * * * *

10:27 A.M.

She couldn't take one more second of these people looking at her.

Annabelle needed to get away. She needed to be someplace where she could be by herself. And here at the hospital that was all but impossible.

Every time the doctors and nurses came to check on her, they looked at her with such pity that it made her want to scream. She was beginning to wish they just looked at her accusingly again like they had when everyone thought she was a killer. Annabelle wasn't used to people feeling sorry for her or fussing over her; she had been self-sufficient ever since she was about five. It made her uncomfortable when people paid her too much attention.

Climbing out of bed, Annabelle didn't even care that she had no clothes to wear, the hospital pajamas would do till she got home.

"Annabelle, what are you doing out of bed?"

Spinning toward the door, her face fell when she saw who was standing there.

"You shouldn't be up." Dr. Daniels came and took her arm, attempting to maneuver her back into the bed.

She shook him off. "I'm leaving," she announced a lot more forcefully than she felt. If she could just get out of this hospital, then she was sure she could sort through the tangle of emotions tying themselves into knots inside her.

"You're not ready to go home yet." The doctor reclaimed her arm and managed to get her halfway back to the bed.

"Well, I'm leaving anyway." Annabelle disengaged herself once more and took a determined step away, hoping that he wouldn't push her too much; she always caved when someone pressured her.

"You know you can't go back to your house," Dr. Daniels changed track, "it's still a crime scene."

She cringed as she thought of the bloody mess her home must be. The home where she had lived her entire life. She still couldn't believe that her parents were dead, and her brothers and her baby sister. That she had been left completely and utterly alone. It just didn't feel real. She kept expecting to wake up at any second.

While she couldn't change what had happened by wishing, she could at least give herself space to deal with it. "I need to go," she didn't have enough energy to hide the begging from her voice. "I need to get out of here. I'm okay now, my shoulder doesn't hurt too bad, I can take care of myself…I just need to be away from here," she finished desperately.

Dr. Daniels wavered. "I don't know, Annabelle." He was studying her with kind blue eyes. "I'd rather you stayed here for another day or two."

"Well, I'm not," she stood her ground defiantly. She was alone now, and she was going to have to learn to stand up for herself. "I'm not asking for your permission. I'll sign myself out, absolve you of any responsibility if something goes wrong, but I'm leaving whether you like it or not." She liked Dr. Daniels, he was nice and he'd been very kind to her, but she wasn't going to let him dictate her life.

"Well, if you're sure I can't talk you out of it, then okay," he sighed reluctantly. "But you'll have to stay in a motel, and I want you to make sure you come back in a week to let me check on your shoulder, and if you have any problems you can call me on this number," he jotted down a number on a scrap of paper. "Any time, day or night."

"Thank you," Annabelle smiled in relief. She wasn't sure she would have been able to fight for what she wanted if he had put up even a little more of a fight. Annabelle hated that she always needed people to be happy with her, even if it meant missing out or backing down if she knew she was right.

"I'll get you something to wear," he eyed her thin hospital pajamas. "Wait here."

"Thank you," she called to the doctor's disappearing back. While she waited, she sat on the bed swinging her dangling legs and keeping her mind carefully empty. She didn't want to think about things right now, because if she did, she was terribly afraid she would lose control and never be able to get it back.

"Here you go," Dr. Daniels appeared in front of her holding out a pair of sweat pants and a t-shirt. "I called you a cab."

"Why are you being so nice to me?" she asked. "You don't

even know me and I'm sure you have hundreds of patients to deal with every day. Why are you looking out for me?"

"Because you're a nice girl who's just been through hell," he answered, his gaze taking on a deadly serious glint that made her turn away. "Call me when you've decided where you're staying."

"Why?"

"So when those detectives come back looking for you, I can tell them where you are."

She was instantly hit by a rocketing wave of rage.

Right now, Annabelle hated those detectives more than anyone else on the planet. She didn't remember what had happened the night her family had been murdered and she didn't know who had hurt her so she couldn't be angry with that person, whoever he may be. She was angry with her parents and her brothers for leaving her alone again. However, they were gone, so being angry with them didn't really do any good. But the detectives had been the ones who had told her that her family was gone and then accused her of doing it, so they were an easy target for her anger to hone in on.

She remembered the last time they had been here, telling her that they had changed their minds and they didn't think she was a killer anymore, acting like she ought to thank them for this change of heart. They'd asked her to help them like she owed them something, and then they'd implied that someone she knew was capable of killing her family in cold blood. The male detective, she thought his name was Xavier Montague, had promised her that he would find the man who had tried to frame her for her family's murders, but she didn't want to find him; she just wanted to pretend that none of this had ever happened.

"I'll let you know when I get there," she answered tightly, taking the clothes from his outstretched hand and slipping into the bathroom. She managed, with some difficulty, to change out of the pajamas and into the outfit Dr. Daniels had scrounged up for her. When she emerged, she was surprised to see that the doctor was still standing in her room.

"You need money for a cab," he held out a wad of cash.

"I can't take that," she protested.

"Of course you can. You didn't ask; I offered," he continued to hold out his hand.

Hesitantly she took it, only because she didn't have any of her own money or credit cards on her. "I'll pay you back," she promised.

"You don't have to."

"I want to, when I come back to let you check my shoulder," she countered adamantly.

"Okay, whatever you want," he smiled at her shyly.

She hoped the doctor hadn't developed a crush on her. The doctor was good-looking; in fact, he was more than good-looking. He was handsome and well built, kind of like a hunky TV doctor. But Annabelle didn't date. Ever. "Thanks again," she gave an awkward smile and made a move for the door.

"Be careful, Annabelle," Dr. Daniels called out. "Don't take any chances."

Catching something in his voice, she froze. "Has something else happened?"

"This guy has struck again," the doctor told her. "Another family killed. This time he left behind the wife."

She felt the blood drain from her head in a rush, leaving her brain feeling like it was floating through the clouds. "He did it again?" she repeated faintly.

"Annabelle," the doctor began anxiously, "you look pale. I don't think it's a good idea for you to…"

Annabelle never heard the rest of his sentence, because she turned and began to jog towards the exit. A couple of minutes later she burst out of the hospital's doors and drank in the fresh air, felt the sun on her skin, and saw the deep blue summer sky.

For a second Annabelle felt like bursting into tears, but she resolutely pushed those feelings away, squared her shoulders, and determinedly faced the world.

* * * * *

1:34 P.M.

"What're you thinking about?" Kate asked Xavier. Her partner had been uncharacteristically quiet today.

Xavier shrugged.

"Let me guess, Annabelle Englewood."

Glaring at her with his piercing hazel eyes, "I was thinking about Annabelle as she relates to the *case*, yes."

"Xavier…"

"We're here," her partner cut her off as he pulled the car to a stop outside a modest two-story house.

The home they'd just arrived at belonged to Lachlan Thompson, Nicole Jenner's father. Kate wasn't relishing the prospect of talking to the man who had just lost his son-in-law, his two grandchildren, and almost lost his only daughter.

"The topic of Annabelle is not closed," she warned Xavier as they both climbed from the car and walked down the short garden path to the front door.

Xavier knocked, and as they waited Kate studied the beautiful garden; obviously Lachlan was quite the avid gardener. The place was full of flowers, most of which she had no idea of the names, but she spotted a couple of roses by the front gate. Her husband, David, was the designated yard tender at their house, but this garden was almost inspiring her to go home and plan something special for her own garden.

"Yes?" The door flew open and a stony face stared back at them.

"Mr. Thompson?" Kate asked.

"Yes."

"I'm Detective Hannah and this is Detective Montague; we

need to talk to you about what happened last night. May we come in?" she added when the man made no move to allow them entry to his home.

"I'm pretty busy at the moment."

Trying not to let her brow crinkle disapprovingly, she knew people dealt with grief in all kinds of ways. "Actually, it's very important that we speak with you now. The man who killed your son-in-law and grandchildren has already done this once before. We're hoping that you might be able to help us establish a link between your family and the previous family that might lead us to who this man might be," she explained patiently.

He exhaled deeply. "Fine." Lachlan Thompson stood back to allow them passage into his house.

The inside of the house, while nicely furnished, was plain. There were no personal touches, no paintings or photos on the walls, no knick-knacks on shelves, no newspapers or magazines lying about, nothing to give any indication of who the person was who lived here. What Kate found most strange, though, was that there was not a single picture of his daughter or grandchildren to be seen. If she hadn't known better, she would have thought this man was completely alone in the world.

Reaching the living room, Lachlan sunk sullenly into a well-worn armchair. "Go. Ask your questions."

She exchanged a discreet glance with Xavier, who nodded, indicating she should continue with the questioning. "We're very sorry for your loss," she began.

"Well, I'm not," Lachlan spat venomously.

Caught by surprise, Kate couldn't stop her mouth from falling open. "I beg your pardon?"

"I never liked that Henry Jenner." His face was dark, his blue eyes cold, and he crossed arms like tree trunks over a chest so muscled his t-shirt barely stretched across it. "And I'm not sorry he's dead."

"He's not the only one who is dead, sir," Xavier spoke up, his hazel eyes hot with anger. "So are your daughter's children."

Lachlan shrugged indifferently, "They're his children, too."

"And they were viciously murdered in their own beds," Kate reminded him. She wanted to add that his daughter was now a widow who had lost her entire family in one night, but she was pretty sure his comeback would be that Nicole was better off without her husband.

"I said I'd answer your questions," Lachlan bit back.

"Have you ever met or heard your daughter mention anyone with the last name Englewood?" Xavier asked.

"Never heard that name before."

"John Englewood is an electrician; do you know if Nicole had any electrical work done at her house recently?"

"I don't know."

"Annabelle Englewood is a teacher; do you know if she's a teacher at the school your grandchildren attend or attended?"

"Not a clue."

She produced a picture of the Englewood family. "Do you recognize any of these people?" Kate asked.

He hardly bothered to glance at the picture, "I've never seen them before."

"You didn't even look," Xavier glared.

Huffing, Lachlan pulled out a pair of glasses, slipped them on, snatched the photo and studied it for a full minute. "I've never seen them before," he repeated, practically throwing the photo back. "Look, I don't have much to do with Nicole's family. We don't have dinner, we don't spend Christmas together, and I don't see them on their birthdays. It's been close to two years since I last saw that man and his children."

"What about Nicole? Do you see your daughter?"

"We have lunch occasionally."

"Can I ask what happened to make you hate your son-in-law so deeply that you're willing to give up being a part of your grandchildren's lives?" Kate couldn't imagine anything coming between her and her family. Neither of her parents had been happy when she had announced at age eight that she was going to be a police officer when she grew up, but they had supported her when she turned eighteen and entered the academy. And when her older sister had dropped out of school at sixteen after declaring she was deeply in love with her eighteen-year-old-ex-con-high-school-dropout-boyfriend, and turned her backs on all of them; they had all been thrilled when she had finally returned. Five years later, with two children in tow, Lisa had realized what a mistake she'd made, and returned to her family because she knew they would help her no matter what. Kate hadn't wanted to settle and start her own family until she'd known that she'd met someone who valued family as much as she did. She knew David was that person.

"Henry Jenner took my daughter away from me," Lachlan answered simply. "My wife died when Nicole was four; I raised her myself. She was my daughter, and she should have stayed here with me, and then nothing like this could ever have happened."

"But he never laid a hand on her or the children?" Kate asked, feeling completely creeped out by this man, and wondering whether Lachlan had attempted to replace his dead wife with his daughter, and just how far he had gone to do that.

"Not so far as I know." Lachlan was quickly becoming even more disinterested in tolerating them.

"Where were you last night around midnight?" Xavier demanded.

Exploding, "I don't have to answer that," Lachlan roared. "It's time for you to leave."

Following him to the front door, "Your daughter's going to need all the support she can to get through this." Kate had to force the words out, not sure how much help this angry, bitter, potentially dangerous man would be to his traumatized daughter. But it seemed as though Nicole still loved her father or she wouldn't continue to spend time with him knowing how much he hated her husband.

"If she admits she was wrong to leave home and marry that man and apologizes, then she can come back," Lachlan announced before slamming the door in their faces.

"You think he's involved?" she asked Xavier as they climbed back into the car.

"I wouldn't put it past him," Xavier started the engine. "He didn't shed a single tear over his dead family or show an ounce of sympathy for his daughter. I don't like him. It's possible that he could have killed the Englewoods as a diversion, make us think it was a serial killer and give him cover to get rid of the son-in-law he hates so his daughter had no choice but to come home."

Kate was as yet undecided about whether or not Lachlan Thompson was involved but she definitely disliked the man as much as her partner.

"How about we grab some lunch," she suggested as her stomach growled loudly, "and then go get some answers from Nicole Jenner."

* * * * *

3:16 P.M.

"You think she'll talk about him?" Xavier asked Kate as they strode through the hospital towards Nicole Jenner's room.

"About her father?" Kate asked.

"Uh huh."

"I guess it depends on how much she loves him versus how obligated she feels towards him."

Xavier was tired, too many days with too little sleep, but he was glad that Kate hadn't peppered him with more questions about Annabelle during lunch. He was thinking about Annabelle enough on his own without having his partner constantly bringing her up. Knowing that she was just rooms away was making his heart thump faster than he'd have liked.

On their way to the hospital, they'd had Lachlan Thompson checked out and it turned out that the guy had quite a temper. He'd had arguments with colleagues that had gotten physical, a few fights at the local bar, and there was an incident several years ago with a sales assistant at a golf store. Xavier wasn't positive that Lachlan was the killer, but he also wasn't positive that he wasn't.

"We're here," Kate announced, coming to a stop outside room 216.

Sensing something in his partner's voice, he stopped, too. "You thinking about her relationship with her dad?"

"Yeah."

"What's wrong?" he asked immediately after catching the slight tremble in Kate's lip.

"I was just thinking how lucky I was to have such a great father," she smiled up at him.

He squeezed her arm, "Is anything else bothering you?"

"It's just sad that so many kids don't have a great dad or mom. I wonder if Nicole Jenner's life would have turned out differently if her mom hadn't died," Kate explained.

He nodded his agreement, but it did no good to speculate, this was the hand life had dealt Nicole Jenner and one way or another she had to deal with it. Remaining unconvinced, though, that it was all his partner had on her mind, he let it go for now and pushed open the door.

A quick flash of Annabelle lying in her hospital room the first time they'd talk to her flashed into his head. He remembered the hate and anger he'd been barely able to control as he'd looked at the woman he'd believed had just slaughtered her entire family.

Focusing his mind on the present, Xavier quietly assessed the woman in the bed. Thirty-four years old, a little chubby, obviously her personal appearance was not too important to Nicole. Still, she was pretty, with big brown eyes and long dark hair. She had milky white skin and little crinkles around her eyes that implied she spent a lot of time smiling.

"Mrs. Jenner?" he spoke softly as he approached, not wanting to startle the woman.

A pair of red-rimmed brown eyes turned to look at him. "Yes?"

"I'm Detective Montague and this is Detective Hannah. We need to ask you a couple of questions about what happened; do you think you're up for that?"

"I guess," Nicole answered uncertainly, her gaze wandering back to the window.

"Did you get a look at the man who hurt you?" Kate asked, taking a seat beside the bed.

Shaking her head, sending tears spilling down her cheeks. "Not really."

"Not really?" he repeated, taking a seat beside Kate. "So you saw something?"

"I'm not sure," Nicole hesitated, her hands moving subconsciously to her eyes.

"Did you see something before he put the tape on your eyes?" Xavier asked gently.

"No, I woke up when he put the tape over my eyes."

Nicole began to tremble and before he realized what he was doing, he had reached out and taken her hand. "But you saw something?" he pressed.

Bobbing her head. "When I woke up and realized someone was in the room, I started lashing out, trying to fight them off…" Her voice hitched but Nicole focused her eyes on a spot on the ceiling and continued. "He put a knife against my neck and I went still. I thought if I kept still he might not kill me but…" She began to lose control again, "…but I could feel something wet and sticky in the bed, I knew it was Henry's blood…"

They let her cry for a moment before Kate rested a hand on the woman's shoulder. "What happened next, Nicole?"

Speaking through her tears, Nicole continued, "He stabbed me, I cried out and he put tape over my mouth. Then it felt like...like he was painting something on my feet." Her eyes met theirs. "Was it my husband's blood? Did he paint my husband's blood on my feet?"

"Yes, he did," Xavier told her truthfully.

She processed that. "Why would he do that?"

"We don't know," Kate told her. "But he's done this before and he's probably going to do it again, so anything you can tell us might help us catch him."

That seemed to give Nicole a purpose, so she steeled herself and resumed, "He hung around for a while. I could hear him; he was breathing really heavily and I kept wondering if he was going to...if he was going to... going to...rape me," her resolve fumbled, trying to hold on to a semblance of composure. "But he didn't. I think that he covered himself in the blood and then danced around."

"Why do you say that?" Xavier asked, trying to block out any thoughts of rape that seeped into his brain. Ever since Julia had been raped and their life together had fallen apart, he had been particularly sensitive to the vicious crime. The thought that Annabelle might have been raped too left him feeling like someone had dumped a bucket of burning coals in his stomach.

"I could feel the bed dipping as he leaned all over it, then I could hear him jumping about, our floorboards creaking. Then I heard him open the curtains before coming toward me, I lay really still, tried to breathe evenly through the pain so he thought I was unconscious. He pulled off the tape, and as he was leaving I peeked..."

"Did you get a look at him?" Xavier hardly dared to breathe as he waited for her answer.

"I couldn't see him well, he was covered in blood, but he was tall and really muscled," Nicole finished tiredly, her energy beginning to fail. "When he left the room, I was so scared that he was still in the house that I didn't get up to check on the kids."

That description could fit her father. "Have you noticed anyone hanging around your house the last few weeks?" Xavier asked.

"No."

"Any letters, emails, phone calls in which you felt threatened, or that seemed in any way unusual?"

"No."

Remembering what Ricky Preston claimed to have seen outside the Englewood house, he asked, "What about a red car parked outside your house?"

"No. Why? Do you think that he was watching our house?"

"Someone reported seeing a red car outside the Englewood home a couple of days before they were killed," he explained. "Do you know anyone named Englewood?"

"I don't think so."

"John Englewood was an electrician; have you had any work done recently?"

"No."

"Kathy Englewood was a bank teller; do you remember anyone with that name at the bank you usually use?"

"No."

"Any teachers at your children's school with the name Annabelle Englewood?"

"No," Nicole's voice hitched this time at the mention of the son and daughter she had just lost.

"Okay," Kate soothed, "have you received any threats from friends or colleagues or neighbors?"

"No."

"What about family?" Kate asked carefully.

Nicole Jenner's eyes grew guarded. "You mean my father? You talked to him?"

"He wasn't very upset about the deaths of his grandchildren," Xavier replied.

"He hasn't been to see me yet," Nicole's bottom lip wobbled and she took on a child-like vulnerability.

"Your father told us your mom died when you were little," Kate pressed on.

"I was four."

"That must have been tough."

Nicole nodded. "I hardly remember her now; I was so young."

"So it was just you and your dad when you were growing up?"

"Yes," she gulped, obviously anticipating where this topic of conversation was veering.

"Did your father ever hurt you, Nicole?"

"He was lonely," she whispered. "I was all he had."

Xavier took that as an affirmative. "Did he hit you?" he asked gently. "Did he make you do things you didn't want to do?"

Her eyes grew shuttered, not wanting to deal with childhood trauma on top of everything else.

"Has your father ever threatened you, Nicole?" he continued.

"He said if I didn't leave Henry and the kids that he would cut me out of his will," she wavered. "He got a huge settlement when my mom died while undergoing surgery, he never spent most of it," Nicole explained. "He's dying of cancer, he wanted me to move back and stay with him until he died."

The fact that he was dying jumped Lachlan Thompson up several notches on the suspect scale. If he was dying, he may be motivated to rid Nicole of what he perceived to be the baggage that prevented her from coming home to him, possibly pushing him into taking drastic action. The fact that he was dying also meant he had nothing to lose.

"My father would never do something like this," Nicole told them seriously.

"Is there anything else you can think of?" Kate asked.

"No, I've told you everything I remember. But I mean it; my dad may not be the nicest person, but he's not a killer. You believe me, right?"

Before Xavier could respond, the door swung open, "I think that is enough for today," Dr. Daniels announced.

Apparently, the man was Nicole Jenner's doctor as well as Annabelle's. "We'll talk to you later," Xavier told Nicole, trying to release his hand from Nicole's grip.

"Detective Montague?"

"Yeah?"

"Are you going to find him? The man who did this?"

"Yeah, we are," he assured the woman, wishing he could stop making promises to victims that he knew he couldn't necessarily keep.

Satisfied, Nicole released his hand and let her heavy eyes fall closed, and both he and Kate followed Dr. Daniels out the door.

"How's Annabelle doing?" Xavier asked once they were back in the corridor.

"Actually, she's pretty exhausted. I don't want you interviewing her today; she needs to rest," Dr. Daniels challengingly arched an eyebrow.

Xavier exchanged a glance with Kate, "We can interview more relatives of the Jenners today and speak with Annabelle in the morning," she proposed.

He nodded his agreement, "Tell her we'll be here early in the morning," he informed the doctor. Once they were out of earshot, he turned to his partner, "Lachlan Thompson is looking pretty good."

Kate nodded, "Let's see if we can get a few more people to corroborate his intense dislike of his son-in-law and maybe we'll have enough for a warrant to get his fingerprints. We get that and we match them to the ones from the Englewood and Jenner homes and we could have our guy before anyone else gets hurt."

"Let's just hope it goes that smoothly." Xavier wanted to give some measure of peace to Nicole and Annabelle. And, as much as he hated to admit it, the first thought that had jumped into his mind was that once they found the killer, there would be nothing left standing between him and Annabelle.

MAY 7TH

7:48 A.M.

"I'd feel a lot better about things if we could find a link between the Englewoods and the Jenners," Kate was saying as they once again plodded their way through the hospital.

"If Lachlan Thompson really did kill the Englewoods to cover getting rid of his daughter's family, then he had to have crossed paths with them someplace. Hopefully Annabelle can shed some light on the how, when, and where." Xavier was hoping that Annabelle had calmed down enough to help them.

"Detectives," Dr. Daniels suddenly appeared before them, "may I help you?"

Xavier was beginning to dislike this man who kept popping up at inopportune times and wondered whether the doctor had been standing outside Nicole's room yesterday listening to their entire conversation.

"We're here to see Annabelle," he informed the doctor.

"Annabelle's gone," Dr. Daniels stated calmly.

Fear spiked his blood pressure. "What do you mean gone?" Xavier demanded. Had her condition changed and suddenly become more serious than they'd thought and she had died? Or had the killer come back to finish her off? Images of every horrible thing that could have befallen the girl rushed through his mind.

"I mean, she's not here," the doctor rephrased.

"Do you know what happened to her?" Kate jumped in to ask calmly before he had a chance to grab the doctor by the collar and shake answers out of him.

"Yes," Dr. Daniels was studying them with a probing stare. "She left."

"Left?" Xavier echoed, overwhelmed by a sense of loss at the prospect he may never see her again. Of course, that was ridiculous on so many levels. As a victim in a case he was working, he would continue to see her until they caught the killer and the case was closed. And even if he never saw her again, that shouldn't bother him. They didn't even know each other.

"Where did she go?" Kate asked.

"She wanted to go home..." Dr. Daniels began.

"Her house is a crime scene; she can't go back there," Xavier interrupted.

"I know that," Dr. Daniels shot him a withering frown. "She went to a motel."

Getting the feeling that the doctor was deliberately yanking them around, Xavier asked, "Do you know which motel?"

"Yes. I called her a cab and lent her some money, and told her to call me when she was settled in case you two came back to speak with her again." The doctor's scowl made it clear he thought they were harassing and not just speaking with Annabelle.

"When did she leave?" Kate queried.

"Yesterday morning."

"Yesterday morning," Xavier spluttered. "Why didn't you tell us that when we were here yesterday afternoon?"

"Because I thought she needed a break," Dr. Daniels' face turned a bright shade of red. "You've already harassed her twice, both times I needed to sedate her. She's just lost her entire family, you accused her of being a killer, then changed your mind, then came back and dumped a truckload of questions on her when she was in no condition to deal with them. She needed a break. I wanted to let her have some time to try to sort things out before you unleashed another tirade on her. *I* knew she was not a killer from the second they brought her in," he announced adamantly. "Anyone with such amazing eyes could never take a life."

He felt a stab of unexpected jealousy that another man was noticing Annabelle's unusual eyes. Xavier was really going to have to let go of this crush he was developing on a woman who he didn't even know and who probably hated his guts.

"You should have told us this yesterday, Dr. Daniels," Xavier reprimanded sternly. "She's a witness in a murder case, not to mention the fact that the man who did this is still out there. What if he were to find her when she was alone and completely unprotected?"

The doctor's face paled at the thought. "I didn't want to put her in danger; I was just trying to protect her."

Xavier was pleased that he had managed to upset the doctor. "She's just been through a major trauma. What if the psychological stress was to get overwhelming and she attempted to hurt herself?" Xavier goaded, even more pleased when the doctor's face paled further. "Have you got the name of the motel where she's staying?"

Sullenly, the doctor answered, "Yes." He fished a bit of paper from his pocket and thrust it in their direction.

"Thank you, Dr. Daniels," Kate smiled. "You take good care of Nicole Jenner."

"I will." The doctor's face switched immediately to fiercely protective.

"Have a nice day." Kate kept her smile in place as the doctor rolled his eyes and hurried off.

"I don't like that guy," Xavier muttered as they backtracked to the car. "He's creepy."

"You think he's got something to hide?" Kate asked.

"I think he's way too interested in Annabelle Englewood."

Kate smirked. "Is that your professional or personal opinion?"

Xavier became serious. "He barged in twice, both when we were interviewing Annabelle and then again with Nicole. I think he was listening to what we were saying, to what *they* were saying. When we were talking to Annabelle the second time and she became hysterical, he came in prepared with a syringe of sedatives. How would he have known Annabelle was hysterical unless he was listening? Maybe he suffers from something like Munchausen Syndrome. Sets up these women to need him and then swoops in as their savior. I don't know," he finished helplessly, wanting a definite direction to move in so he could finally feel like he was doing something. "I just think we should keep an eye on him."

* * * * *

8:36 A.M.

"Thanks so much for coming." Annabelle didn't know what she'd do without Ricky.

"Any time," he smiled at her, his blue eyes twinkling comfortingly. "Anything else you need?

"No, I think you've got me everything." Annabelle wondered how she was ever going to repay her neighbor, Ricky Preston, for everything that he'd done for her. When she'd arrived at the motel yesterday, she'd placed a call to her friend and asked him if he could lend her a little money, just until she'd gotten her purse back from her house and had access to her accounts and credit cards again.

Annabelle had felt embarrassed turning to him for help, but Ricky had assured her it was no problem and turned up at her motel room a couple of hours later with food, toiletries, and clothes. Overwhelmed by his generosity, Annabelle had been mortified to find herself bursting into tears. Ricky hadn't seemed to mind; he'd just held her as she cried, and then made her something to eat.

They'd chatted all through the afternoon and for a while it had felt like old times with her friend, and Annabelle had been almost able to forget what had happened.

She remembered what her brother, Paul, had told her one day

not that long ago, that he thought their neighbor had a crush on her. Annabelle had been embarrassed. Had protested that she and Ricky were simply friends, but to herself she had prayed it wasn't true. Ricky was about her only friend and she didn't want to lose him if he found out she wasn't interested in him that way.

Throughout the afternoon, Ricky had been nothing but a kind and generous friend, nothing in his behavior or attitude indicated that he thought of her as anything more. When he'd made a move to leave, Annabelle had found herself absolutely terrified at the prospect of being alone. Ricky had seemed to sense that and offered to let her stay in his spare bedroom until she sorted things out.

Of course, she had refused; she hadn't wanted to lean on anyone for support. She was, after all, a self-reliant girl. In the end, though, her fear of being alone had won out and she'd asked if he'd mind spending the night on the couch here at the motel with her. Ricky had happily obliged and spent the night on the couch. The comforting sound of his snoring had been all that had gotten her through the night.

"Oh no," Annabelle groaned. Through the window, she caught sight of two people approaching her room.

"What is it?" Ricky asked, instantly concerned.

"Those detectives are back," she replied.

"The ones who accused you of being a killer?" Ricky's face grew dark. "I met them. You want me to get rid of them for you?"

She sighed. As much as Detective Montague and Detective Hannah were the last people on the planet she wanted to see right now, she knew it would only be putting off the inevitable to refuse to see them now. "No, that's okay," she assured him.

"You want me to stay with you?" Ricky asked as a knock sounded on the door.

Taking a deep breath, she said, "Thanks, but I can manage." Drawing up every ounce of strength she could muster, she opened the door. "Good morning, detectives."

"Good morning, Miss Englewood," Detective Montague returned formally, his face completely passive, but his eyes assessed her carefully.

"We were wondering if we could ask you a few more questions," Detective Hannah explained.

"Of course," she held the door open wider to allow them entry.

"Are you sure you don't want me to stay with you, Annabelle?" Ricky asked.

"No, I'm fine," she replied, noticing how Detective Montague froze when he noticed the man in her room.

"All right, I'll be going then." He crossed to her and held her by the shoulders, careful to avoid her injured one. "You call me if you need anything, or if you want me to spend the night again. And the offer still stands, my spare room is available for as long as you need it."

"Thanks, Ricky," Annabelle smiled, wondering whether she'd take him up on his offer but knowing she most likely would not.

"You're welcome," he grinned, and gave her a tender kiss on the forehead, before turning to catch the detectives in a glare. "You take it easy on her, she's been through hell," he warned them as he headed for the door.

"I thought you said you weren't involved with Ricky Preston," Detective Montague spoke tightly once they were alone.

Annabelle saw the look his partner shot him and wondered with horror whether Detective Montague was interested in her. If he was, then he was in for some bad news; Annabelle didn't date.

Ever.

No matter how hot the guy was. And Detective Montague was even better looking than Dr. Daniels.

Even if she *did* date, right now this man was the focus of all her pent up anger, so any hope he had of becoming involved with her was absolutely and completely futile.

"I'm not," she answered simply. "I told you we were just friends. I called him yesterday and asked if he could lend me some money until I got my purse back. I was intending to go shopping myself but Ricky brought me clothes and food. We spent the afternoon talking, and then he slept on the couch because I was scared to stay by myself." She tried to keep her voice as emotionless as possible, desperately wanting to avoid stirring up her turbulent feelings.

Relaxing a little, his jealousy floated away. "We have a couple of potential leads," Detective Montague explained. "May we sit?"

"Sure," Annabelle gestured to the small sitting area of the motel room where two battered sofas faced one another, a tatty table in between. She took the couch farthest away, hoping the detectives would sit together on the one opposite. Unfortunately, Detective Montague planted himself beside her, way too close for comfort. To make matters worse, her pulse began to thump wildly in response to the close proximity of such a gorgeous man.

"Another family has been killed in circumstances identical to what happened to your family," he told her gently.

"I know," she nodded. "Dr. Daniels told me."

Jealousy clouded his face again. "What else did Dr. Daniels tell you?" Detective Montague demanded.

"Nothing, he just told me to be careful." She remembered the kind look in the doctor's eyes and the shy smile he'd given her. She never usually attracted the attention of men, and now she was worried that Ricky, Dr. Daniels, and Detective Montague were all more interested in her than they should be. "He was nice to me. He was the only one who was always nice to me."

Flinching slightly, he said, "Annabelle, we were only…"

"I know, I know," she cut him off. "You were only doing your jobs."

"Annabelle, did Dr. Daniels ever do anything inappropriate to you?" Detective Hannah asked.

"What? No," she exclaimed. Then suspicious, "Why?"

"Did he tell you that he's also treating the survivor from the other family?"

She wasn't really sure why that was relevant, but answered, "No."

"Did he ask you any questions about what happened to you?"

"No, not really." She tried to think but she didn't remember much of what people had said to her or what she'd said to them while she was in the hospital.

"What does 'not really' mean?" Detective Montague demanded sharply.

Annabelle shrugged, "He'd just ask how I was doing."

"Have you remembered anything about the night of your attack?" Detective Hannah asked, changing the subject.

"No," she replied adamantly. Annabelle didn't want to remember that night; she wanted to forget all about it. "Why were you asking me questions about Dr. Daniels?" Her eyes grew wide as she realized what they were implying. "Do you think that Dr. Daniels is the killer?"

Her face must have paled because Detective Montague grabbed her uninjured shoulder and shook her gently. "Annabelle?"

"I'm fine," she uttered weakly. Dr. Daniels couldn't be a killer; he had been so nice to her.

"We don't have any evidence that he's involved," Detective Montague assured her.

"Then why are you asking questions about him?"

"Because he's been paying a little too much attention to you," he replied. "Is there any reason he might have to be overly interested in you?"

Thinking of the way he'd looked at her, at her suspicions that he wanted to be more than just her doctor, but she had done nothing to encourage his interest, she answered, "None."

He released her shoulder, "Do you know anyone by the surname Jenner?"

"Is that the other family?"

"Yes, do you know anyone by that name?"

"No, I don't think so, it doesn't sound familiar."

"This is a photo of them," Detective Hannah handed her a picture.

Reluctantly, she took it and studied the four people smiling up at her. Two brown-haired kids, a girl who looked about eleven or twelve, and a boy a couple of years older. The parents were standing behind them, a pretty looking woman with her hands on her son's shoulders, and a man with a scruffy beard and an easy arm around his daughter. She thought of her own family, of the portrait they had had taken last Christmas. The picture hung above her parents' bed. Deliberately, she pushed those images away.

"I've never met any of these people before," Annabelle told them slowly. "Did you talk to her?"

"To who?" Detective Hannah asked, confused.

"To the wife."

"How do you know she was the survivor?"

"Dr. Daniels told me," she replied before she could stop herself, realizing she'd probably given them more ammunition against the doctor.

The detectives let it go and produced another photo. "Do you know this man?" Detective Montague asked.

Studying the next picture, this one was of a gruff man, probably in his mid to late fifties, with piercing blue eyes and a head of dark hair. The man looked surly and cross, glaring at the camera. Her hands were shaking badly, "Is this the man you think is the killer?"

"Right now he's just a person of interest," Detective Hannah told her.

"You think he's the man who killed my family." All of a sudden, Annabelle desperately needed to be on the move. Standing, she began to pace up and down the room. "You think this is the man who framed me for murder?"

"Have you seen him before?" Detective Montague asked, coming to stand before her.

Unable to rip her gaze away from the photo, it seemed to draw her eyes to it against her will. "No," she whispered.

He extracted the picture from her hand. "His name is Lachlan Thompson; do you know anyone by that name?"

"No." It was beginning to feel like the walls were closing in on her; she wanted the detectives to go now. She *needed* them to go now.

"Are you sure?" Detective Hannah persisted.

"I'm sure." Annabelle breathed deeply; she could feel her emotions starting to surge forward but she didn't want them to come bursting out while she had company.

"Annabelle, we have to ask you something difficult." Detective Montague took her arm and tried to lead her back to the couch, but she pulled free.

"What?"

"I know you said you don't remember anything about what happened that night, but...but..." the detective trailed off helplessly and turned to his partner for support.

"Is there any chance that the man who attacked you might have hurt you in another way?" Detective Hannah stood and came to join them. "Do you think that man may have raped you?"

"What?" Dots began to dance in front of her eyes. That couldn't have happened, could it? She would know if someone had done that, wouldn't she? But she didn't remember a single thing about that night. How was that possible? How could she have forgotten it all?

"Whoa," Detective Montague caught her as her knees buckled. "You okay, Annabelle?"

She wanted to answer, but there didn't seem to be enough air in her lungs to produce any sound. She was as helpless as an infant to do anything as Detective Montague lifted her up. For some reason, his touch stilled the violent tremors wracking her body, and she relaxed into him. He carried her to the bed and set her down on it gently. Finally, she found her voice, "That man didn't rape me," she insisted.

"Are you sure?" Detective Hannah pressed.

"I'm sure," she repeated more forcefully.

"Okay." Detective Montague was watching her closely, "Do you want us to call an ambulance?"

Annabelle didn't want to be around people right now, she wanted to be alone. "No, I'll be okay."

He hesitated, then said, "I don't think we should leave you alone right now."

"It's all right, I'm used to it," she murmured, closing her eyes, rolling over onto her stomach and burying her face in the pillow.

The detectives quietly collected their things and left. When she heard the door close behind them, Annabelle expected the tears to flow, but nothing came. Instead, she just curled herself up in a ball and tried to figure out why the man who had killed her family had left her behind.

* * * * *

6:21 P.M.

"You two have a productive day?" David asked as they walked through the front door of her home.

"Not really," Kate sighed, pausing to kiss her husband, who deepened the kiss and for a moment Kate forgot all about the case.

Xavier cleared his throat and rolled his eyes at them.

"Sorry," Kate grinned, tingling when she thought of what she and David would spend the night doing once her partner went home.

"No closer to getting a warrant for your suspect's fingerprints yet, huh?" David asked.

Growing serious, Kate explained, "Everyone we talked to was full of stories about what a horrible guy Lachlan Thompson was," Kate explained. "And everyone knew how much he hated his son-in-law. He blamed Henry Jenner for stealing his daughter and didn't even attend the wedding. He hated his grandkids almost as much as Henry, because he saw them as his son-in-law's kids, not his daughter's. But while everyone knew he hated them, no one heard him expressly threaten them, so…"

"Bottom line, we don't have enough for a warrant." Xavier's grim face brightened, "What's for dinner?"

Kate smiled at her partner, "Your favorite, of course; nice, big juicy steaks."

"Yum," Xavier's face grew even brighter.

"Barbecue's already fired up," David informed them, heading for the kitchen. "Dinner should be ready any minute. Oh, and I made a salad," he added as he began tending the meal.

More often than not, her husband was the one to cook the meals in their house, if she was even home to eat with him. David was a dentist, with nice stable working days, and always the possibility of an early finish if someone cancelled at the last minute. Although she sometimes envied him his easy working life, Kate wouldn't trade jobs with him for all the money in the world. From the first time she'd met a police officer at the age of eight at a car accident that happened outside her home, she had known that it was what she was destined to do.

When the food was ready, they made the most of the pleasant evening and took a seat at the table in their yard, and for most of the meal, they chatted aimlessly about their days, old friends, and the hot weather they'd been having so far that hinted at a long summer to come.

As much as she was enjoying hanging out with her husband and her best friend, Kate couldn't relax. There was something she needed to tell Xavier—something she'd been putting off for weeks—but she couldn't make herself say the words.

"So, Xavier, anyone new in your life?" David asked, sliding over to be closer to his wife, wrapping his arms around her waist.

"Not really," Xavier shifted uncomfortably.

She thought back on the look on her partner's face earlier today when he'd held Annabelle Englewood in his arms. For a second he'd looked just like the old Xavier, the way he used to look before Julia's assault. Back then Xavier liked to hang out till all hours of the morning with his friends; Julia did not. One night when she'd been home alone, someone had broken into the house and raped her.

Kate knew that Xavier blamed himself for not being home to protect his wife when the intruder had broken in, and for what had happened next, even though none of them had known that Julia had been sexually assaulted until it was too late. She also knew that although Xavier was desperate to move on and find happiness again, he thought to do so was betraying Julia, letting her down all over again.

"It would be great if you had a date for our anniversary party next week," David pushed. Her husband was almost as enthusiastic about setting Xavier up as she was.

"I can't believe it's almost been a year since our wedding." Kate ran a hand through David's thick brown hair, temporarily forgetting about Xavier and Julia and Annabelle.

David's eyes heated, "It feels like only yesterday that we said our 'I do's' and I got to kiss you for the first time as your husband," he dipped his head and pressed a hungry kiss to her mouth.

Xavier cleared his throat and stood, "I think that's my cue to leave." Xavier couldn't quite hide the jealousy and longing from his smile.

"I'll walk you out," Kate stood, as well, shooting David a quick glance to let him know she wanted a minute alone with her partner.

"I'll start on the dishes," David began to collect the plates and cutlery.

When they reached Xavier's car, she laid a hand on his shoulder, "Xavier, what happened with Julia wasn't your fault. You know that, right? Even if you'd known about the rape, it doesn't mean things would have worked out differently. Julia could have told you what happened, she could have told me what happened, she could have told anyone what happened. She chose not to; she chose to try to deal with things on her own. Even if you *had* known, it doesn't mean things wouldn't have ended the exact same way."

"I know all that," Xavier nodded calmly.

"You just don't believe it, huh?" Before her partner could respond, she continued, "Look, when we find the guy who's killing families," emphasizing the when because she had to believe that they would indeed find him, "and if you still feel a connection to Annabelle, then ask her out. Maybe she'll say yes, maybe she'll say no, but either way at least you'll know." Kate still wasn't sure that Xavier dating Annabelle was a good idea for either of them, but it was great to see him finally ready to think about moving on.

"Yeah, I'll think about it." Xavier gently pulled free from her grasp. "I'll see you in the morning."

"In the morning," Kate echoed as she watched her partner's car disappear down the street and wondered whether Xavier would ever get over what Julia had done.

"Everything okay?" David slipped his arms around her, pulling her close against his chest and resting his chin on the top of her head.

"Yeah," she leaned back against him.

"Did you tell him?"

"No," she admitted guilty.

"You're going to have to tell him eventually," David reminded her. "This kind of secret can't stay secret forever."

"I know," she assured him. "It's just that Xavier's so confused and scared right now because he's developing feelings for one of the victims in our case. And it just feels like everything is changing." She wiggled around to rest her head on her husband's chest. "I'm a little scared, too. I've wanted to be a cop my whole life, I *have* been a cop my whole adult life, it's going to be weird having to take a break from work. I'm happy, but every time I think about telling Xavier I just chicken out, but I'll do it. I promise, the next time I see Xavier, I'll tell him about the baby."

* * * * *

9:42 P.M.

Annabelle couldn't believe that this cold, dark house was her home. The home she had grown up in. The only home she had ever lived in.

It had been a mistake coming back here so soon.

She hadn't really intended to. All through the day she had been adamant that she was ready to spend the night alone, but then when darkness had fallen, her resolve had cracked. She'd tried calling Ricky to ask him to come and spend the night at the motel with her again, but she hadn't been able to reach him. Knowing that sometimes he went out the back to work in his shed, Annabelle decided she would head over there and maybe take her friend up on his offer to stay in his spare room.

However, she hadn't gotten that far yet.

She took a cab to Ricky's house, and as soon as she'd stepped out into the warm night she caught sight of her home. Now it had probably been close to half an hour that she had been standing in the street staring at her home and wondering how this horrible looking house could be the place she had lived in just days ago.

It wasn't that this house had always been a happy home. Growing up, she had spent many a day hiding out in her room as her parents had another one of their screaming matches. She'd spent many a day playing on her own because her brothers were too busy with each other. And many a night she had cried herself to sleep, feeling all alone in the world.

Annabelle didn't hate her parents; she just hated that they had spent the majority of her life forcing her to play referee in their fights. She didn't hate her brothers either. She just wished that they had been closer, that she hadn't always felt like the third wheel. And as for Katherine, Annabelle just wished that she had felt more like the little girl's big sister and less like her mother.

She'd resented the fact that she had been the one to keep her family running. As well as working full-time she did the cooking, the cleaning, the shopping, and cared for Katherine, while the rest of her family swanned around having fun and living their own lives. Annabelle was sad that her family was gone, but she wasn't sure if it was because her loved ones were dead or because she had been left all alone or a combination of the two.

She thought of the visit from the detectives this morning, and how safe and secure she'd felt in Detective Montague's arms. But it was an illusion. Nothing more. She wasn't safe. The man who had hurt her was still out there. The man who had murdered her family was still free to kill more people.

In a trance, she crossed her front lawn, ignoring flashes of memories of playing out here on weekends when she was little, of climbing the big tree, of running through the sprinkler. Barely noticing the police tape that crisscrossed the door, she entered her home. In a daze, she wandered from room to room, surveying everything, but downstairs everything appeared to be as it usually was. Drawing a deep breath, she faced the stairs.

Step by step she made her way up, coming to a stop when she reached the hallway.

She shouldn't be doing this.

She shouldn't be here in her home on her own.

What she should do was walk back downstairs, out the front door and straight to Ricky's house. Annabelle almost did it, but something was pulling her onwards. Almost against her will, she walked down the corridor. The doors were all open, and passing Katherine's room she halted immediately, shocked at the blood that stained the floor and walls.

There was so much blood.

Too much.

Katherine was only seven; there was too much blood for such a little girl. The bed had been stripped of sheets, blankets, pillow—all gone—but Annabelle guessed it, too, had been drenched in Katherine's blood.

Shaking badly, she wanted desperately to leave, but her feet had other ideas as they traipsed her across the hall and into her own room.

The last thing she remembered before waking up with Detective Montague hovering above her was falling into bed uncharacteristically exhausted.

When she caught sight of the blood staining her own mattress, the reality of all that had happened crashed down upon her.

The tears that had refused to come earlier today now flowed freely as she burst into hysterical sobs and turned and fled the room. Almost tripping over her feet as she took the stairs two at a time, Annabelle headed straight for her father's study, tucking herself away in the corner between his desk and the filing cabinet. Bringing her knees up against her chest, she wrapped her good arm tightly around them, and buried her head.

It might have been minutes or hours that she sat there crying, but a sharp rapping on the door sent her instantly still.

"Annabelle?"

It was Detective Montague. The last person she wanted to see right now. What was he doing here anyway?

"Annabelle, it's Detective Montague. I know you're in there. Open up."

Maybe if she stayed quiet, he would assume he was wrong and leave. What gave him the right to know where she was anyway?

"Annabelle, are you okay?"

Why couldn't he just leave her alone?

"Annabelle, I'm coming in."

A moment later she heard the door creak open and footsteps searching the house. Remaining as still and quiet as possible, she squeezed her eyes closed and prayed the detective would give up and go.

When several minutes passed without another sound, Annabelle slowly crept out of her hiding place, grateful that at last something had gone her way. Intending to leave and go straight to Ricky's, she hadn't made it more than a step when she caught sight of a family portrait perched on her father's desk. The portrait was old, taken just after Katherine was born. In it her mother cradled her youngest child; ten-year-old Julian, thirteen-year-old Paul and her father had dressed in matching outfits; and Annabelle herself, aged sixteen, was smiling with the hope that a new baby would finally bring her family peace.

The sight of the picture sent her into another fit of tears and she dropped to her knees. Baby Katherine hadn't brought the Englewood family peace and now nothing ever could. She would never have an opportunity to make her family happy, or to tell them that she loved them. And she did—she did love them, she really did—no matter how crazy they drove her.

"Come here."

Someone's hands wrapped around her arms, drawing her to her feet. At first she thought it was Ricky, who had realized that she was here and that she needed him, and he'd come to help her, but then the voice clicked.

It was Detective Montague again.

He hadn't left like she'd thought.

She didn't want this man here, in her house, even if it had been ruined beyond repair. Wildly she fought against him as he tried to embrace her, her sobs growing louder.

"Shh, it's okay, Annabelle," Detective Montague refused to let go of her. "It'll be okay; we'll make it okay. Try to calm down. Everything will be all right, Belle."

Hearing him call her Belle immediately turned her to stone. Something from a long time ago, long since forgotten, sprung into her head.

* * * * *

10:10 P.M.

Annabelle slumped silently in the passenger seat of his car.

Xavier knew this was a bad idea and yet he was making no move to stop.

Back at the Englewood house, when he'd gone inside, he hadn't been able to find where Annabelle was hiding. So he had remained quiet, hoping she'd think he had left, until she'd crept out from a corner of the study.

Xavier had watched as she caught sight of something in the room and collapsed to the carpet in a flood of tears. Without hesitation he had gone to her, pulling her up off the floor and into his arms. She had fought at first, beating at him with her small fists, but when he'd called her Belle she had gone completely still. He'd wondered whether that was perhaps a nickname her parents had used; but whatever the reason, it had worked like a charm.

Holding a woman in his arms again after three long years had stirred up all sorts of feelings and longings that he had repressed. He'd enjoyed the way her forehead pressed against his chest and the soft whoosh of her breath against his neck, the sweet scent of her shampoo tickling his nose.

Eventually he had pulled away and offered to take her back to the motel, but Annabelle had freaked out and begged him not to leave her alone. Instead she'd asked him to take her next door to her friend's house, but when he'd thumped on the door, there was no answer.

By the time he had decided Ricky Preston was either a very heavy sleeper or out, Annabelle had looked dead on her feet. So he'd taken her arm and led her back to his car, helped her into the passenger seat, buckled her in, and headed for his house.

Casting a surreptitious glance in Annabelle's direction, Xavier found himself admiring her thick, chocolate brown locks. Her hair hung to her shoulders and framed her pretty face. It looked so silky, so soft, that the desire to run his fingers through it was nearly overwhelming.

What Kate had said tonight was all true. Xavier did *know* that what Julia had done wasn't his fault, but sometimes knowing and believing were two different things. The fact that Julia had been hurt in the first place, however, most definitely was his fault. He should have made more of an effort to go home on the nights when he wasn't holed up at work. If he had been at home, then Julia would never have been raped and the rest of those tragic events would have never happened. But Julia was gone now, she was no longer a part of his life. Annabelle, on the other hand, was right here, and she needed someone whether she wanted to admit it or not.

All day he had been unable to forget how right it had felt cradling Annabelle in his arms when she'd almost fainted back at the motel this morning. He hadn't wanted to leave her alone and had even contemplated calling her friend Ricky to go and check up on her.

As he'd left Kate and David's after dinner, pondering Kate's words, he had driven around in circles for close to an hour before biting the bullet and heading for the motel. He hadn't planned on staying long, or even necessarily letting Annabelle know he was there, he was just worried about her and wanted to check to make sure she was hanging in there. When he'd found her room empty, he had known exactly where she would be and driven straight out to the Englewood house.

Xavier honestly felt like he was losing his mind.

It made no sense for him to feel anything other than the usual compassion he felt when dealing with a victim of a violent crime. And yet, there was something about Annabelle Englewood that just wouldn't leave him alone.

Pulling into his drive and inside the garage, Xavier climbed out of the car, flipped on the light and then went to retrieve Annabelle. As he opened her door and unbuckled her seatbelt, she turned to look up at him with her enormous white eyes and his heart froze. This was a bad idea. It had to be. What was he thinking bringing her to his house?

Too late to back out now, he forced himself to keep moving, he slid an arm under her knees and his other behind her back and lifted her from the car. She didn't protest; in fact, she curled into him, wrapping her good arm around his neck and burying her face in the crook of his shoulder.

Carrying her inside and upstairs, he kicked open the door to the spare bedroom opposite his room, and settled Annabelle on the bed. Xavier slipped off her shoes and tucked her in, brushing a tendril of hair off her forehead. He wanted to kiss her but knew it was a bad idea.

"My room is right across the hall," he told her. "If you need anything, just yell out and I'll be right here."

He was just straightening up when she grabbed his hand. "Please don't leave me alone," she whispered.

Squeezing her hand, he responded, "Okay, I won't leave you," he assured her. "I'll sleep in the chair." He started to release her hand but she clung on.

"Could you talk to me?"

"About what?" he asked, puzzled, wondering whether she wanted details on the case.

"Can you...can you tell me about your childhood?" Annabelle asked, her bottom lip trembling.

Catching the sad longing in her voice, Xavier wondered whether her childhood had been an unhappy one. "Sure," he agreed. Fetching his desk chair, he brought it right over by the bed. As soon as he was seated, Annabelle reached for his hand once again, clutching it firmly.

"Well, I was the product of a one-night stand," he recounted. "Both my mom and dad were married to other people. They both had families, and one night when they were each going through a rough time they got drunk and had a one-night stand. In the morning they both regretted it, wanted to make things work with their respective partners, but it was too late, I had already been conceived. My mom and dad both confessed their indiscretions and remained with their families, but they both wanted to be a part of my life. So, growing up I spent half my time at my mom's house with her and her husband and their four kids, and the other half with my dad and his wife and their two kids."

"Your mom and dad both loved you?" Annabelle asked sleepily, struggling to keep her eyes open.

"Yeah, they both loved me a lot."

"And your brothers and sisters loved you, too?"

"Yeah, them too." Although he had never been particularly close with any of his siblings, something that he regretted more and more the older he got. "It took them a while, but when they realized I wasn't a threat to their families they learned to love me. I grew up knowing I was loved, but it didn't mean that I wasn't lonely or that I didn't often feel left out. I knew I was a constant reminder to my parents and my stepparents and my siblings of my mom and dad's infidelity. I missed birthdays and other special occasions bouncing back and forth between homes. I always felt like I never really belonged anywhere, like wherever I was that everyone was always making a special effort to love me and keep the peace. I guess I just wanted for once to not be the constant reminder of what my parents had done."

Xavier wasn't sure why he was telling Annabelle such personal information. He'd never confessed his feelings about his childhood to anyone before. Not his parents or siblings or friends, not even to Julia. But with Annabelle he sensed that she needed to hear that she wasn't the only one who had felt out of place in their own family.

Looking down, he saw that Annabelle had finally fallen asleep. Disengaging his hand and rearranging the covers around her, Xavier then stretched out in the chair and knew that for the second night in a row he was going to have good dreams.

* * * * *

11:31 P.M.

This time her stupid parents were not going to ruin things.

Vanessa was still beyond mortified and embarrassed and horrified that her parents had found her and Vince naked in her bed. They had gone absolutely bananas, screaming and screeching so loud they had woken the neighbors.

Who exactly did her parents think she was, anyway?

It wasn't like she was still a little girl.

She was seventeen; Vince was nineteen, and what they chose to do in the privacy of her room was none of her parents' business.

Not only had it been humiliating that her parents had barged in right as she and Vince were about to make love, but they had also seen her naked. Vanessa knew they'd seen her naked as a baby, but this was different, she was a woman now, and she felt like her privacy had been completely violated.

After they had pulled Vince off her and thrown his clothes at him, insisting that he get dressed and get out before they called the police, they'd looked in horror at the skimpy lingerie she'd bought for her special night and pulled some regular pajamas from her closet.

Then Vanessa had been forced to sit on her bed, her cheeks flaming red from anger and humiliation, and listen while they droned on and on for hours about how immature she was, and how could she give up her virginity to the first boy who came along? Then they'd moved on to all the risks associated with sex. Her mom had cried as she'd asked whether Vanessa was ready for motherhood if she ended up pregnant.

Throughout the tirade, Vanessa had sat there silently seething. When her mom and dad had finally run out of words, she coldly showed them the door, climbed back into bed and burst into a flood of tears. That was two days ago. Since then, she had made a point of refusing to speak to her parents.

But Vanessa wasn't going to let them ruin things for her.

She'd been so worried that Vince would hold her parents' actions against her. That he would be so upset about her mom and dad busting them naked in her bed that he would never want to see her or talk to her ever again. Luckily, Vince really did love her and had called her the morning after to assure her that he still wanted to make love to her more than anything else in the whole entire world.

And that was exactly what Vanessa planned to do.

It was now close to midnight, and everyone ought to be asleep. It was the perfect time to sneak out. Vince would be waiting for her in his car, just around the corner, ready to make her the happiest person on earth.

Slipping down the stairs, checking to make sure no one was following her, she was at the front door when they sprung her.

"Where do you think you're going, young lady?" her father demanded.

Vanessa stared back at him sullenly.

"We told you that you are not to see that boy again," her mother added sternly, flipping on the living room light.

"Still giving us the silent treatment," her father looked disappointed. "Do you think by doing that you're showing us that you're mature enough to date?"

It annoyed her that her dad had a point. "I'm seventeen now," she reminded them.

"Which is not old enough to be having…doing…" her father stammered, not wanting to put her and sex in the same sentence. "Doing *things* with some college kid."

"Vince and I are in love," she shouted.

"Honey, you're too young to know what love is," her mother spoke softly. "You've only been on a couple of dates, you have a lot of growing up to do before you should be even begin thinking about sleeping with someone."

"How would you know what I'm feeling?" she shrieked. "I told you I *love* Vince and he loves me."

"Vanessa, we are your parents, we're just looking out for you. It's our job." Her father gave her a sympathetic smile, "But I'm sorry to have to tell you that most boys Vince's age have only one thing on the brain. Sex. It's not about the girl, it's not real love for them, they just want to brag to their friends about how many girls they've slept with. I know, I was a young man once."

"Vince isn't like that," Vanessa protested. "He really loves me, he told me he did."

"Maybe he was just telling you what you wanted to hear," her mom suggested sadly. "He's older than you, honey, he's probably been with girls more experienced than you are. Maybe the idea of taking a girl's virginity appealed to him."

"How could you say that?" Tears began to stream down her cheeks. "You're making me sound like some immature little girl. I'm seventeen years old, and I know how I feel and I feel like Vince is the man I want to spend the rest of my life with."

"I'm sure you feel like that now, but one day you're going to meet someone who loves you with their whole heart." Her mom tried to embrace her in a hug, but Vanessa jumped away.

"Vince *does* love me," she insisted adamantly. "And we're going to spend the rest of our lives together and there's nothing you can do to stop me."

"That's where you're wrong, young lady," her father took on

his stern voice. "You are already grounded due to the other night's activities. You are not leaving this house tonight or tomorrow or any other day for the next two months."

Vanessa knew she was treading dangerous territory with her dad and yet she pushed on anyway, "Two months?"

"You had a naked boy in your bed; you were planning on having sex with him. I think under the circumstances, two months is very lenient."

"No," she shook her head. "I am not grounded."

"Yes, you are." Her father took a warning step toward her. "Now up to bed."

"You're not the boss of me." Vanessa held her ground, even though her insides were quaking. "I'm going out with Vince tonight, and we're going to make love, and it's going to be the most special night of my life and you can't stop me."

"Oh. Yes. I can." He took another menacing step forward.

"I hate you," Vanessa screeched. "I wish you weren't my parents. I wish you were dead." With that, she threw open the front door and ran down the path to the sidewalk, ignoring her father's orders to return and her mother's pleas that they loved her and only wanted what was best for her.

As Vanessa ran through the dark, quiet streets, tears still trickling down her cheeks, heading straight for the safety of Vince's arms, she was so consumed by her problems, that she didn't notice the shadowy figure watching her from a car parked across the street from her house.

MAY 8TH

1:06 A.M.

Rawlin Rankling enjoyed this time of night.

It was about the only time of the day left where he could really take some time for himself. At seventy-four years of age he really treasured those moments because he never knew how many of them he would have left.

He couldn't deny that retirement had not turned out to be what he'd thought. This year would be the fifteenth anniversary of his wife's accident. Fifteen years since their lives had been irrevocably changed forever when two joy-riding teenagers had slammed into their car. While he had walked away with relatively minor injuries, his wife had not been so lucky. Lorraine had spent three months in a coma. Three long agonizing months. When she had eventually regained consciousness, Rawlin had learned that she had suffered severe brain damage and lost the use of her body and a lot of brain function.

With no children, Rawlin had managed his wife's condition mostly on his own. He had been lucky enough, though, to have the full support of the wonderful young doctor who had been involved in Lorraine's case since the beginning. Plus the support of one of his neighbors who had gone above and beyond the call of duty. Even though the man had moved away more than ten years ago, he still gave up one day a fortnight to come and look after Lorraine.

Rawlin's love for his wife had not diminished after her brain injury, and yet, he couldn't deny that he was tired of looking after her. Lorraine was bound to a wheelchair, able only to move her arms and legs in jerky, uncontrolled spasms. She could breathe on her own, and she was able to eat, although she had no control over her bladder or bowels. Fifty-nine at the time of the accident, Rawlin had retired from the job he loved as a junior high school math teacher, to take care of his wife full time.

As much as he loved Lorraine, he desperately missed all the things they used to do together—picnics, cooking, skiing, sitting up till all hours of the night talking about anything and everything. Rawlin missed talking to her the most. Although Lorraine could eat, she couldn't speak. She could, however, blink her eyes or tap her finger to answer yes or no questions, and Rawlin had learned to be satisfied with that.

He bustled about the kitchen, busying himself preparing a meal from one of the hundred or so cookbooks that he and Lorraine has amassed over the first half of their marriage. Every evening after he had settled his wife down for the night, he came down to the kitchen to cook. As he did, he'd picture Lorraine standing beside him—the old Lorraine, the one she'd been before, and it was these times when he felt the closest to her.

There had been so many things he and Lorraine had wanted to do. So many dreams left to make come true. Upon their retirement, he and Lorraine had planned on taking a trip to Paris, of studying cooking and opening their own restaurant, or moving out to the country and starting up a bed and breakfast. Those dreams had died that day when he'd lost a part of the woman he loved.

Rawlin remembered those hours sitting beside her in the hospital, praying that she would wake up, that she wouldn't leave him. All that time, the doctors had taken great pains to remind him that, even if Lorraine awakened from her coma, she would more than likely never again be the woman he had known. He'd assured them he understood, had really thought he had, and yet when Lorraine had woken up and he had learned the extent of her injuries, it had still come as a complete shock. A part of him had believed that if she would just open her eyes, then everything would be okay.

It was the second time in his life he had suffered a horrible psychological blow. As most young couples do, following their wedding he and Lorraine had planned to have a big family. They were both only children and the idea of having lots of kids had appealed to both of them. After years of trying and no luck, they'd sought help and been told that they would most likely never have a child of their own. He and Lorraine had slowly come to accept that children were not in the cards for them and adapted their life accordingly.

Until the conception of their first child.

Upon discovering that Lorraine was pregnant they had gone immediately to their doctor, who had warned that they would probably miscarry and they had readied themselves for this to happen. But the months had continued to tick by and when they reached the seven-month mark without suffering a miscarriage, they finally began to believe that they were about to become parents.

As their excitement grew, they bought baby furniture, thought up names, and began to dream of their future. Rawlin had imagined what it would be like to have a daughter, the little girl sitting on his knee, him proving to her that he was the one man she could always trust, then eventually letting her go to the man who would take his place. Or a son, playing baseball, watching sports, going fishing and camping, and teaching his little boy how to grow into a man.

Then tragedy had struck. At eight months, Lorraine had gone into premature labor. The baby, a beautiful tiny little girl, was stillborn. The doctors had no explanation as to why their daughter had died, and he hadn't realized how much he'd wanted to be a father until he held that small body in his arms.

Together he and Lorraine had worked through the heartache, just as they had faced everything else. What was killing Rawlin now was that he wasn't sure how much longer he and Lorraine could remain together. He was getting old now, no longer able to cope with the physical requirements of caring for someone in Lorraine's condition. The thought of moving his wife into a nursing home ate at him day and night, and he wasn't sure how he would ever be able to do it. At their wedding, they'd promised until death parted them and anything less seemed…

"What kind of person is cooking at one-thirty in the morning?"

Even though he knew it was impossible, for one second Rawlin thought it must be Lorraine, but then common sense kicked in, and with it a sense of foreboding.

"What are you doing here?" he asked, relaxing a little at the familiar face.

"Unfinished business."

"It's the middle of the night," Rawlin was confused.

"That's the best time for my kind of business."

"What kind of business is . . .?" he trailed off as he caught sight of the knife, and instantly, he knew what was about to happen. "It's you," Rawlin frowned accusingly. Funny enough, he didn't feel the teensiest bit scared; instead, he almost felt relieved at the thought of death, infinite rest. "You're the one who killed those other families. Why? Why did you do it?"

"I told you. Unfinished business."

"Lorraine…" Rawlin couldn't bear the thought of his wife being left all alone, and that was what had happened to those other families. One of them had been left behind, and in this case, he knew it wasn't going to be him.

"You'd already decided to put her in a home."

"I hadn't…yet," he protested.

"Yes, you had. You just couldn't bring yourself to admit it." He took a menacing step forward. "I'll do it quick. It won't hurt."

As much as Rawlin welcomed the thought of infinite rest, he couldn't allow himself to go without a fight. Lorraine needed him, and that thought was enough to spur him into action. He made a dive for the knife he'd used to peel potatoes. Before he reached it, there was a burning rip in his throat, and something wet began to drip down chest.

Rawlin Rankling's final thoughts lay with his wife.

* * * * *

5:16 A.M.

The third family killed in four days.

Kate stifled a yawn as she and Xavier traipsed once more through the hospital; it was beginning to feel like they lived here. She'd hardly gotten any sleep last night. After Xavier left, she and David had started their anniversary celebrations early, and it had been close to one before they'd finally fallen asleep. The call had come in around quarter to two.

Another family destroyed.

This time the victims were an elderly couple.

The rest of the MO was the same. When a call had come in to the 911 operator with no one on the other end, a call had also been placed to her and Xavier. They had arrived at the Rankling house just minutes after the responding officers to find seventy-four-year-old Rawlin Rankling dead on the kitchen floor, hands and eyes and tongue removed, and his disabled wife Lorraine bleeding in an upstairs bedroom.

The Rankling house had blood everywhere. At the Jenner house the killer appeared to have covered himself in blood and danced around the master bedroom. It seemed he had done the same thing here. Only this time he hadn't just danced around one room; this time, it looked like his romp had included the entire house. Blood splatter covered the floors and some walls of each of the downstairs rooms, and a trail led up the stairs and down to Lorraine Rankling's bedroom.

Since she and Xavier had already been inside the house, they hadn't bothered to wait until Diane and her team were finished; instead, they had spoken with a few of the neighbors and then headed straight over here to the hospital to see Lorraine. The killer hadn't injured the woman badly, perhaps because she was already physically and mentally disabled that it had seemed pointless. Whatever the case, the wound to Lorraine Rankling's left shoulder was much less severe than the wounds to both Annabelle and Nicole Jenner.

Casting a glance at Xavier, her partner was particularly quiet and withdrawn this morning. He'd barely spoken two words at the Rankling house or on the drive over here. Something was definitely up with him. Kate hoped he wasn't upset with her about their conversation at her house last night.

"Xavier, are you mad at me?" she asked.

"What?" Xavier looked genuinely confused.

"I didn't mean to upset you last night. I thought I was only telling you stuff you already knew. I know that you still love Julia, but…"

"I'm not mad at you, Kate," he assured her, his hazel eyes serious.

"Well, something's going on with you." She narrowed her eyes at him. "You've spent all morning looking at your phone. Are you waiting for a call?" She wondered what Xavier had gotten up to last night.

"No," Xavier's voice wavered.

Stopping abruptly, she demanded, "What is going on?"

Sighing guiltily, "I didn't go straight home after dinner last night."

"You went to see Annabelle," she sighed too. "Well, how did it go? Did she even let you in the door?"

"I went to the motel, she wasn't there," Xavier explained. "I thought she'd be at her house. She was, she was crying."

"Please tell me you didn't do anything stupid." Kate had a feeling her partner had indeed done something stupid.

"Not stupid exactly," he stammered.

"Xavier, what did you do?"

"She was hysterical, I didn't want to leave her alone, we tried Ricky Preston's house but got no answer, so I took her back to my place. She slept in the spare room," he added defensively. "She was still asleep when I left. I left her a note, but I was wondering whether I should call and make sure she's okay."

"You are stupid," she snapped, but before she could say more a doctor approached them.

"Detectives?"

"Yes, I'm Detective Hannah, and this is Detective Montague, we're here to speak with Lorraine Rankling."

"I'm Dr. Pedding." The woman shot them a grim look, "You know Mrs. Rankling is mentally and physically disabled, right?"

"We were at the house earlier," Kate assured her, remembering Lorraine's empty eyes staring at them as they tried to assure her everything would be okay.

"There's something else you should know," Dr. Pedding stopped them as they tried to bypass her. "When we were examining her, we found evidence that she may have been being abused."

"Abused? By whom?" Xavier asked.

"Husband is the primary caregiver," Dr. Pedding shrugged.

"He's also seventy-four." Kate couldn't imagine the old man harming his wife.

"Stress gets to everyone eventually. It's been almost fifteen years of looking after a disabled wife, mostly on his own. That's got to be tough on him. Maybe hurting her was the only way he could get through the day. It wouldn't be the first time…"

"Rawlin would never hurt Lorraine," an outraged voice insisted.

Kate could practically feel Xavier's eyes roll when they turned around to see a red faced Dr. Daniels glaring at them.

"What are you doing here?" Xavier demanded.

"I'm one of Lorraine Rankling's doctors," Dr. Daniels snapped irritably.

"You ended up treating *another* victim of the same serial killer?" Kate asked, wondering whether there could be something to Xavier's jealous suspicions.

"No," Dr. Daniels was quickly becoming agitated. "I was one of her doctors after the car accident. Rawlin would never ever lay a hand on Lorraine; he loved her more than life itself." That comment seemed to remind him that Rawlin Rankling no longer had a life, because for a second he faltered.

"You've kept in touch with the Ranklings?" Kate asked.

His cheeks heated in embarrassment. "Lorraine was one of my first cases. Rawlin reminded me of my father; I got more attached to him than I should have. Over the years I've stayed in touch, helped him out by looking after Lorraine every now and then to give him a break. Once again, I have to tell you all that if someone was abusing Lorraine it was not Rawlin," the doctor eyed them all defiantly.

"Do you have any idea who it could be then?" Xavier inquired.

"No. Now I'm going in to see Lorraine," Dr. Daniels barged past them.

"Dr. Daniels," Xavier stepped in front of him to block his path. "Lorraine is a victim of a violent crime. We need to ask her a few questions."

"Good luck getting answers, she won't be able to tell you much. And what makes you think she even saw anything? Annabelle and Nicole didn't."

"The killer didn't use drugs or tape to cover her eyes this time," Kate told him. "That means Lorraine could have seen the man who killed her husband and two other families."

"She can maybe give you hair and eye color," Dr. Daniels informed them. "But height, weight, age, facial features, she won't have a clue."

Glancing at Dr. Pedding for confirmation, the other doctor

nodded. "And you'll have to phrase everything as a yes or no question," Dr. Pedding added. "She can respond by tapping her finger or blinking her eyes."

"And you'll take it easy on her," Dr. Daniels ordered. "Does she know Rawlin is dead?"

"She knows." Kate had been able to tell the second they'd found Lorraine in her bed that she already knew her husband was dead. "I think the killer told her before he stabbed her."

"I'm going in with you." Dr. Daniels didn't wait for their consent; he simply turned and barged into Lorraine's room.

"I told you I didn't like that guy," Xavier muttered as they followed the doctor through the door. "He's now connected to all three cases."

Inside, the doctor had pulled up a chair close to Lorraine's bed, he was holding her hand and leaning over her. As they got closer, they could see the affection shining in both Dr. Daniels' and Lorraine's eyes. It was pretty obvious that the two were very close, making Kate doubt that the doctor was involved.

"Mrs. Rankling?" Kate came up beside the bed. "My name's Detective Hannah, remember we met at your house earlier?"

Lorraine blinked twice.

"That means yes," Dr. Daniels supplied.

"I need to ask you some questions, is that okay?"

Two blinks.

"Did you see the man who hurt you?"

Two blinks.

"Do you think we could talk about what he looked like?"

Two blinks.

"Did he have brown eyes?"

One blink.

"Blue eyes?"

Two blinks.

"Okay on to hair color. Did he have dark hair?"

One blink.

"Light hair?"

One blink.

"Red hair?"

One blink.

There were no other hair colors left. "Do you know what color hair he had, Mrs. Rankling?"

One blink. This time tears glistened brightly in her eyes.

"Are you sure she can't give us more?" Kate directed this question to Dr. Daniels.

"Lorraine has the mental capacity of a child around the age of four, to her everyone looks old and tall and big, anything she gives you won't be reliable," the doctor informed them.

"Lorraine, did you know the man who hurt you?"

A hesitation.

"Lorraine, do you know who he is?"

Another hesitation followed by two blinks.

"Can you tell us?" Kate wasn't sure how to get that information out of the woman and wished they had a photo of Lachlan Thompson on them.

Her eyes darted around the room before settling on Dr. Daniels, and Kate wondered if maybe Xavier had been right after all.

* * * * *

10:42 A.M.

"What'd you get?" Xavier asked Kate as he set the phone down. They were at their desks, trying to find any links between the Englewoods, Jenners, and Ranklings. For the moment they were looking for anything that might link the families to their two prime suspects: Lachlan Thompson and Dr. Bruce Daniels.

He'd taken Dr. Daniels and Kate had taken Lachlan and for the last hour or so they had worked away, trying desperately to find a link that might point them in the correct direction. Now it was time to compare notes and see what they came up with.

"All right," Kate shuffled the mess of papers on her desk and settled more comfortably into her chair. "I couldn't find anything linking Lachlan to Rawlin and Lorraine Rankling, but I did find out that John Englewood did some electrical work at Lachlan's favorite bar. Maybe he saw the guy there, it sparked an idea, he didn't think the family would be able to be linked back to him because of the flimsy connection, we might not ever have even found it if we hadn't specifically asked. Oh, and Lachlan drives a red Toyota."

"Dr. Daniels drives a red Nissan, so I guess that makes them even on that score," Xavier added.

"What'd *you* get?"

"Okay, Dr. Bruce Daniels is forty-six years old, currently single and never been married, and like I said, drives a red Nissan. No criminal record, but I did find something interesting in his past at the hospital. Apparently several years ago there were some allegations against him that he was poisoning children who came into the ER with young mothers. There were four cases where he was accused of doing something to kids, only ever when there was a single mother. He'd examine the child, who would get dramatically worse, then he would come swooping in to attempt to save the day, and would be overly interested in the moms. These were only allegations, because they couldn't find any evidence of what he was doing to the children, so in the end, they had to let it drop. But they insisted he get some counseling. After the accusations and the order to get help, there were no more recorded suspicious cases."

"That could fit with our Munchausen theory." Kate looked thoughtful. "Did you find any links to our families?"

"Well, we know he was one of Lorraine Rankling's doctors, so I checked to see whether anyone from the Englewood or Jenner family had recently taken a trip to the hospital. About a month ago, Katherine Englewood fell off her bike and split her head open; Annabelle took her to the hospital. About six weeks ago, Nicole Jenner took her daughter in when Callie had a bad case of food poisoning. Dr. Daniels was not the treating doctor in either case, but he was on shift both times, so he could have seen them there and had access to their charts."

"Maybe he learned his lesson from last time and decided to pick people who weren't his patients." Kate's smile faltered. "But we're still no closer to pointing the finger at which guy it is. All of this is circumstantial, and it could just be coincidental. We don't have any actual proof that either Lachlan Thompson or Dr. Daniels is involved. It could still be someone else and this could all be completely random."

"Even if it is random, he still has to have seen them somewhere." Xavier didn't get the feeling this was random though; it felt like their killer had a purpose.

"It doesn't feel random." Kate seemed to read his mind.

"No, it feels like he picked these particular families for a reason. We just don't know what that reason is."

"If he's choosing these families for a reason, he's not studying them very well to get a sense of their routines. Rawlin Rankling was killed in the kitchen, which is different than the others. If the killer had been planning this out properly, he would have known that it was Rawlin's routine to settle his wife down for the night and then start cooking. By approaching Rawlin while he was awake, the man could have fought back, and that was a big risk to take…"

"Maybe a calculated one, though," Xavier contemplated. "Rawlin is seventy-four, probably no match for our killer. Plus, the killer could have surprised him from behind, slashed his throat before he even knew someone else was in the room. Or, maybe the killer was someone Rawlin knew and didn't see as a threat." He began thinking of the way Lorraine's eyes had settled on Dr. Daniels when they'd asked her if she knew her attacker. "There was no break in this time, either," he reminded his partner. "So the idea that it was someone the Ranklings knew and had given a key to is looking good."

"I think we need to talk about Annabelle," Kate announced suddenly, studying him with a probing blue stare. "Are you going to tell Rob that she spent the night at your house?"

"In the spare room," he reminded his partner, but considered her question. He knew their lieutenant would go bananas if he found out that one of his detectives had brought a victim from an active case home to spend the night, no matter how innocent his intentions had been.

"Xavier, are you really serious about Annabelle, or do you just think she has unusual eyes?"

"It's not that her eyes are unusual." He tried to explain what he was feeling. "It's what's in them. I don't know, I just feel some sort of connection."

"Well, you have to decide whether you're going to do something about it or not, because if you start up with her and then change your mind, you don't want that to be the straw that broke the camel's back with her and push her over the edge..."

"Like I did with Julia," he inserted.

"No, not like what happened with Julia," Kate contradicted firmly. "Julia didn't tell anyone that she was raped, and there's no way you could have predicted that she would have wound up doing what she did. You have to let that go, Xavier. I know it's hard, but you can't let Julia's mistakes rule your life. You didn't know what Julia was planning to do. If you had known, you would have stopped her. If you really think something could develop between you and Annabelle, then go for it. I'll support you, but right now your priority has to be finding this killer."

"I know that, Kate," he assured her. "I know that I need to let go of Julia, but unfortunately, it's a lot easier said than done. I don't know if anything's going to develop between me and Annabelle. All I know is I can't stop thinking about her, and that hasn't happened since Julia…"

"Who's Julia?"

* * * * *

11:09 A.M.

"Who's Julia?" Annabelle repeated, curious about the woman Detective Montague had neglected to mention last night when he'd been telling her about his family.

"Annabelle, what are you doing here?" Detective Montague looked a little sheepish.

"You have my keys," she informed him, wondering whether he'd taken them on purpose so she couldn't get back home. "If you'll just give them to me, I'll get out of your hair, go back home and get my things, and then see if Ricky will let me stay with him for a while."

"How did you get here?"

"Took a cab from your house." If Detective Montague's partner was surprised to hear that she had spent the night with him, she didn't show it.

"I don't want you going back there alone," Detective Montague informed her.

"Fine," she turned around to leave.

"Wait," Detective Montague grabbed her arm and held her in place. "Where are you going?"

"Ricky's. My parents might have given him a key to our house." Annabelle tried not to think about her parents or her house right now. As much as she dreaded going back there, she had to get her wallet and license, the keys to her car and some of her clothes.

"Annabelle, we need to talk," Detective Montague held onto her arm.

"I'll go pay the cab driver." Detective Hannah excused herself and disappeared.

Annabelle yanked herself out of Detective Montague's grip once he'd guided her into an empty room. "Who's Julia?" she repeated her earlier question, wanting to keep the attention off herself. She hadn't heard his whole conversation but she had heard him say that he wasn't sure if anything was going to happen between them but he couldn't stop thinking about her, and apparently he hadn't felt that way since someone called Julia had been in his life.

"Julia was my wife," he replied uncomfortably.

"Why didn't you tell me you'd been married last night when you were telling me about your family?" she demanded, knowing it was none of her business. But focusing on someone else's business meant she could forget about her own for a while.

"Why were you eavesdropping?" he asked, instead of answering her question.

"I wasn't eavesdropping," Annabelle protested. "I was coming to get my keys and happened to hear what you were talking about. Why didn't you tell me that you had a wife?" She wasn't sure why the knowledge that Detective Montague had been married bothered her so much. No matter what he was thinking about her, it wasn't mutual. She didn't want a boyfriend.

"Why would I have told you?" He looked annoyed now. "You're just a victim in a case I'm working."

She had to admit she was hurt when he said that. She didn't want to admit it, but it had felt nice having someone take care of her last night. She didn't understand why if he was interested in her, he didn't just say something, then she could let him down gently and move on. Despite her resolution that she wasn't interested, when she spoke she couldn't quite keep the tremble from her voice. "If I'm just a victim in your case, then why did you come looking for me last night? Why did you take me back to your house and sit with me for hours so that I wouldn't be alone? Why did you hold me in your arms while I cried? And why do you keep looking at me with those longing glances?"

"I...uh...I don't...I mean, I..." Detective Montague stammered awkwardly.

"Look, it doesn't matter anyway," she sighed sadly. "You actually seem like a pretty nice guy, well except for the accusing me of being a murderer thing, but I don't date. Ever."

Now the Detective looked hurt. "Julia and I were married for two years, but three years ago she was raped. She didn't tell anyone, including me, what had happened until it was too late. She did something that almost destroyed all of our lives. It's hard for me to talk about her—to move on from her—but I want to. For the first time in a long time, I want to move on from her."

Annabelle was shocked when a wave of desire to run her hands through Detective Montague's silky light brown hair washed over her. She didn't think about men that way. She made sure she didn't. And she didn't really think she felt anything for this man she didn't even know. It was probably because she had just lost her family, she didn't really have any friends, she felt scared and lonely, and Detective Montague kept popping up and staring at her like she was somehow important to him.

To keep herself on track, she took another shot at anger. "You tricked me last night. You broke into my house, made me think that you'd left, and waited for me to come out. You took advantage of my vulnerability to get close to me, because for some strange reason that I can't fathom you think you have feelings for me."

"Technically, I didn't break in; I had a key," he made an attempt at joking, saw she wasn't amused and changed track. "I was just trying to help you. I was worried about you after everything you'd been through, and when I went to the motel and didn't find you there, I thought you might have gone back to your house. I knew it would be hard for you. I didn't mean to trick you, and I definitely didn't want to take advantage of the fact that you're vulnerable right now. I *really* just wanted to help you."

"If you *really* wanted to help me, then why did you leave me to wake up alone in your house with nothing but a note to explain that you'd gone to work?" It had been terrifying to wake up from the grips of a nightmare all by herself in a strange house.

"I'm sorry," he said immediately. "I should have woken you to tell you, but you were finally sleeping soundly, and I didn't want to wake you—you needed to rest."

"I was scared," she whispered, hating that everything left her fearful these days.

"I'm sorry. I didn't intend to do it, but we got a call that another family was killed."

She was instantly crestfallen. "Another one?"

"Yes, I'm sorry, Annabelle."

"How many?"

"Two, an elderly couple. The wife was disabled, he left her alive, even let her see him."

She closed her eyes for a second, trying to take it all in. She was aware of a presence right in front of her even before his hands rested lightly on her shoulders, careful to avoid the injury on her left one. Detective Montague didn't speak, just waited until she was ready.

"Their names were Rawlin and Lorraine Rankling. Do you know anyone by that name?" he asked, when she finally opened her eyes.

She shook her head because she didn't trust herself to speak right now.

"Did you take Katherine to the emergency room recently?"

His question surprised her. "Yes, about a month ago. She fell off her bike and hit her head, she had to get stitches."

"Do you remember seeing Dr. Daniels there that day?"

"Dr. Daniels didn't treat Katherine, and I don't remember seeing him, but I wasn't paying attention to anything but my sister. Katherine is…" Realizing her mistake, "I mean *was*," steadying the hitch in her voice, "a bit of a wimp. She was screaming and crying the whole time we were there. I don't remember anything else. Why are you asking me questions about Dr. Daniels again?" She didn't want to believe that the doctor who had been so nice to her was in any way involved.

"Right now we're pursuing several leads," he told her vaguely.

Annoyed, she wiggled free from his grip. "That's a terrible answer."

"Well, it's all I can give you at the moment," he replied unapologetically.

"You keep sending me mixed signals," she groaned. "Sometimes you're really nice and sometimes you're almost cold. Are you interested in me or not?"

"I'm..." he started to answer as the door swung open.

"Xavier, Rob wants to see us, now," Detective Hannah announced, then disappeared as quickly as she'd come.

"We're not finished talking," Detective Montague informed her as he headed for the door. "Wait for me at my desk. When I'm done, I'll come get you and we'll grab some lunch."

"Detective Montague, I don't think that's a good..." Annabelle protested immediately.

He interrupted, "Xavier," he corrected. "Please, Annabelle, wait for me."

"Fine," she agreed reluctantly, not sure why she would consent to go on a date with this man, and hoping that she didn't like it. Once he was gone, she gathered herself and breezed out into the main room, located Detective Montague's desk, and sat. Feeling very conspicuous, Annabelle began to fiddle with the pile of pens on the desk. She didn't think it was a good idea to start calling Detective Montague by his first name. They weren't dating—they weren't even friends—and he had been completely accurate when he'd said that she was just a victim in a case he was working.

Yet she knew he wanted it to be more than that.

And she didn't.

Well, at least she thought she didn't, but he had called her

Belle.

When she'd been a lonely, sad little girl she had had a dream where her prince charming had come riding in on a big white horse and carried her away to live in a big beautiful castle, where she would never be sad or lonely ever again. Her prince charming had called her Belle. No one else had ever called her that. Not her parents or her siblings or any of the few friends she'd had, just the man who would love her and care for her forever and ever.

As a little girl, Annabelle had thought it was so special for her prince to call her Belle, and in her head, she had grown to connect the name Belle to the man who would love her like no one else ever had.

It was stupid.

She knew that.

It was just a coincidence that Xavier had called her Belle. She was letting her childhood dreams cloud her judgment. Whatever Xavier saw in her wasn't really there. He would quickly realize that and forget all about her, and she would forget all about him, too.

Only she knew that was never going to happen. In her mind, Detective Montague had already morphed into Xavier.

She was attempting to spin one of his pens around her fingers, when it flew across the desk and into a stack of papers instead. Reaching out a hand to retrieve it, she accidentally sent the papers scattering. Distracted, she began to restack the pile when she saw a photo of her house. These must be the crime scene pictures. Against her better judgment, Annabelle began to rifle through them. She didn't expect to see anything she hadn't already because she'd already been back to her house and seen all the blood.

Then her hand froze.

It was a photo of her parents. Only they weren't her parents anymore.

Well they were, only someone had slashed their throats, ripped out their eyes, cut out their tongues, and chopped off their hands.

Rifling quickly through the stack, she found one of her brother

Julian, and one of Paul.

Their bodies had been mutilated, too.

Hesitating before she continued, surely there couldn't be one of Katherine. No one could do this to a seven-year-old child. But the very next picture showed her baby sister's lifeless corpse, minus hands, tongue, and eyes.

How could any person have this much hate for another human being that they could mutilate them so horribly?

Her hands began to shake uncontrollably.

Someone had done this to her family and Detective Montague, who had pretended to be so understanding and thoughtful, had accused her of doing this.

Feeling her whole body begin to quake, she dropped the papers on Detective Montague's desk and fled for the elevator.

"Annabelle?"

Spinning around, she found Detective Hannah watching her worriedly.

"You look pale? Is everything okay?"

"Fine," she managed to croak out, then fled before the detective could pepper her with more questions. With tears pricking the backs of her eyes and a sob catching in her throat, Annabelle desperately sought refuge. The only problem was she didn't know where to go to find it.

* * * * *

12:36 P.M.

"Kate? What's up?" Xavier was looking from his empty desk to his partner who was staring intently at the elevator. He hoped that Kate hadn't said anything to Annabelle to upset her. He had felt like he was finally making progress with her when she agreed to go out for lunch with him.

"Annabelle just ran out of here like the place was on fire."

Kate turned to look at him, and he saw the genuine concern there.

"Did you say something to her?"

"No, she was already at the elevator when I came in," Kate explained. "I just asked her if she was okay. She said she was fine, but she looked pale—something really freaked her out."

"I asked her to wait at my desk until we were done with Rob, then we were going to have lunch." Xavier was already half way to his desk and when he was close enough, he saw immediately what had upset Annabelle.

"Xavier? What is it?" Kate came up beside him.

"She saw these." He held out the crime scene photos from the Englewood house, struggling to draw a deep breath as he pictured how Annabelle had felt seeing what had been done to her family.

"Oh…" Kate looked horrified. "Well, that certainly explains the look on her face."

"I've got to go and find her." He'd already made the mistake of leaving her alone this morning; he wasn't going to do that again.

"Go," Kate nodded. "Wait, Xavier, you don't know where she is. Do you want me to put out an APB on her?"

"No, I know where she'll be." He grabbed his jacket, keys and cell phone, positive that he knew where Annabelle would have fled.

"Okay, call me when you find her," Kate called to his back as he took the stairs down to the parking garage.

Xavier hardly remembered the drive to his house. All he could think of was that he hoped he was right and Annabelle had sought sanctuary at his house. And that she hadn't done anything stupid.

Thoughts of Julia couldn't help but infiltrate his mind.

He remembered the fear he'd felt that night as he'd sped home, unsure of what he'd find when he got there. The scene that met him when he arrived was chaotic. Police officers everywhere, the blood, the screaming, the feeling of wondering how he could be married to someone and yet know so little about what went on inside their head. That was the night he'd found out Julia had been raped. That was the night he'd found out just how far gone Julia really was. That was the night that he'd lost her forever.

He couldn't go through that again.

Whipping his car into the driveway, he didn't bother to lock it as he flew through the front door. Immediately he let out a breath when he heard the shower running; at least he had been right about where he'd find her.

Satisfied she was there, he slowed his pace. Annabelle was upset, she'd just seen the pictures of what someone had done to her family, of what she had been accused of doing, and the last thing he wanted to do was startle her.

Plus, he was also pretty sure that some of her anger would be directed at him. She knew he was interested in her, and he knew she would be upset that he hadn't told her about the post-mortem mutilation, and that he had thought her capable of such a heinous act.

Reaching the bathroom, he heard the sound of sobbing mingle with the pounding water. Edging the door open, he saw her huddled on the floor of the shower. Her knees were drawn up to her chest, her head tucked in, and her arms encircled her body like she was physically holding herself together.

Without a second thought, Xavier stripped off his shirt, dropped his pants and boxers, and opened the shower door. Annabelle didn't notice him until he sat behind her and pulled her against his chest.

He expected her to fight him, but instead she came into his arms willingly, resting against him as she cried. When her sobs ceased, Xavier held her for a moment longer, and then gently tugged her to her feet. Again, she came willingly and stood still while he poured some shampoo into the palm of his hand and began to wash her hair. Annabelle leaned into him as he massaged her head, pressing against him, and he had to struggle to reign in his desire.

When he was done, he turned off the shower and drew her out

behind him. Rubbing her dry with a towel, Annabelle barely seemed to register him; her white eyes were still glazed with shock. Throwing his clothes back on, he wrapped her in a fluffy towel and carried her to his room, setting her down on the bed as he went to find her something to wear. In the spare room, he dug out some of Julia's old clothes he hadn't been able to part with yet, which were still packed away in boxes.

Returning to the bedroom, he saw Annabelle's eyes were closed and he assumed she had fallen asleep, but at his touch they popped back open. She didn't move while he slipped the sweatshirt over her head and tugged her arms through the sleeves, carefully trying to avoid causing pain to her injured shoulder.

He needn't have bothered; Annabelle seemed to have retreated from the world to hide inside herself. Probably a trick she had employed many times over the years and would likely employ many more before this was over.

The sweat pants he slipped her legs into were way too long. Julia had been a good five inches taller than Annabelle, so he rolled them up. After dressing her, he tucked the covers up around her chin and stretched out beside her, surprised and pleased when she immediately curled into him, nestling her face against his neck.

Soaking in how amazing it felt to be holding Annabelle in his arms, for a few minutes Xavier just allowed himself to enjoy it. However, he knew it couldn't last, he and Annabelle needed to talk about what she had discovered. Gently he began to stroke her hair. "Belle, I think we should talk."

"Why do you call me Belle?" came the soft reply.

"I don't know, why?" he answered, surprised with the question.

"It's stupid."

"You can tell me anything." He slid his arm out from under her and propped himself up on his elbows so he could see her better.

"When I was little, I used to dream that the man who would love me called me Belle," she answered dully, her unfocused gaze staring unseeingly through him.

He was touched by the sadness and longing in her voice. "I'm sure your family loved you," he assured her, knowing what it was like to grow up sure, and yet not quite sure that your family loved you.

At that, tears began to trickle down her cheeks again. "How could someone do that? How could someone chop off the hands and rip out the eyes and tongue of another person? It's so horrible. Wasn't killing them enough? What kind of monster did this?"

"I don't know," he answered her truthfully. "I don't know why he did it, but I think that it means something to him, and that's a good thing. If he's doing this for a specific reason, then it means we can find him."

"How could you think that I could do that?" she whispered desperately.

"It wasn't that I wanted to think you did it, that was what the initial evidence suggested," he explained. "I *am* sorry, Belle, really sorry," he assured her, hoping that she would be able to forgive him.

"Why didn't you tell me?" her voice was flat, more disappointed than accusing.

"Because I didn't think you needed to know."

"You didn't think I needed to know?" she repeated, with only a hint of incredulity. "My parents and brothers and sister were mutilated, and you didn't think I had a right to know that?"

"I didn't think you could deal with it right now; I would have told you when you were ready to hear it." Xavier wasn't sure he would have ever told her unless backed into a corner.

"Do you really think Dr. Daniels could be the killer?" Annabelle was still steadfastly refusing to meet his gaze.

"Maybe, but he's not the only person we're looking into at the moment."

Annabelle pressed her body closer against his. "Xavier, I know you have to work, but would it be okay if you stayed here with me for a little while?"

Ignoring the burning desire pulsing inside his body, Xavier told himself that Annabelle needed his support right now, nothing more. "Of course." His hand cradled her head against his chest, his face in her hair. "I'm not going to leave you," he promised. "Just try to get some rest. I'm gonna call Kate and tell her I'm not coming back in today and I'm going to stay right here by your side for as long as you need me to."

He deliberately did not add that he hoped that would be for a really long time. Annabelle was in no frame of mind to be committing to a relationship right now. She needed a friend, someone to help her with no strings attached. He would be that person for her, and if when this was over, she decided she wanted more, then great; and if not he'd walk away. As hard as he knew it would be, if him walking away was what Annabelle wanted, then he would do it.

He tenderly kissed her forehead, then the tip of her nose; hesitating, his lips hovered above hers. Xavier wanted more than anything to kiss her but Annabelle was vulnerable right now, and she'd already accused him of taking advantage of her once. He didn't want to ruin things between them before they even started by doing it again.

Then Annabelle's eyes met his for the first time. In them, he saw acknowledgment of what he wanted to do and permission to do it, and ever so slowly he brought his mouth to hers. Ensuring the kiss was soft and light, Annabelle didn't return it, but she didn't shrink away from it either.

When he pulled back he met her hungry eyes, and she laced her fingers in his hair and pulled his mouth back down upon hers. This time, her kiss was hard and fiery and the next thing he knew she had released his hair and her fingers were fumbling at his belt.

Breaking off the kiss, he caught her hands and stilled them. "Belle, wait." He stopped her. "If and when we do this, I want it to be perfect. I want it to be something we're both going to remember for the rest of our lives. I want it to be something that you *want* to do, not something you think will make you forget about everything you've been through. I'm sorry, I don't want to hurt you."

Annabelle nodded, her face growing sad once more, and as he lay back down beside her, she immediately folded into him. With his arms encircling her, he resumed stroking her hair, and in less than five minutes, he felt her relax against him, sleep taking hold.

Reaching out a hand to grab the phone from his bedside table, Xavier hoped that when he found this killer, Annabelle would give him a chance, give *them* a chance, and not ask him to walk away.

MAY 9TH

7:02 A.M.

"I have bad news," Diane entered Rob's office with a grim face.

"More bad news?" Xavier didn't want anything to spoil the high he'd been riding since yesterday afternoon. Although he'd laid awake for close to two hours holding Annabelle in his arms as she slept, he had eventually dozed off, awakening in the early evening to Annabelle's whimpering. Drawing her closer, she had immediately settled back down, and another hour passed before she had awakened in a panic.

Xavier had been concerned that when Annabelle awoke, her numb and flat mood would have been replaced by one of anger and resentment, and that she would immediately begin to push him away. But Annabelle had allowed him to comfort her as she was held in the grip of her nightmare, and when he'd suggested dinner she had willingly followed him to the kitchen, watching absently as he prepared something for them to eat.

After dinner, they'd watched a movie. Sitting together on the couch had reminded Xavier of all those good times with Julia just after they had been married. He'd missed simple pleasures like that and wondered why he had kept himself out of circulation for so long. He loved being in a relationship.

When darkness had fallen and he told her it was time for bed, he had waited with bated breath for her to make a decision when he'd asked if she wanted to sleep in the spare room or his room. Without much hesitation she had chosen his room, so once again he had fallen asleep with a woman curled up in his arms.

This morning he had refrained from making the same mistake as the previous day and awakened Annabelle to inform her that he had to go to work. Unsure about leaving her alone, he didn't think that she would do anything stupid but she was still in shock and shouldn't have to be alone right now. He had even bitten his tongue and offered to call her friend, Ricky Preston. Annabelle had insisted, though, that she didn't mind staying alone, and that she wouldn't mind some peace and quiet to process things. So he had reluctantly left her in his living room, curled up in a corner of the couch looking small and scared, and come in to work where apparently more bad news awaited them.

"What've you got, Diane?" Rob asked tiredly, none of them wanted to hear more bad news on this case.

Diane cast him a concerned glance that made his heart beat uncomfortably hard. "What's going on?" Xavier asked.

"It's about Annabelle." Diane now avoided his gaze.

"What about her?" He didn't like the fact that Kate wasn't the only one who seemed to know that he was attracted to Annabelle.

"I was finishing up with the evidence we collected from the Englewood house. I was going through the things from Annabelle's room, and…" she trailed off.

A horrible feeling brewed in his gut. "Don't tell me you think Annabelle is involved in this…"

"No, no, no," Diane assured him, then took a deep breath. "I think Annabelle was raped."

Everyone gasped, which Xavier thought was odd since he couldn't breathe at all. The fact that everyone was staring at him with thinly veiled concern wasn't helping. "We asked Annabelle and she said she wasn't," he protested weakly, pictures of Julia floating through his mind.

"Actually, Annabelle said she doesn't remember anything about that night," Kate corrected gently.

"I found semen and vaginal secretions on the sheets," Diane explained. "I'm sorry, Xavier."

"Why are you apologizing to me?" he asked hollowly, not liking everyone's sudden interest in his personal life. "Maybe she had consensual sex."

"I also found evidence of vaginal bleeding," Diane continued awkwardly. "I think Annabelle was a virgin."

No one said anything, and Xavier knew they were all waiting to see his reaction. He also knew that if Rob found out how personally involved he was making himself in this case, then he would be yanked off it faster than the speed of light. He forced himself to maintain control. "We wondered why he drugged the Englewoods but no one else," he said at last, pleased when his voice came out cool and calm. "Maybe it wasn't because the Englewoods were his first and he was nervous, maybe it was because he wanted to sleep with Annabelle."

"Maybe." Rob looked relieved that he was holding it together. "Okay, let's look at our suspects, try to decide on a direction to move in."

"Well number one, we have Lachlan Thompson," Kate began. "Motive would be to get rid of his son-in-law and grandchildren so there would be nothing stopping his daughter from coming back home to care for him. If it was Lachlan, that might explain why only Annabelle was raped," she faltered a little and shot him another worried glance. "He didn't rape his daughter or granddaughter, and perhaps he didn't realize Lorraine Rankling was disabled until he saw her."

"Although we do believe that Lachlan sexually and possibly physically abused his daughter throughout her childhood," Xavier inserted, recalling the look in Nicole Jenner's eyes when they'd asked her if her father had hurt her.

"Okay, so we have a possible motive but no evidence," Rob's eyebrows waggled as he spoke.

"No one heard him make any direct threats to his daughter's family. But he does drive a red car, and Ricky Preston said he saw one parked out in front of his house in the days leading up to the

Englewood murders," Xavier added. "Plus, Kate found out that John Englewood did some electrical work at the bar where Lachlan likes to hang out."

"And then we have Dr. Bruce Daniels," Kate continued. "He's been a doctor involved in Lorraine Rankling's case since the beginning. Dr. Pedding said that someone has been abusing Lorraine, and apparently Dr. Daniels is regularly alone with the woman, which would give him the opportunity to do that. Plus, both the Englewood and Jenner families recently visited the emergency room while Dr. Daniels was working. Since he has a history of making patients sicker so he can swoop in and save them, it's not so big of a jump to believe that he might have branched out and started creating his own problems where he can be the hero to traumatized women."

"We also just found out that four months ago, Dr. Daniels got dumped by his fiancée of two years," he informed everyone. "After the accusations that he was poisoning little kids and he was sent to counseling, he fell for his therapist. She asked for him to be transferred to a colleague so she and Dr. Daniels could start dating. They dated for a while, then Dr. Daniels proposed. It seems she dumped him about a week before the wedding, announced it while he was at work, told him that she had been cheating on him throughout their entire relationship and was pregnant with her lover's baby."

"So, Lachlan Thompson just found out he's dying and Bruce Daniels just got dumped, both traumatic occurrences that could have pushed them into taking drastic measures to get what they wanted," Rob mused.

"I think we should add Ricky Preston to the list of suspects," Xavier announced.

"Xavier, just because you think…" Kate shot him a warning glare.

"No it's not because I'm jealous of him," he denied adamantly, catching the tightening in his boss' jaw. "Just listen to me for a moment," he urged them, and when no one objected, he plowed on. "The night the Ranklings were murdered, Annabelle wanted to go and stay with him, she went to his house, knocked on the door, called out but she couldn't get any answer from him." He deliberately left out his own attempt to contact the man.

"Maybe he's a heavy sleeper," Rob suggested dryly.

"Annabelle said he's not."

"Or he could have been out walking," Kate put in. "He told us he's been having trouble sleeping."

"He offered to let Annabelle stay with him, and she tried calling him but never got an answer, why would he then ignore her when he said he'd be there for her?" Xavier couldn't give up on this; Ricky Preston creeped him out.

"There could be any number of reasons why he didn't answer." Diane looked doubtful.

"Yes, there could be," he admitted, "but all I know is that Annabelle hammered on the door, yelled out, there was no noise from a TV or radio, and no response."

"Annabelle hammered or you hammered?" The look Rob shot him indicated he already knew that he'd been there that night.

Xavier forged on. "The way he looks at Annabelle, he's interested in her."

"Annabelle said there's nothing going on between them," Kate reminded him overly patiently.

"I know, but that doesn't mean there isn't something one-sided there." He was positive that Annabelle wasn't interested in Ricky Preston, she'd told him she never dated. "You saw him, Kate, the way he looked at her, the way he talked about her. Even if Annabelle doesn't realize it, Ricky likes her."

"Kate?" Rob looked to her for her opinion.

"He does look at her like he likes her," Kate agreed reluctantly.

"Maybe that's why he raped her," Xavier had to force the words out. "Maybe this was all just a bid to isolate Annabelle and then get her to rely on him, and before she knows it he springs on her that he's in love with her. The Jenners and Ranklings could just be collateral damage."

"Anything else to add to your theory?" Rob didn't look convinced that Ricky could be involved.

"He has a broken arm, and yet he drove all around town buying Annabelle clothes and food while she was at the motel." That was all he could come up with for now. And it didn't even make any sense.

"You can drive with a cast on," Kate contradicted. "Not at first, but when your arm stops hurting."

Xavier huffed and narrowed his eyes at his partner. "Ricky Preston is…" He was searching for the right words to articulate what he was feeling. "Look, I don't know how to say it, but my gut says something's not right with that guy."

"I won't count him out," Rob told him seriously, "but I'm also not counting him in. If you can find some connection between him and the Jenners and Ranklings, we'll talk more. Right now I think Annabelle is the most useful tool we have…"

"She doesn't remember anything," Xavier reminded his boss.

"She thinks she doesn't," Rob contradicted. "He drugged her; she might have seen or heard more than she knows, and she might be subconsciously blocking something out. Take her back to her house and see if it prompts her to remember anything."

"She's already been back; it didn't go well," he confessed.

Rob arched a brown brow. "I know, but this time you'll go with her."

"We also have to tell her what happened to her while she was unconscious," Diane reminded them.

All eyes turned to him once more. "I'll tell her," Xavier sighed, knowing it would be best coming from him but dreading having to say those words to her.

"All right, good, we have a plan." Rob looked pleased; he always liked it when they had a concrete plan of attack.

Filing out of Rob's office, Xavier hoped that his boss' plan of attack ran smoothly and produced results.

* * * * *

9:21 A.M.

"I'm not sure I can do this." Annabelle was squashed up against the passenger door in Xavier's car.

"I'm going to be right by your side," he assured her.

She was still doubtful, recalling the other night when she'd gone back inside her home, that had been a disaster and she hadn't even known at the time all the facts about what had happened to her family. "I really don't think I can go back in there," she insisted again. Already the closer they got, the more she started to shake uncontrollably.

"You can do it, Belle," Xavier told her confidently. "You can do it because we're going to do it together. I'm not going to leave you."

Xavier had said that to her yesterday and he had been true to his word.

Annabelle had been mad at Xavier right up until the second he had joined her in the shower. When she'd fled the police station despite her anger at Xavier she had headed straight for his house. As a little girl, the shower had been her place of solitude; curled up in the steam, she would cry her little eyes out. And yesterday when she'd been pushed to her limits, she had reverted back to that scared and lonely child.

When Xavier's arms had encircled her, she had been too thrilled that she wasn't alone that she hadn't had any energy left to stay angry. In fact, she hadn't had any energy left for anything. She had allowed Xavier to wash her hair, then dry her off and dress her as though she were an infant.

Even though it terrified her to admit it, Annabelle had enjoyed the feel of his strong arms holding her, his warm body against her, and when he kissed her she hadn't protested; in fact, she'd kissed him back. He had wanted to take things further, she'd known that, literally been able to feel it, and for one delusional second she had been ready to go along with it, but Xavier had stopped her and this morning she was glad he had.

At least he hadn't made the same mistake as last time she spent the night. This morning he had woken her up to tell her he was leaving for work; he'd even cooked breakfast for her and delivered it to her on a tray so she could eat in bed. She hadn't wanted to stay in bed alone though and had wandered through to the living room, curling up on the couch and staring aimlessly at whatever nonsense was on TV.

She had still been doing that when Xavier had returned to his house an hour ago. Although he only lived about fifteen minutes from her house it had taken him three quarters of an hour to coax her as far as the car.

Annabelle didn't want to ever set foot inside her house again, but Xavier had wheedled and begged. He was eventually able to get her to agree, because she wanted to help stop this man before another family was destroyed. If going back to her house might help that to happen, then—as much as she hated it—she had to do it.

"I keep telling you I don't remember that night," she shuddered as they pulled to a stop outside her house.

He turned to face her. "Your family was different, Belle, and we don't know why. But, so far, your family has been the only one that was drugged. That means maybe you did see something and you're just blocking it out because it's too much to deal with at the moment."

"Why was my family different?" she demanded.

"Well, we thought it might be because you were first. Maybe he wasn't too confident about killing so many people at one time and he thought it would be easier if you were all out cold."

"So he drugged us," she repeated. "That's why at the hospital you were asking about who cooked dinner." She remembered that conversation well because it happened right before Xavier told her that he thought she was a killer. "That means he was in our house before that night; he had to be to drug the food. Do you think that's the only reason we were drugged and the others weren't? Because we were first and he was nervous, that's why we were different?"

"I don't know, Belle."

She read something hidden in his tone. "No more secrets, Xavier, please," she begged. She'd already lost enough control over her life.

Shifting uncomfortably, Xavier reached for her hands. "I'm afraid I have bad news," he began solemnly. "I don't know how to tell you this, Belle…"

"Just say it," she steeled herself, not liking the look on Xavier's face one little bit.

"We think that he…uh…that he…raped you." Xavier looked devastated and she remembered that his wife had been raped.

But Annabelle just felt numb.

She felt nothing at all.

Which she thought was odd. She was a virgin; well, she *had* been. She should feel horrified to learn that she had just lost her virginity to a rapist. And not just a rapist, but also the man who had slaughtered and mutilated her family and framed her for his crimes.

She was about to ask Xavier what was wrong with her when she realized that she couldn't see. Everything had gone black.

"Annabelle." Xavier's sharp voice echoed inside her head. "Belle, come on, open your eyes," he commanded.

Were her eyes closed? She thought she'd just gone blind.

"Belle, wake up." A hand slapped lightly at her cheeks. "Open your eyes."

Struggling to comply, she managed to force open her eyes to meet Xavier's panicked hazel gaze.

Xavier sighed with relief. "You fainted. Are you okay?"

"I think so," she mumbled.

"I'm going to take you to the hospital. I'm sorry; this was too much." He turned the engine back on.

"No, Xavier, I don't want to go back to the hospital. I'm okay, really, let's just get this over with." She threw open the door and climbed from the car, stalking determinedly across the yard toward her front door.

"Annabelle." Xavier caught up to her, grabbed her arm and spun her around to face him. "I think we need to talk about this."

"I don't want to." She couldn't deal with that right now, but she could ignore it.

"Belle…"

"I mean it. I can't do that now."

He examined her carefully. "Do you have a key that you keep hidden somewhere in case someone gets locked out?"

Confused, she asked, "What?"

"Your house wasn't broken into," he continued, "do you keep a key someplace where someone might find it."

Catching on to what he was trying to do, she let him distract her. "Yeah, we have one under my mom's bird feeder." She paused at the bird feeder on the way to the door. "Do you think that's how he got in without having to break in?"

"Maybe." Xavier held out a bag for her to drop the key into. "We'll check it out. Does anyone know you keep it here?"

"I'm not sure."

Slipping his hand around hers, he began to tug her along behind him. His hand tightened around hers as he drew her through the front door. "I want you to walk me through everything you did that night."

"You really think I might have seen something?"

"I don't know, Belle, but so far we don't have a lot else to go on." He stooped to kiss her forehead before straightening. "Okay, I want you to start from the very beginning, from when you first got home."

She pushed her mind back to that afternoon. "Katherine and I came home about four o'clock and I sent her to her room to change her clothes. While she was changing, I put on a load of laundry." Once she began, everything started to come back. "Katherine came back down about ten minutes later and we made the cookies. Katherine had been bugging me for days to make some with her..." She trailed off as she thought of her little sister's begging. Katherine had just lost her two front teeth and the effect added to her cuteness, making it almost impossible to say no to her.

"What happened next?" Xavier asked gently, taking her hand again and squeezing it supportively.

She brushed at her eyes. "By the time the cookies were done, everyone was home. I put the washing in the dryer and started on dinner while Katherine did her homework. Then we ate together, but after dinner we all got kind of tired." Her brow furrowed in concentration. "I forgot about that. I guess it was the drugs; we thought we were coming down with the flu or something. I don't know what the others did, but I sent Katherine straight to bed. I could hardly keep my eyes open, so I followed her. I don't know what happened after that. I'm sorry."

"Okay," Xavier said softly, "I'm going to take you to your room. Can you handle that?"

Giving a shaky nod, she answered, "If you stay with me."

"I'm not going anywhere," he promised, slipping an arm around her waist as he guided her up the stairs.

Her steps slowed as they got closer to her bedroom, but she plodded determinedly on.

"Hanging in there?" Xavier asked at the door.

"Uh huh," she said, before she took a step inside.

"All right, I want you to close your eyes and take a deep breath," Xavier's voice was soft, almost hypnotically quiet. "You got into bed, you were tired, not feeling well, did you open a window?"

Surprised, she'd forgotten about that. "Yeah, I did. How did you know? Oh, that's right; you were here. This is never going to work, Xavier. After going to bed, I don't remember anything until I woke up with you hovering over me."

"Give it a try." He sat her down in her rocking chair. "So you opened the window and got into bed. Did you think about or worry about anything before you fell asleep?"

"I did worry about something. One of the kids in my class, his parents just split up and he's been acting out and I've been trying everything I could think of to get him to open up to me. And then after that, someone was standing beside me, but I don't think it was you." Her eyes popped open and grew wide. "I remember someone being in here with me."

"Do you remember what he looked like?"

Annabelle concentrated really hard, trying to make the fuzzy edges smooth into something recognizable. "Tall, muscled, blue eyes." She became frustrated, "But I can't see his face properly, it's all hazy."

"That's okay," Xavier assured her, "you're doing great. Does he say anything?"

Closing her eyes once more to help herself focus. "Yes, he says...he says..." trying to force the words to become clear enough to hear. "He says 'Annabelle, I've been waiting a long time for this.'"

* * * * *

10:11 A.M.

He wasn't pleased Annabelle had come back here with that Detective Montague. The man was nosy, a busybody, an interferer, a snoop, a prier, meddlesome, and he couldn't afford to have someone like that hanging around until everything was complete. He was getting there; he'd already done three of the families on his list, and now he was almost done. But almost wasn't completely, and since he'd come this far, he couldn't let his plan be derailed.

As he watched them through his binoculars, he could just make out their figures in Annabelle's bedroom, and he remembered being in there with her that night. She had looked so beautiful lying there, and he was so glad he had decided to go with the drugs for the Englewoods. He had wanted Annabelle from the moment he'd met her. That thick chocolate brown hair, those white eyes, her sweet nature—his desire for her was overwhelming and he'd been pleased that he had gone with the newer version of the plan.

Originally, he had been going for the complete annihilation of each of the families on his list. But the more he'd thought about it, the more he realized that it wouldn't be enough to satisfy himself. He needed them to suffer. And so he'd decided leaving one alone would work so much better. He had to admit that Annabelle had played a large part in that decision. The framing thing he'd just added in at the last minute to amuse himself.

That night with Annabelle had been incredible, even if she had been barely conscious at the time. It was a night he would never, ever forget. He was pretty sure that she had seen him, and probably heard him too, but it didn't matter, if she knew it was him she hadn't said anything to anyone. Perhaps she'd blocked out what he'd done to her. Or perhaps thoughts of her new admirer had pushed everything else from her mind.

Nicole Jenner didn't do anything for him, and never had, so he hadn't bothered with her. And he'd already had as much fun with Lorraine Rankling as was possible. Those visits with her had always been entertaining. Rawlin was so desperate to get away for a little while that he never paid attention to how edgy his wife got whenever she saw him. Rawlin was so relaxed when he returned home that he never noticed his wife's pained eyes. He was careful to only ever hurt her in places where no one would find the tiny wounds unless they were looking. And Rawlin Rankling was too naive to think that another human being would hurt his disabled wife.

Still, thinking about Annabelle was not going to accomplish anything. Maybe when it was all finished, he would come back for her. But right now he needed her and her police officer boyfriend otherwise occupied.

He needed a diversion, and he had the perfect one in mind.

With a gleaming smile, he lit the match.

* * * * *

10:35 A.M.

"Annabelle, why don't you date?" Xavier was watching her closely; he knew she was near her breaking point. An hour in this house—after what had happened to her and her family here—was almost more than she could bear.

"What?"

"The other day you said that you never date. Why?" He was curious to know why she didn't date when she was so beautiful. Her features were so delicate, her eyes so exquisite, that he couldn't imagine that she hadn't had men falling at her feet her entire adult life.

Shrugging uncomfortably, she asked, "Who would want to go out with someone like me?"

He wondered what kind of childhood she'd had that had her so lacking in self-esteem. "What are you talking about?" he demanded. "You're beautiful, your hair is gorgeous, your eyes are amazing, you're sweet and thoughtful, you take care of your family. You're perfect," he finished a little breathily and took a step towards her, hoping she wouldn't back away. She didn't, and when he took another step closer she came to meet him, tilting her face up to meet his. When he hesitated, she took his face and pulled it down, kissing him lightly before letting go and fleeing to the other side of the room.

"I'm not perfect," she told him seriously.

Disagreeing, Xavier thought she was amazing. She hadn't fallen apart even though she'd lost her whole family in one foul swoop. She hadn't fallen apart when he'd told her she'd been raped. She had agreed to come back here even though it terrified her because she didn't want any other family to go through what she had. "Belle, did your parents ever hurt you?"

"No," she answered quickly, a little too quickly. "Why?"

"Because someone's given you the impression—the wrong impression—that you're not worth anything, and I don't like that."

"There's nothing remotely appealing about me. I don't know why a guy like you would even be the least bit interested in me."

Pleased that she was thinking about him at all, maybe she wasn't as set on her no dating philosophy as she claimed. "A guy like me?"

Her cheeks turned an endearing shade of bright pink. "You're, you know...hot, and really kind, and..." she trailed off, clearly embarrassed.

He was encouraged by the fact that she thought he was hot, and even more that she thought he was kind. "You're not the only one who feels self-conscious and has things about themselves they don't like," he told her. "I hate my name."

"Xavier Montague? It's a fine name."

"Xavier is my middle name. My parents thought that since my father's last name is Montague it would be cute to name me Romeo."

Annabelle attempted to stifle a giggle. "Romeo Montague? Like from Romeo and Juliet?"

"Yep." Seeing Annabelle's mood lighten made him actually not hate his name for the first time since he was about nine. It had been fourth grade where one of his peers had finally gotten the connection between his name and one half of perhaps the best known fictional lovers in the world. Ever since, he had hated his name. He refused to use it, and started going by his middle name instead.

"That's funny." Annabelle relaxed a little.

"Then there's my eyes," Xavier continued, enjoying seeing Annabelle so relaxed. He wished she could be this way all the time.

"Your eyes are beautiful," Annabelle protested.

Putting a finger to his left eye, he removed the contact lens, revealing his green eye. "I have heterochromia, one hazel eye and one green eye." Kids had teased him since preschool about his different colored eyes. As he got older, the teasing stopped but the staring didn't. Eventually he'd gotten so sick of all the stares and questions that he'd started wearing a hazel contact lens over his green eye.

"That's even more beautiful," Annabelle smiled shyly.

"Just like I think your eyes are beautiful," he told her, closing the distance between them once more. "You're beautiful, Annabelle, whether you know it or not. You are a very special woman."

Blushing, she stared deeply into his eyes for a long moment, then took a step backward. But it was too late. Xavier had seen the desire in her gaze, the attraction between them was mutual, even if Annabelle wouldn't admit it.

Uncomfortable, she headed for the door. "I need to go to the bathroom." Throwing the door open, she froze, her eyes growing wide. "Xavier, fire, the house is on fire."

Springing to her side, he saw the hallway filled with smoke. Hurrying to the top of the stairs, he looked down, he could see red and yellow and orange flames dancing wildly.

"Oh my gosh, we're going to die," Annabelle's voice was high with panic and she clung tightly to him.

"We're not going to die," he assured her. "I'm going to go down, try to see how bad it is, maybe there's a way out. You stay here." Gently he pried her hands from his arm and gave her a quick kiss. Ever since he was a kid, Xavier was always good in a crisis; as long as he had something concrete to do, he was fine.

He descended the stairs to assess how bad things were. The heat down here was almost overwhelming and he could barely even make it to the bottom of the steps. Downstairs, the flames consumed most of the living room and he could see no safe passage through them that would lead him and Annabelle outside.

Returning to the second floor he found Annabelle frozen in place, right where he'd left her. "We can't get out down there," he informed her.

"We're going to die," she murmured again, her eyes glassy with shock as she began to cough from the thick smoke filling the hallway.

"We are not going to die," he repeated, grabbing her hand and pulling her back into her bedroom, closing the door behind them. "We'll go out the window."

"Out the window?" she squeaked, going even paler than she'd already been. "Xavier, I'm afraid of heights."

"Fire's too strong for us to get through it; it's not going to be long before the floor caves in and your whole house goes up. We need to get out of here now." He yanked open her window. "We can jump to this tree and climb down it." Xavier had noticed the huge tree outside Annabelle's window earlier because it reminded him of the one that had stood outside the window of his room at his dad's house. As a child, he spent hours climbing up and down it, he'd hung a swing from it, and even worked with his dad to build a tree house in it. He was halfway out the window before he realized Annabelle hadn't joined him. "Come on, Belle." Already smoke was filling the room.

"I can't, I'm sorry, Xavier, I can't, I can't," she was quickly becoming hysterical.

Xavier knew he didn't have time to persuade her. "Does your dad have a ladder?"

Shaking her head, tears spilled out. "No, but Ricky does."

"All right, you stay here, stay down low. I'll climb out, get the ladder, and come get you, okay?"

She was quaking violently now. "Okay," she agreed.

"Belle, I mean it; I'll be back." He grabbed her fiercely, ignoring her wince as he inadvertently squeezed her injured shoulder, and kissed her passionately. Then he lined himself up at the window and leapt, connecting with the branch closest to the window with a thud. Years of practice under his belt, he shimmied down the tree in no time, and was just about to hurdle the small fence between the Englewood home and Ricky Preston's when he heard the squeal of tires. He looked up just in time to see a red car rocket off down the street. He should have run after it, tried to get a plate number, or at least a make and model, but all he could think about was Annabelle still trapped inside her burning house.

Beelining straight for the shed in the back right-hand corner of Ricky's backyard, he barged through the locked door, grabbed the ladder and hightailed it back to the house.

"Detective Montague?" Two of the neighbors they'd interviewed a few days ago met him on the lawn.

"What's going on?" another demanded. "Is someone still in there?"

"Annabelle," he replied, resting the ladder against the side of the house.

"Annabelle's still in there?" The first shot a horrified glance at the fire that was quickly consuming the house.

"Not for long." Xavier was already scampering up the ladder, reaching the top in seconds. "Belle?" he called. The room was now filled with smoke and visibility was down around zero. He climbed back through the window. "Belle?" he yelled again, a little more frantically this time. "It's Xavier, where are you?" He circled around the edges of the room, he was about to give up and wondered if Annabelle had fled to another room farther down the corridor to escape the smoke, when he saw her huddled in a corner. She laid still, eyes closed, and he uttered a prayer that she was okay. Dropping down beside her, his hand clenched and shook her shoulder.

She roused immediately at his touch and began to cough. "You came back," she spluttered, attempting to smile at him.

"Of course I did," he admonished. "Come on, let's get out of here."

Annabelle tried to stand, but she was weakened by the smoke and she struggled to make it to her feet. Wrapping an arm around her waist, Xavier dragged her up and over to the window. He breathed in mouthfuls of the fresh air before readying himself for the climb down.

"I can't do it, Xavier," Annabelle's faint voice whispered, breaking into another coughing fit as she choked on the smoke.

"Yes you can, honey," he encouraged as the most beautiful sound ever echoed in the distance. Sirens. Help was almost here.

Hoisting Annabelle over his shoulder, he managed to maneuver out the window and awkwardly down the ladder, relieved when a pair of steadying hands gripped him. Reaching solid ground, he refused to release Annabelle to her well-meaning neighbor, instead rearranging her in his arms, as someone guided him away from the burning house and across the street.

Clutching Annabelle tightly, Xavier sunk to the ground, knowing that he intended to never let her go again. The killer was still out there, and clearly he regretted leaving Annabelle alive. He was going to hunt this man down if it was the last thing he ever did, and then he was going to make sure that Annabelle knew just how special she was.

* * * * *

11:17 A.M.

"Xavier, are you okay?" Kate jumped from her car and ran over to her partner who was hovering in the middle of the street.

"I'm fine," he assured her.

Giving him a once-over, his voice was a little croaky and he smelled like a smokehouse, but other than that, he seemed all right. "You scared me half to death," she admonished shakily. She hadn't been able to stop shaking since Xavier had called her ten minutes ago to inform her of his and Annabelle's near deaths.

"Kate, I'm really okay," he patted her shoulder.

She turned her attention to the still smoldering Englewood house that the firefighters almost had under control. "You were lucky to make it out of there alive," she murmured.

"Someone didn't like that we came back here." Xavier's gaze shifted to the ambulance a few yards away. "I'm just gonna go check on Annabelle."

Kate followed him to the back of the ambulance where Annabelle was lying on a stretcher. Her face was pale, eyes closed, and even with an oxygen mask over her mouth her breathing was still labored.

Xavier took Annabelle's hand and stroked her hair. At his touch her eyes fluttered open to gaze up at him, and Kate could see immediately that things had changed between her partner and Annabelle.

"We're ready to leave for the hospital," one of the medics announced. "You coming with us, Detective?"

"No, I'm fine..."

"Xavier," Kate began to protest, the medic looking like he was about to join her.

Cutting her off, he said, "Really, I'm fine. I wasn't in there as long as Belle was."

"You're not coming with me?" Annabelle's eyes flared with panic as she pulled off the mask.

"I'm going to be there really soon," Xavier soothed, gently extracting the oxygen mask from her hand and positioning it back over her nose and mouth. "I just need to talk to Kate first, and your neighbors, see if anyone saw anything, but the second I'm done I'm going to come straight to the hospital, okay?"

"Okay," Annabelle's small voice whispered, her eyes drifting tiredly closed.

"Hey," Xavier shook her gently, waiting till she was looking at him. "You are amazing, always remember that."

Annabelle smiled up at him and Xavier kissed her forehead tenderly before climbing down from the ambulance, watching it intently as it drove off down the street.

Kate was watching her partner just as intently. "She remember anything?"

Tearing his eyes away from the corner where the ambulance had just disappeared, he answered, "Actually, yeah. She remembered someone hovering over her during the night—tall and muscled with blue eyes, but she said his face was fuzzy and she couldn't see it properly. Same description we got from both Nicole Jenner and Lorraine Rankling. And she said he spoke to her. Apparently, he called her by name and told her he'd been waiting a long time for this." Xavier's jaw clenched as he repeated what the killer had said to Annabelle right before he raped her.

"So the killer definitely knows his victims," she mused. "But that he said he'd been waiting a long time for her makes Lachlan Thompson look less plausible as our killer. If his motive was to free up his daughter, and the Englewoods and Ranklings were just collateral damage, then it wouldn't make sense for him to be fixated on Annabelle."

"But it doesn't count out Dr. Daniels or Ricky Preston." Xavier looked from the Englewood house to its neighbor.

"Did you see anything when you got here?"

"I wasn't paying attention." Xavier shook his head. "How useless is that?" He brushed her off before she could say anything.

"Annabelle was scared of going back into her house. When I told her she'd been raped, she fainted. When she came to, she went charging off toward the house. I wasn't looking out for anything but her."

"So you didn't see anyone watching you and Annabelle or the house?" she pushed, hoping he'd seen more than he remembered he had.

"I don't remember seeing any cars or people loitering in the street. But..." he drew it out for dramatic effect, "...after we realized the house was on fire and there was no way out through the downstairs, I told Annabelle we'd have to go through the window. She was scared, said she was afraid of heights, so I left her in there and climbed down the tree. I was going to get the ladder from Ricky Preston's shed when I heard tires squeal." He turned, gesturing to the black marks on the road. "It was rocketing off down the street, and I didn't even bother to go after it. Annabelle was still in there."

"Xavier, you did the right thing," she consoled. "Annabelle could have died if she was in there much longer. Did you get the car's color?"

"Red. If he was telling the truth about that, then Ricky Preston was right," he sighed tiredly and rubbed at his red eyes. "We get anything on the fire yet?"

"No, fire's still going, so no one's been in, and I haven't spoken to anyone yet." Kate already knew the answer but asked anyway, "We're thinking it was him?"

"I don't see who else it would be. It was definitely arson, and it would be a pretty big coincidence that Annabelle and I come here to try and get answers, and a random stranger sets her house on fire. Come on, let's talk to the neighbors and see if anyone saw something useful; then we can go to the hospital."

Trailing behind her partner, Kate hoped that he was going to be able to keep his personal and professional responsibilities separate. It wasn't going to do Annabelle any good if he was distracted and that led to the killer slipping away.

She also hoped that Xavier was serious about Annabelle, and not just caught up in the romanticism of being her white knight. If, when all of this was over, Xavier still had feelings for Annabelle, then she'd support him any way she could.

However, Xavier still had unresolved issues with regards to Julia, and he hadn't told Annabelle all that had happened between him and his wife. Kate was pretty sure that if he didn't rectify that mistake soon, then his foundling relationship with Annabelle would be over before it even began.

* * * * *

12:54 P.M.

"It was the middle of the day, most people were out at work and school," Kate consoled him as they headed for Annabelle's room.

These days Xavier felt like they practically lived at the hospital, but he had never been so anxious to walk into a hospital room. He was disappointed that none of Annabelle's neighbors had seen or heard anyone hanging around, but one or two had seen the red car parked in the street. However, the whole time he and Kate had been interviewing the neighbors, all he had been able to think about was Annabelle. Maybe he should have gone with her to the hospital; he didn't like to think of her alone and scared.

"Can we slow down a little?" Kate asked, having to jog to keep up with him.

"We sure can." He shot her a grin as they reached Annabelle's room.

"Xavier, wait," Kate stopped him. "So, things are a go between you and Annabelle?"

"I'm not sure," he answered honestly. "I hope they are, and she's opening up to me little by little, but she told me that she doesn't ever date, so I'm not sure. Maybe I'm just a rock to lean on while she's going through hell or maybe she feels something too. I think she does, but maybe it's just wishful thinking—you know, seeing what I want to see. I don't know." At the moment, he was trying not to think long term, just focusing on the here and now.

"Xavier," Kate stopped him once again, "she feels something for you. The look in her eyes when she gazes at you, the way she panicked when she heard you weren't staying with her—she feels something, I know she does. Which is why you have to tell her about Julia. It'll look bad for you if she finds out about it from anyone else, and if you're serious about her, then she has to know at some point."

Xavier knew Kate was right, but he didn't want to think about Julia right now. He wanted to focus all his energy on Annabelle. So with that in mind, he threw open the door and drank in the sight of her. It didn't matter to him that she looked utterly worn out, that her eyes were closed, her breath still catching despite the plastic tube looped from ear to ear that helped to deliver oxygen to her smoke-filled lungs.

At the sound of the door opening, her head turned, her white eyes opening to meet his, a faint smile lighting her pale face. "You came."

"You can't keep saying that with such surprise," he admonished gently, crossing the room to sit on the bed beside her. "I told you I'd be here as soon as I could be, and I'm a man of my word."

"I'm sorry," she apologized immediately, a scared little rabbit look wiping away her smile.

"Don't be sorry." He took her hand, and with his other stroked a tendril of hair off her cheek, tucking it behind her ear. He didn't like how panicked she'd looked when she'd thought he was upset with her. He was getting the distinct impression her life so far had not been a happy one. "We need to talk about where you're going to stay when they discharge you later this afternoon," he informed her. "The killer is still out there, and he's following us—or you at least. He set fire to your house. It looks like he regrets leaving you alive, and he wants to change that. I don't want you left unprotected; I want you to stay with me until we have him in custody." He held his breath, awaiting her reply.

"What about the others?" she asked. "The two other women he left behind."

"We've organized protection for them, but I want *you* to stay with me," Xavier repeated. He could see indecision battling in her eyes. "During the day when I'm at work, I can drop you off at the precinct; there'll be no safer place for you to be."

"I'm not sure that's the best idea, for me to stay with you," she looked disappointed but adamant. "Considering that you're interested..." she trailed off to look at Kate.

"Kate already knows that I'm interested in you, Annabelle," he told her, disappointed although not surprised at her hesitation to agree to move in with him until this was all over. "I need to know that you're safe..."

"Annabelle!" The door burst open and Ricky Preston came running in. "I just heard what happened; I'm so sorry I wasn't there for you."

"Ricky." A smile lit Annabelle's face as her friend crushed her in an embrace.

"Are they bothering you again?" Ricky demanded when he pulled away.

Her cheeks heated slightly with embarrassment. "No, they're not bothering me. Xavier was just saying that he thinks I need protection, that the killer might come after me again."

"Xavier?" he arched a brow. "Since when are you and the police officers who called you a murderer on a first name basis?"

"Ricky," she rested a calming hand on his arm, "Xavier and I... he's been really great to me, he's helped me a lot."

Ricky sighed, "You really think she's in danger?" He held

Xavier in a probing stare.

"Yes, I do," he answered honestly. "Annabelle and I went back to her house to see if it would help prick her memory…"

"Did it?" Ricky directed his question to Annabelle.

"A little." She shivered. "I remembered his face and that he spoke to me."

Ricky took Annabelle's free hand. "I'm really sorry I haven't been there for you the last few days. I know that I promised to let you stay with me if you needed to, but then I got a call from my mom. She's sick, so I rushed off to help her. I called you to let you know I'd be out of town."

"I didn't get your call." Annabelle's brow creased.

"I left you a message on your cell."

"My cell phone is still in my house," she reminded him.

Ricky slapped his head at his own stupidity. "I'm sorry, Annabelle. I didn't even think about that. I was in a hurry, I was worried, I wasn't thinking straight. I'm sorry," Ricky repeated.

"That's okay," Annabelle consoled him. "I'm glad you're here now."

"You'll stay with me," Ricky insisted firmly.

Xavier cleared his throat, "Actually, as I was saying…" Xavier couldn't help but frown at Ricky Preston; he was not liking the man any better despite his apparent concern about Annabelle. "…the killer must have been following us. How else would he have known that Annabelle was at her house again? And then to set fire to the house with us inside. He wants to stop us, and he's probably regretting leaving behind live victims. If he makes another attempt on Annabelle's life then I want her someplace safe, and no offense, Mr. Preston, but you're not a police officer and you're currently in no condition to fight off an attacker."

"I'd lay down my life for Annabelle," Ricky protested fiercely. "Besides, we're friends, she'd be more comfortable staying with someone she knows rather than a complete stranger."

Xavier winced at the barb, he didn't feel like he and Annabelle were strangers; he'd shared more with her about his childhood than he had with any other person, including Julia, and he could see she was on the verge of sharing her own secrets with him. Blocking out Ricky Preston, he leaned over Annabelle, taking her face in his hands and softly tracing his thumbs along her cheekbones. "Annabelle, right now all I care about is keeping you safe. Yes, I like you, but keeping you alive is the most important thing in the world to me at the moment. I want you to be safe, and I think staying with me is my best option of keeping you safe. I promise if you agree to stay with me, I am not going to do anything you're uncomfortable with."

"Well…" She was wavering; her white eyes were staring at him longingly.

"Annabelle, you'll still be safe with me." Ricky tugged on her hand until she shifted her gaze to him. "I'll hire you a bodyguard—whatever it takes. Don't let him pressure you into doing something you don't want to do."

"I'm not pressuring her," Xavier contradicted with a scowl in Ricky's direction. "I'm a police officer. Could there be a safer place for Annabelle to stay? But it's up to you, Annabelle. You do whatever you feel comfortable with."

Uncertain, at last she turned to her friend. "I'm sorry, Ricky."

"Annabelle," her neighbor protested immediately, "this guy is using you."

"No, he's not," she assured Ricky patiently. "And he's right; I *will* feel safer with him than anywhere else."

"Fine," Ricky pouted sullenly.

Xavier resisted the urge to gloat. "Why don't you get some rest," he suggested to Annabelle. "It's been a really rough day and you're exhausted."

"Yeah," she agreed, but looked apprehensive at the prospect of being alone again.

"I have to make some phone calls, but I can do that here," Xavier looked to Kate, who nodded.

"I'll go back to Annabelle's house and see if CSU got anything helpful. Feel better, Annabelle. Mr. Preston, I'll walk you out." Kate offered Ricky Preston an innocent smile.

Annoyed, Ricky remained at Annabelle's side. "I can stay as long as you need me to."

"I'm pretty tired, I'm probably just going to go straight to sleep." Annabelle smiled gratefully at her friend. "But thanks so much for the offer."

"Fine, if you change your mind about staying with *him*," Ricky spat out the word viciously, "then call me." Before anyone had a chance to say more, Ricky barged out of the room at a brisk stalk.

"I guess he doesn't want to walk out with me." Kate pretended to look hurt.

"I'm sorry." Annabelle was struggling to keep her eyes open. "We're friends. He's still mad about you accusing me of being a…you know."

"Okay, I'm out of here. Xavier, I'll call you later. Annabelle, try to get some rest, and I'm sure my partner here will be only too happy to try to make you feel better." Kate grinned at both his and Annabelle's reddening cheeks and then blew out of the room.

Once they were alone, Xavier studied her seriously. "You know we need to talk about some of the things I told you today." Her refusal to discuss her rape worried him. He knew it was a lot to deal with on top of everything else, but he needed her to start accepting it. He couldn't let it consume her until he lost her like what had happened with Julia.

"I know, but not now. Please." She stifled a yawn.

"All right, sleep now, we'll talk later." He tucked the covers up around her chin.

"Xavier?"

"Yeah?"

"Could you hold my hand until I fall asleep?"

"Of course, I can." He reached for her small hand and clutched it between both of his, absently rubbing it.

"When I was really little, and I'd get sick, my mom used to sit beside my bed, holding my hand until I went to sleep. I liked that," Annabelle murmured, more to herself than to him. "It made me feel safe, loved."

The way she said that made him understand that feeling loved was not something Annabelle was used to. It also strengthened his resolve to make sure she never again felt like no one loved her.

* * * * *

9:48 P.M.

Vanessa was giddy.

That was a funny word. Giddy. She liked it. Liked the way it rolled off her tongue, liked the way it seemed to tingle in her ears—but even more, she liked it because it reminded her of Vince.

Vince was the reason that she was so giddy.

After running out of her grandparents' house two nights ago, she had found Vince waiting for her just as he'd promised. He had taken her into his strong arms and held her while she cried, then he'd settled her in his car and driven them to a fancy hotel where they had spent the night making love. It had been every bit as beautiful and amazing as she had dreamed.

Waking up entangled in his arms the next morning had been wonderful, too. Vince had ordered them room service and they'd spent the morning in bed and the afternoon having fun in their private hot tub. Vanessa ignored a couple of dozen phone calls from her parents, and when Vince asked her to stay a second night, she readily agreed.

However, when Vince had asked again for her to spend the night with him, she had declined. As much as she loved being with him, and every second they weren't together made it feel like her heart was being pulled apart, Vanessa knew that she needed to go home. Not because she was anxious to see her mom and dad, but because she was dying to inform them of just how wrong they'd been about her and Vince. They'd treated her like a baby, telling her she didn't even know how she was feeling, and that Vince was just using her, and she wanted them to know just how incorrect they had been.

As she teetered up the front path, on legs she was sure had never been this wobbly before, and with a stomach that seemed to swing from side to side, Vanessa thought perhaps it would have been better to confront her parents when she wasn't drunk. She was about to turn back around and go back to Vince's hotel room when the porch light flicked on, practically blinding her.

"You've got a lot of explaining to do, young lady," her father's harsh voice boomed through the opening door.

"Barney, we agreed we were going to remain calm." Her mom appeared at her dad's side. "Give her a chance to explain to us what's been going through her head lately."

She stumbled up the porch steps. "No, that's okay, Mom. I want to explain everything." Vanessa marched as fiercely as her wobbly legs allowed her to through the front door and into the living room, where she planted herself in one of the chairs and waited for her parents to join her.

"We're listening." Her dad tapped his foot impatiently.

"Vince and I are in love," she began.

"Not this again," her father growled. "Really, Vanessa, that's all you've got to say for yourself? You stormed out of this house in the middle of the night, you don't call to tell us where you are or that you're okay, you ignore calls from both me and your mother, and you think that 'I'm in love' is going to cut it? I am appalled at your recent behavior, and if I find out that you've been shacking up with that boy..." Her father let his tirade trail off, awaiting her reply.

"I was with Vince," she answered defiantly. "And we are in love, and I did make love to him, and there's nothing you can do about it."

Her mother looked devastated. "Vanessa, how could you? I thought we talked about waiting until you were married."

"That was what *you* wanted me to do," she corrected her mom. "I told you, Vince and I love each other and we are going to spend the rest of our lives together. If you can't accept that, then I'm moving out." She attempted to stand resolutely, but her shaking legs didn't want to support her weight and she swayed unsteadily.

"Are you drunk?" her father demanded.

"I had a couple of glasses of champagne with dinner," she replied haughtily.

Her mother was shocked. "You're underage," her mom exclaimed, "and so is that boy."

"It was just champagne, Mom, and it's not like we were hanging around some sleazy bar or a club or anything. We were at a hotel. A nice hotel," she added. "Vince isn't just some cheap loser, you know. He's really rich, and he really loves me a lot, and he makes me happy, and I love him too, and I'm glad that I lost my virginity to such a wonderful, loving, sensitive guy…"

"That's it!" Her father exploded, angrier than she had ever seen him. "I didn't want to have to do this. I was hoping that you would come to your senses on your own, but obviously, that's not going to happen…"

"Barney," her mom interrupted, "I'm not sure that…"

"No, Hilda," her dad cut her off firmly, "this is our only option before she runs off the rails completely. Vanessa, you are still a minor and as long as you're under your mother and my care, you will do as we say. As of next week we will be placing you in a boarding school, an all-girls boarding school, far away from young Vincent Abrams."

"You can't do that," Vanessa screeched, shocked and outraged—her rolling stomach and blinding headache only made things worse.

"I can and I have," her father was dismissing her. "Now up to bed. I don't want to hear another peep out of you tonight."

"You can't do that," she repeated, incredulous.

"Goodnight, Vanessa."

"Mom," she protested.

"Barney, maybe we could just talk to her a bit. Try to get her to understand…" her mom pleaded on her behalf.

"No, Hilda, I'm done talking and she isn't listening to a word we're saying. Come on, we're going to bed now."

Vanessa watched as her dad took her mom's arms and led her from the room, her mom casting her one last disappointed look before they disappeared up the stairs. Vanessa would have protested more, would even have run back off to find Vince and seek comfort in his big, strong arms, but her stomach was pitching forward, and she could only manage to just make it to the downstairs bathroom before she threw up.

As she splashed water on her face, she studied her reflection in the mirror. "I hate them, too," she consoled herself. "I hate them and I am not going to let them ruin the rest of my life by taking Vince away from me."

MAY 10TH

His diversion had worked perfectly.

The police had wasted an entire day investigating the fire, probably coming up with all sorts of theories as to why he'd done it. He didn't really care what the police thought as long as they were preoccupied with that and not with trying to figure out what he was going to do next.

Chuckling to himself, really it was *who* he was going to do next.

Letting himself inside house number four, he headed for the kitchen, not because he expected to find anyone there but because he suddenly found himself overwhelmingly hungry. Opening the refrigerator, he rummaged around, then settled on some cold risotto and fixed himself a snack. Pouring a glass of soda, he took his snack and settled on the softest, spongiest sofa he'd ever sat on and began to chow down.

He had never thought of himself as serial killer material.

Growing up, he had been happy and well adjusted. His dad had been absent, but he and his mom had been happy together. At school he'd been popular, smart, and good at sports. He'd had plenty of friends and, thanks to his good looks, plenty of girlfriends.

In his past, no shrink would find any of the so-called indicators of a serial killer. He hadn't been abused as a child, his father had abandoned him but his mom had never been the domineering kind. Instead, she was kind and gentle and he had loved her deeply. His family had no psychiatric, alcoholic, or criminal history, and he had no trouble holding down a job. He hadn't been bullied as a child, he hadn't wet his bed, or been interested in sadomasochistic pornography or fetishes. For enjoyment as a child he hadn't tortured animals or started fires, and he hadn't ever been involved in committing petty crimes.

He had become who he was now because of what others had done to him.

If it wasn't for the actions of those on his list, then he would never have turned into a murderer.

It was on them.

They had created this side of him, and although he would never have thought that taking a human life could be anything other than horrific, now that he had tried it, he realized how much it invigorated him.

Now he was a murderer in every sense of the word.

All he could think of was his next kill. Of the sight of the blood. Of the feel of it on his skin. Of the feeling of control and power that flushed through him as he took the life of another human being.

He liked killing. And even though he'd started this plan to get revenge on those who had ruined his life, he now knew that he was never going to stop. Even when this was finished, he was going to keep killing.

He finished off his snack. As fun as it was pondering how he had become this monster, a lot more fun was awaiting him upstairs. Prancing up the stairs, he pulled his knife from its sheath in the belt around his waist. Pausing at the window at the top of the stairs, he lifted his knife to catch the moonlight on its smooth blade. Tonight was going to be different than the others.

Tonight was going to be a lot more fun.

* * * * *

2:39 A.M.

Annabelle was too restless to sleep.

Already she had lain awake for a couple of hours, staring at the ceiling and trying to figure out if she knew anyone who hated her or her family enough to do all of this. She wasn't quite sure whether the possibility that some complete stranger had targeted her family randomly, or that she might actually know and trust the killer, was scarier. And the more she thought about it, the more afraid she became.

Not for the first time, she was glad of Xavier's solid presence in the bed beside her. It was so comforting to have his arms wrapped loosely around her, his breath whooshing across the back of her neck, and knowing that if she awoke from another nightmare he would be there to hold her until she stopped shaking and crying.

Annabelle didn't know how she would have gotten through the last few days without him. She wasn't happy about that, but neither did she want to do anything about it. She knew it wasn't a good idea to get too attached to Xavier, because even though he was interested in her, and she was even starting to become interested in him, it didn't matter because when this was over, when he had found the killer, then she would walk away.

It made her sad to think of not having Xavier in her life anymore, even if she had only known him less than a week, and they hadn't gotten off to the ideal start. Even though it scared her to admit how dependent she had become on him, she had to admit that it was nice to know that there was someone she could count on.

She was also going to miss days like the pleasant afternoon they'd had. At the hospital, Xavier had held her hand until she fell asleep, and he'd been right by her side when another bad dream had ripped her from sleep. Annabelle wondered whether she'd ever be able to sleep through the night again. When the hospital had released her, Xavier had taken her out for dinner before bringing her back to his house, where he had been true to his word to not do anything that made her uncomfortable. Once again, he'd put on a movie, and although he'd sat beside her on the couch, he had been careful to keep his distance. In the end, it had been she who slid closer and initiated physical contact. He had responded by lightly placing his arm around her shoulders, but she had felt him shudder when she'd nestled her head against his neck.

This time he hadn't bothered to ask her which room she was spending the night in. When the movie was over, he simply took her hand and led her to his bed. Annabelle knew that Xavier had lain awake for hours, wanting to be ready to console her when she woke from another nightmare. Even though she hadn't wanted to fall asleep, the fire had exhausted her and before she'd known it, she had drifted off to sleep.

She hadn't slept for long, and when she had awakened, she'd found that Xavier had finally fallen asleep. She didn't want to wake him, but she needed something to do to occupy her mind. Annabelle was so tired of thinking about that night, trying to perfectly recall the man's face and voice, of picturing her family's bodies, of reliving the terror of being trapped inside her burning home. She wanted to think of something else.

As carefully as she could Annabelle wiggled out from underneath Xavier's arm, trying hard not to disturb him, and pattered down the hall. She fixed herself some hot cocoa and flopped down in a chair in Xavier's den, her eyes roaming the room in search of a distraction. Her gaze settled on his computer, and the wheels in her head began to turn.

Annabelle felt exposed, both physically and emotionally, in front of Xavier. Not only had he seen her naked, but he knew so much about her. He had talked to everyone who knew her—her neighbors, colleagues, friends—in the course of his investigation into her family's murders and he had learned a lot about her. Yet she knew next to nothing about him. Maybe if she knew a little more about him, who he was and how he had become that person, she might feel a little better about things. Plus, it would give her something to do.

Taking her drink with her, she switched the computer on and waited. There was only one thing from Xavier's past that she could think of that might reveal to her more of who this man who was interested in her really was. There had to be a reason why Xavier would take an interest in her, not only a complete stranger but also a victim in one of his cases, and she was pretty sure what that reason was.

Julia.

His wife.

His wife who there was pretty much no trace of anywhere in the house. In the few days she'd been here, Annabelle hadn't seen any of the little indicators that a woman had once lived here. There were no pretty pictures hanging on the walls, no decorative pillows on the couches, or ornaments on shelves, and there was not a single photo of Julia anywhere. It was like the woman had completely disappeared off the face of the planet and out of Xavier's life. Whatever Julia had done, it was like it had caused Xavier so much pain that he now had to pretend that she had never existed at all.

Annabelle was almost positive that if she could find out everything that had happened with Julia, then she would come to understand Xavier's attraction to her. He had told her that he and Julia had been married for two years and that she had been raped.

At the thought of rape, Annabelle had to stop and take several deep breaths to keep from passing out. She knew that at some point she was going to have to deal with what had happened to her, but right now she couldn't. She just couldn't.

Pushing that away, she returned her thoughts to Xavier's wife. He had said that after her rape Julia had done something. Apparently Julia hadn't told anyone that she had been sexually assaulted, not even her husband, and she had done something horrible. Something so horrible that Xavier had been unable to move past it.

What had Julia done?

Had she committed suicide? Had she tried to exact her own revenge on the man who had hurt her? Had she lashed out at her husband and blamed him?

Whatever it was, Annabelle intended to find out.

Jumping onto the World Wide Web, she opened up Google and typed in Julia Montague. From there, it didn't take her long to start connecting the dots as all the pieces of the puzzle fell into place. And she had to admit that she could see why Xavier had described Julia's actions as ones that had almost destroyed all their lives.

Within minutes, Annabelle had a pretty good understanding of just what Xavier was hoping to accomplish by instigating a relationship between the two of them. She was so absorbed in taking in all of this information that she hardly registered the ringing of the phone. Nor the footsteps that sounded as Xavier searched the house for her. It wasn't until he entered the room that she managed to kick her brain back into gear.

"Annabelle, everything okay?"

"Fine," she stammered breathlessly, just managing to bring up a new window as he came up beside her.

"Are you sure?" he hooked a finger under her chin and nudged her face up. "You look pale; did you have another nightmare?"

"No, I just couldn't sleep," she forced herself to smile. "I hope you don't mind me using your computer, I was just looking for something to do to take my mind off things."

"Of course I don't mind," he assured her with only a hint of reproach.

"Was that the phone ringing?" she tried to shift the conversation away from herself.

"Yeah." His intent hazel gaze becoming apologetic.

She sighed, "He's killed again?"

"Yes."

"When is this going to end?"

"I don't know, honey." His hand left her chin to cup her face, gently stroking her cheekbone with his thumb. "But Kate and I will find this man, and even though it won't fix things, it will at least give you the peace of knowing he's not out there anymore."

She nodded, but what Annabelle really wanted was for Xavier to leave. She needed to sort out in her head what she'd just read and what Xavier wanted from her.

"Are you going to be okay here?" he continued. "An officer is coming over to keep an eye on you. I don't want you alone."

The possessive way he said that made her tingle, but she reminded herself of his ulterior motives. "I'll be fine," she assured him.

"All right then, I have to go. I'll call to check on you later." He dipped his head to kiss her then pulled away when she didn't return it. Puzzled and concerned, he asked, "Are you sure you're okay?"

"I'm okay." She was fighting back tears now. "Go, Xavier."

He remained unconvinced. "Call me if you need me."

Watching him go, Annabelle waited until she heard the front door close before she let herself cry. She had allowed herself to start to fall for Xavier, even though she'd known it was a mistake, even though she'd continued to tell herself that she didn't date. She had let herself start to dream of a future with the prince charming she had wished for as a little girl.

Now she didn't know what she was going to do.

One thing she was sure of, though; she was not about to let herself be used to assuage someone else's guilty conscience.

* * * * *

3:17 A.M.

"Either this guy is losing it or he's enjoying killing people way too much for my liking." Diane met them at the front door of the Littleton house.

"It's worse than the last one?" Xavier was trying to focus, but he couldn't get Annabelle's face out of his head. Something had been wrong when he'd left, and he wished he'd had more time to figure out what it was.

"It's not even in the same category," Diane replied.

Entering the house felt like entering hell.

The killer had painted huge, grotesque love hearts on every wall. "Is that...?"

"Blood?" Diane inserted. "Yes, it is."

"The Littletons?" Kate asked.

"We'll test it, but my guess is yes."

"How did he get so much of it?" Xavier couldn't help but stare at all the blood on the walls.

"You'll see when we get upstairs," Diane answered grimly.

"It looks like he had fun down here." Kate pointed to the dozens of bloody footprints that crisscrossed the room. Tiny drops of blood splattered the carpet around the footprints. It looked like the killer had covered himself in blood and then ran races with himself around the house.

"He had even more fun upstairs." Diane reluctantly began the hike up the steep staircase that branched off from the kitchen.

Almost as reluctantly, he and Kate followed, carefully avoiding treading on the bloody marks left behind as the killer had marched up and down the stairs. Xavier wondered how the killer had managed to top himself this time. When he stepped off the last step, it was instantly evident how their guy was increasing his own enjoyment with his sick game.

They were standing in a square room around which five doors sat open. The space appeared to be used as a home theatre room with a huge TV screen against one wall, a set of shelves were stacked with movies, and thick curtains hung at the windows that Xavier was pretty sure would completely block out light. Four of the five open doors led to bedrooms. Ken and Kitty Littleton's room was the first on the left. The next one belonged to their oldest daughter Kaitlin, aged 17. The room on the far right belonged to youngest daughter, thirteen-year-old Kerralyn. Next was middle daughter Koral's room; the fifteen-year-old had spent the night at a friend's and had yet to be notified of the fate of her family.

Perched in front of each open bedroom door sat the lifeless body of the room's occupant. Ken, Kitty, Kaitlin and Kerralyn were all missing their eyes, hands and tongues just as the previous victims had been, only this time the missing body parts hadn't been left with the bodies.

That wasn't the only thing the killer had done differently this time. This time he had been a lot more elaborate in his treatment of the bodies. Yes, he had slit their throats, Xavier was pretty sure that would end up being cause of death, but this time the killer hadn't stopped there. This time he had sliced off their clothes and repeatedly stabbed the bodies. Not just in the torso, but all over. There were knife wounds to the legs, arms and head, probably dozens of them.

Not only had the killer gone berserk on the bodies, but he had also used them to further his seeming enthrallment with blood. Each member of the Littleton family was covered in streaks of dried blood, and from the splattered patterns on the floor, it looked like the killer had painted his victims in blood and then rolled them around.

"There's more in the bathroom." Diane led them to the middle of the five doors.

Inside the bathroom there was a pile of electrical tape by the door, it was spotted with blood and when he bent to look at it, Xavier could see brown hairs stuck to the sticky side. One of the glass walls of the shower had been shattered into a thousand tiny glass raindrops, and in front of the bath there was a puddle that he guessed to be urine.

The bath itself was filled with blood. It dripped down the sides and pooled on the floor. On the sides of the bath he could see what looked like brush marks and he understood what Diane had said downstairs.

"This is where he got the blood." Xavier took a step closer. "He must have killed them in the bath to catch the blood so he could use it to decorate the house."

"Then painted it all over the Littleton family so he could play with it some more," Kate added.

"This is one sick guy." Diane looked disgusted.

"He's also getting more brazen." Kate looked around the room. "He killed them all in here which meant that this time they were awake and aware of his presence and what he was planning to do."

"I think he started with the youngest daughter, Kerralyn." Diane led them out of the bathroom, past the teenager's body and into her room. "Signs of a struggle," she indicated the mussed bed and the lamp and clock that had been knocked off the bedside table.

"Looks like he used her to coerce the others into doing what he wanted," Xavier thought aloud. "He picks the smallest and weakest, wakes her up, maybe holds the knife to her throat, drags her into the other rooms, threatens to hurt her if the others don't obey him."

Kate picked up the thread, "Then he takes them all into the bathroom," Kate continued, "because he wants to collect the blood and the bath is the best place to do that." She retraced her steps to the bathroom, he and Diane following. "Maybe he gets the mom or dad, or the other daughter, to tie up the others with the tape. Then he makes them watch while he kills them one by one." She indicated the puddle of urine on the floor by the bathtub.

"There's urine on the pajamas Kaitlin was wearing." Diane pointed to an evidence bag containing a pair of Winnie the Pooh pajamas.

"So he slits their throats," Xavier resumed the narrative. "Catches as much blood as he can, then once they're all dead he paints them in blood and rolls them around before propping them up in front of their rooms."

"Where he cuts off the hands and tongue and rips out the eyes, which instead of leaving with the bodies he places inside the bedrooms on each person's bed." Kate was staring at the bodies.

"Then for some reason, he uses the rest of the blood to paint giant love hearts on every single wall downstairs." Xavier was struggling to get a handle on this guy; he seemed all over the place. "He didn't bother to paint their feet this time, and although he left the middle daughter alive, he didn't really have a choice since she wasn't home…"

"Yeah, but did he know that in advance, or did he only find out when he got here?" Kate pondered.

"He's certainly escalating with each family," Xavier mused. "He drugged the Englewoods; he didn't bother with sedatives at the Jenners but he started to be fascinated by the blood. The Rankling house was covered in blood, but this time he took it a step further and didn't just put it on himself and dance around, he also painted it on the walls."

"He still called it in himself. The nine-one-one operator said this time he could hear laughter in the background," Kate added for Diane's benefit.

"It still feels like all of this has a purpose, that he's choosing each of these families because they mean something to him. But it also feels like the fascination with blood caught him by surprise and he just went with it. I don't like it, Kate. This guy is still out there, and we have no solid proof that it's any of our suspects, and we have no idea how many other families he's planning on doing this to. Plus, he's already made one attempt on Annabelle's life, and we don't know if he's going to come back and try again with her and the other victims he left behind."

"The real problem," Kate shot him a dismal glance, "is that we really don't know anything. Four families, thirteen people dead, four left behind, three suspects, and we still don't really know anything."

* * * * *

2:48 P.M.

It had taken her twelve hours just to garner enough courage to get here. And now that she was here, she was super close to backing out.

Annabelle knew that for once in her life she had to stand up for herself and confront Xavier about playing with her emotions. She was mad, but she wasn't good at being mad. Annabelle hated it when she knew someone was angry with her and she was pretty sure that Xavier was going to be pretty angry when he found out she had investigated him behind his back. If he was really interested in her, he should have told her everything about Julia himself. Then again, she reminded herself, he wasn't really interested in her.

Taking a deep breath to calm her nerves, she set out determinedly for Xavier's desk. His partner, Detective Hannah, caught sight of her first and gestured to Xavier that they had company.

"Annabelle." He didn't look that surprised to see her. "Is everything okay?"

"Is there someplace we can talk?" She didn't want to have this conversation in a public place; as it was, she was embarrassed enough about her behavior the last few days.

"Sure." Looking concerned, Xavier took her arm and guided her to the room they'd spoken in last time she was here. "What's wrong?" Xavier asked the second they were alone.

She took a deep breath, steadying her resolve. "I know about

164

Julia," she informed him.

"What?" Xavier's face completely drained of color.

"This morning, I couldn't sleep and I didn't want to wake you because you were exhausted." If she could stick with the facts, then she could do this. "I needed something to do to keep my mind off everything, so I got on your computer and…"

"And you decided to invade my privacy?" he demanded angrily, his pale face turning bright red.

"You should have told me that after your wife was raped, she went off the deep end and killed a couple so she could steal their baby." Annabelle still couldn't believe what Julia had done.

A mixture of frustration and guilt covered his face. "There was more to it than that."

Annabelle raised a suspicious brow. That was all the information she had been able to garner from the Internet.

Reluctantly, Xavier flopped down into a chair. "Like I told you earlier, Julia never told anyone that she was raped, so I didn't know there was anything wrong with her, plus I was busy with work and not home a lot. Then Julia was pregnant, and I was really excited. I couldn't wait to be a dad, give my child the family I always wanted as a kid. I was so wrapped up in the baby that I didn't notice that Julia wasn't even slightly excited…"

"The baby was her rapist's?" Annabelle asked with shocked horror.

"Julia wasn't sure. Her whole pregnancy, she was terrified that the child she was carrying didn't belong to her husband but the man who had raped her."

"That's awful, why didn't she say something to you?"

"I don't know," Xavier shook his head dismally. "I didn't find out until I got the call that Julia had a bloody baby in our house and that there were two dead people in our front yard. I dropped everything when I got the call, and rushed straight home. When I got to our house, there were police everywhere and blood all over the lawn. They wanted me to try and talk Julia down so we could get the baby out safely."

"Did you?" she asked with bated breath, forgetting that she'd already read that he had indeed saved the innocent infant.

"When I went in, Julia was sitting in the nursery we'd prepared for our baby—our daughter who had died. The umbilical cord had wrapped around her neck during birth and strangled her. Anyway, Julia was covered in blood, the baby was covered in blood—her mother's blood. She'd been in her mother's arms when Julia shot the woman. The baby was screaming, but Julia didn't seem to notice, she just kept saying that she was sorry. She told me that she'd been raped and that she hadn't known until the baby was born that it was mine and not her rapist's. She told me that during her entire pregnancy she had prayed that the baby would die because she thought it wasn't ours, but when our daughter was born she knew it was our child. She blamed herself for our daughter's death because of what she'd wished, and she knew how devastated I was not to get to be a dad anymore, so she wanted to make it up to me. She thought that she had let me down, so she killed two people to steal their baby, to give it to me, so I would be a dad again."

"I'm really sorry, Xavier." Annabelle wanted to rest a comforting hand on his arm, but she was too shy.

"When I took the baby from her arms, she started screaming." Xavier's voice had dropped to a whisper. "She asked me how I could not notice that something was wrong with her. She asked what kind of husband I was."

"You didn't know because she didn't tell you," she reminded him.

"I didn't know because I didn't want to," Xavier corrected. "I was too busy with my own life, work, friends, the baby—I was too preoccupied to notice that Julia was falling apart."

For a while they both lapsed into silence, Xavier stuck back in time three years ago, Annabelle debating whether to push to get answers to her questions or let it go. She bit the bullet before she could back out. "Xavier, when did you find out I had been raped?"

"What?" his glazed eyes looked up to meet hers.

"Did you know all along that I had been raped?" she demanded. "Is that why you developed an interest in me, because I represent a chance to do things right this time?"

"No!" he exclaimed. "I didn't know that you were raped until just before I took you back to your house. I swear, I told you as soon as I knew. I didn't want to, but I knew that you needed to know. Annabelle, I am not interested in you because I think I can do things better with you than I did with Julia. I made a mistake with Julia, I should have been paying more attention, but what I feel for you has nothing to do with Julia."

"I disagree," she shook her head adamantly. "I think that you still love Julia and that's why you didn't tell me about what happened with her."

"I didn't tell you about Julia because it's hard for me to talk about." He thumped his fist on the table. "I feel guilty about her destroying her life, I feel responsible for the couple she killed and for the child that has to grow up without her parents. I'm a police officer and my wife was raped, murdered two people and abducted a baby, and I should have been able to do something to stop that from happening."

"You keep all of Julia's things in boxes in your spare room," she reminded him. "It was your wife's clothes you gave me to wear at your house after I found out what had happened to my family." While working up enough confidence to confront Xavier, Annabelle had gone rummaging through his house in search of something that might prove he really was interested in her; instead, all she had found was box after box of Julia mementos.

"You had no right to go through my house," he snapped fiercely. "And for your information, Annabelle, I have gotten rid of most of Julia's things."

"That's another thing," she clung to the last tiny spark of her anger at being used, she felt sorry for everything that Xavier had gone through but that wasn't an excuse for him to use her. "You have to decide if it's Belle or Annabelle."

He shot her a tiredly puzzled frown.

"At first you called me Annabelle, then when you realized I wasn't a killer you started using Belle, especially after I told you what the name meant to me. Then I told you I don't date and you went back to Annabelle. In the fire you called me Belle, and now that you're mad at me again, it's Annabelle. You have to decide what you want."

"You had no right to go behind my back and look up all about my past," he ignored her comment completely.

"You know everything about me," she countered. "You spoke to everyone I know; you went through my life with a fine-tooth comb."

"That was different," he protested. "We were trying to find someone who hated you or your family enough to commit murder."

"I'm sorry I was nosy, but I wanted to understand what would possess you to take an interest in me, and now I do." Annabelle couldn't deny it made her sad to think she wasn't anything special to Detective Xavier Montague, that she was nothing more than a means to an end. "You were just using me, right from the beginning, you used me to assuage your guilt over Julia. You played with my emotions, and that's not fair, considering everything that's happened the last few days."

"If you really think that I would use you, then you don't know me at all," he scowled crossly then stalked to the door.

"I really don't," Annabelle agreed to his departing back.

Once Xavier had gone, she sunk down into the chair he'd just vacated and tucked her knees up to her chest, retreating inside herself as she had done on many a night as a lonely little girl. She didn't want to let herself cry, but tears were pricking relentlessly at the back of her eyes, and a sob was building quickly in her chest.

Making sure to keep quiet, she allowed herself to let the tears fall.

* * * * *

3:26 P.M.

Every day on this case made her feel worse and worse.

Kate couldn't get the picture of Koral Littleton's shocked and horrified face out of her head. It felt like the image had been burned into her brain. Joining it were Annabelle, Nicole Jenner, and Lorraine Rankling's faces, all painted with the same look of surreal disbelief at the nightmare they had been thrown into.

Upon leaving the Littleton house this morning, she and Xavier had gone to inform the fifteen-year-old that she no longer had a family. For a young girl, Koral had handled the news very maturely. She'd cried, she'd attempted denial, she'd been scared about what would happen to her, but all in all, she had managed to hold it together pretty well.

They'd asked her the usual questions about whether she remembered any strangers hanging around her house, or her or anyone in her family, to which she'd answered no. She had also answered no when they'd asked her if there had been any suspicious phone calls, emails, or letters. They'd asked her if there were any neighbors, colleagues, friends or relatives who may want to hurt her or her family; Koral had said she couldn't think of anyone. Then they had asked if she knew anyone from the Englewood, Jenner or Rankling family, to which she had once again said no. Neither had she recognized Dr. Daniels, Lachlan Thompson, or Ricky Preston.

When they had deposited the teenager—her face still a mask of wide-eyed shock—in the care of her maternal grandparents, she and Xavier had returned here to begin another fruitless search for something substantial to point them in the right direction.

Kate had thought she was making some progress when she'd

found that Kitty Littleton's mother had been a patient of Bruce Daniels when she'd been admitted to the emergency room following a stroke a few months back. With connections now found between Dr. Bruce Daniels and each of the four families, she was pretty sure that would get them a sample of the doctor's fingerprints to use to compare to the unidentified ones from each of the crime scenes.

Before she had been able to tell her partner what she'd found, she had noticed their silent guest. Indicating to Xavier that Annabelle was there, she'd been intrigued about what was going on between them when they'd hurried off to talk in private. Still, it didn't look like she was going to have to wonder much longer. Xavier came stomping over to his desk, his face dark, hands shoved deep into his pockets.

"What's up?" she asked as he plopped heavily down into his chair.

"Annabelle investigated me," he raged tightly, attempting to keep his voice down so as not to attract the attention of their colleagues. "She knows about Julia."

Surprised and impressed, she hadn't thought sweet little Annabelle had it in her to go and research Xavier's past. "How much does she know?" Most of the articles at the time hadn't filled in all the details of Julia's crimes.

"Everything," he hissed.

"Everything?" Kate repeated, arching a brow and assuming that meant Xavier had filled in the gaps.

"Yes, I told her the rest," he snapped, catching on. "I wanted her to know why Julia shot a woman who was cradling her baby in her arms."

"I knew you should have told her about Julia; I was worried if you didn't, it would all end in disaster."

"Annabelle thinks I'm still in love with Julia."

"Are you?" Kate honestly wasn't sure whether her partner was still in love with his wife or not, neither was she sure if Xavier himself even knew the answer to that question.

"Of course I'm not," Xavier huffed.

She caught a slight glint of uncertainty that sparked in his hazel eyes. "I think you need to be sure of that before you pursue anything with Annabelle," she cautioned.

"Pursue things with Annabelle?" he repeated incredulously. "How can I ever trust her after this?"

"You researched her, what's the difference?"

"Annabelle said that," he huffed.

"Well, she's a smart girl and you're an idiot. You should have told her yourself; no wonder Annabelle thinks you're still in love with Julia."

"I need some air," Xavier glared at her.

"You should talk to Annabelle."

"I will," his glared deepened. "I just need some air."

Kate rolled her eyes. "Where's Annabelle?"

"Still in there," he gestured to the room he'd just left before stalking off.

Annoyed at Xavier's stupidity, she wanted to see him happy, not ruin things before they even got off the ground. Deciding her partner was a lost cause for the moment, Kate thought Annabelle would be the easier one to talk some sense into.

She halted at the door when she heard Annabelle crying. Kate didn't want to intrude, but after a minute or so it became clear that Annabelle had a lot of tears still left to spill. Entering quietly, she pulled up a chair and placed a tentative hand on Annabelle's shoulder.

Immediately Annabelle's head popped up, surprise and embarrassment flying across her face. Quickly, she brushed away her tears. "I didn't know you were there," she mumbled.

"Xavier told me you investigated him." Kate couldn't help but smile, she was still amused and impressed by Annabelle's spunk.

She shrugged. "He's pretty mad about it."

"He doesn't like to talk about Julia."

"Because he's still in love with her." Annabelle tucked herself up even tighter. "He has all her things still packed in boxes at his house."

Kate hadn't known that. "Xavier blames himself for Julia's actions," she explained.

"He said that."

"Part of him knows that Julia made her own choices and she has to live with them. But the other part keeps telling him that if he had spent more time at home, then Julia would never have been raped in the first place; and even if she had, things wouldn't have gotten out of control."

"What was Julia like?"

"Well," Kate had to admit that she had never made the effort to get to know Julia that well. She had been a little jealous of the woman for getting Xavier to fall so hard and fast. "Julia was quiet, kind of old-fashioned, very different from what Xavier was like back then. She didn't like to hang out with him in the middle of the night or have huge parties. She liked to sit at home and watch movies or read or just talk. At first, Xavier tried to do that with her, but it didn't last. He loved being surrounded by people, not stuck at home. But he really loved Julia and he was determined to make his marriage work. And then when she got pregnant he was so excited about the prospect of being a daddy, and he kept raving on and on about what a great mom Julia would be. He was so devastated when their daughter was stillborn, and then when Julia killed those people so she could have their baby. Xavier lost everyone he cared about all at once. Kind of like you did," she added gently. "He never had a chance to get closure and properly deal with his feelings."

"Is Julia in a psychiatric hospital?"

"No, she's in jail."

"But she wasn't in her right mind when she did those things, right?" Annabelle looked perplexed. "I mean, she'd been raped and then she thought she was pregnant with her attacker's baby, then she lost her baby…"

"Xavier tried to get Julia to plead out and go to a hospital, but she wouldn't do it," Kate explained, remembering just how hard Xavier had fought for Julia.

"Are they divorced?"

"Yes."

"Does Xavier still love his ex-wife?"

Wanting to tell Annabelle what she wanted to hear but knowing how devastated Xavier had been when Julia had served him with divorce papers, Kate struggled to respond. "I don't know," she answered honestly.

"Well, I know that he doesn't really feel anything for me; he was just using me, trying to make up for what he thinks were his failures with Julia."

"That's not true," Kate countered firmly. "Do you know how many times I've tried to set Xavier up with someone? How many times he refused to go on the dates, or went on them and deliberately acted like an idiot so they wouldn't call him back? Even when we thought you were a killer, Xavier couldn't help but think about you."

"Really?" A tiny ray of hope lit Annabelle's white eyes.

"Really. Xavier doesn't believe in love at first sight, but he *does* believe that you can instantly form a connection with someone, and then get to know them and fall in love. Xavier feels a connection to you and he wants to get to know you; he really likes you, Annabelle. I haven't seen him look at anyone the way he looks at you. He's interested. The real question is, are you?"

Annabelle hesitated, battling indecision, her eyes clearly said yes she was, but presumably her brain was telling her otherwise.

"Xavier said you told him that you don't ever date. May I ask why?"

Annabelle met Kate's gaze directly for the first time. "Because I'm scared," Annabelle replied.

"Scared of what?"

"Scared that no one could ever love me," Annabelle answered awkwardly.

"Why would you think no one could ever love you?"

"What is there to love about me?" Annabelle began to drum her fingers on her knee. "I don't think anyone could ever be interested in me, so rather than get my feelings hurt, I just avoid relationships."

"I would tell you that that is absurd," Kate couldn't help but smile. "That you're beautiful and that you seem to be a thoughtful, caring, loving, sweet young woman, but I don't think it'll do any good. You'll realize it yourself in time. Just don't give up on Xavier. He's mad now because he feels exposed and vulnerable, but he'll get over it, and maybe once we find this killer both you and Xavier will finally find what you've been looking for."

Kate was halfway to the door when Annabelle stopped her, "Detective Hannah?"

"It's Kate, and yes?"

"Are you sure that Xavier is interested in me?"

"Positive."

She seemed to be mulling it over. "Okay, thanks."

Kate paused at the door. "Can I tell you a secret?" she turned back to face Annabelle.

"Of course," the young woman peered back seriously.

"I'm pregnant." Finally uttering those words to anyone other than her husband felt like a weight had been lifted off her shoulders.

MAY 11TH

8:59 A.M.

"We now have a warrant for Dr. Bruce Daniels' fingerprints and DNA," Rob announced.

Xavier sighed with relief. "Good. What about one for Lachlan Thompson?"

"Not yet." Rob shook his head. "We can't find any connections between him and either the Rankling or Littleton families."

"At least we'll be able to either positively identify or exclude the doctor once we get his fingerprints." Kate couldn't wipe the grin off her face.

"We certainly have plenty to compare it to," Diane spoke up. "We collected nice clear prints from the phones at all three of the houses where he called it in himself. Plus, we have the DNA from Annabelle's sheets." She shot him another apprehensive glance.

Dismissing it, Xavier wasn't going to think about Annabelle until he'd had a chance to sort out his feelings. Otherwise he was only going to continue to drive himself crazy and probably make things worse than they already were between him and Annabelle. "What'd you get from the Littleton house?" he asked, directing the question to Diane.

"Looks like he woke Kerralyn first, then used her as leverage to keep the others under control. We found fingerprints belonging to Kaitlin on the tape, so he probably forced her to tie up her family. One piece of tape had Kerralyn's fingerprints on it so once he had the parents under control he was willing to release her to get her to finish off the job."

"He use any tape on Kerralyn?" Kate asked.

"No, no marks on her whatsoever. Well, not from the tape," Diane stammered, no doubt picturing the bodies of the Littleton family covered in stab wounds. "Probably killed her first, then the parents, then Kaitlin."

"So it was obviously important to him this time to see his victims suffer first," Kate mused. "Whereas the previous times he's killed them while they were asleep."

"Except the Ranklings," he reminded her. "If he expected Rawlin to be asleep when he got there, then found him in the kitchen and had to kill him while he was fully aware of what was about to happen, maybe he liked that, decided it added more fun and excitement, and decided to deviate from his original script."

"It feels like he didn't expect to like killing as much as he is," Rob proposed.

"That could make sense if it was either Dr. Daniels or Lachlan Thompson; neither have ever committed murder, at least that we know of. And if the allegations of the doctor poisoning those kids were true, he didn't intend for them to die; he simply wanted attention," Kate agreed. "Maybe he didn't realize what a rush it would give him until he started."

"It doesn't seem to bother him that he's leaving evidence behind; it's like he doesn't care if we figure out who he is."

"So long as he can finish what he's started," Kate added. "Leaving behind so much physical evidence is a big risk to take. If we find out who he is too early, then it disrupts his plans; he might be caught before he's finished."

"It would be great to know how many other families he has on his list…"

"I think I can answer that question," Billy Newton slunk into the room.

"You get something in the autopsies?" Rob demanded.

"Yes," Billy squirmed in his chair.

"Well," Rob prompted irritably.

"Well, first off, I thought you'd all like to know that the stab wounds were inflicted post-mortem. I think he just did it to drain as much blood out of the bodies as he possibly could manage so that he could do his, uh…" trying to come up with an appropriate word, "…painting."

"That's good news, but it doesn't tell us how many other families he has in mind to slaughter," Rob snapped. The lieutenant was not in a good mood today.

"He left us a message." Billy's eyes were darting around the room, not resting on any one place for more than a second.

"On the bodies?" Kate asked.

"In the bodies," Billy corrected.

"In the bodies? What does that mean?" Xavier asked, positive that whatever it meant it wouldn't be good.

"While I was doing the autopsy on Kitty Littleton I was checking for signs of sexual assault, since we knew Annabelle had been…" Billy trailed off uncomfortably, refusing to even glance in his direction. "And I found a piece of paper inserted in her vagina."

"A piece of paper?" Diane's face had drained of all color.

"What was on it?" Kate asked, her face only slightly less pale than Diane's.

"It."

"It what?" Rob frowned.

"It, as in the word," Billy elaborated. "Since that didn't make a lot of sense, I checked the girls, and he'd done the same to both Kaitlin and Kerralyn."

"What did the other notes say?" Xavier asked.

"Kaitlin's said 'is' and Kerralyn's said 'finished.' 'It is finished.' That's his message. I think he's telling us he's done, that the Littletons were the last family on his list, that whatever he had in mind, he's achieved it."

Xavier was surprised. "You think he's done?" he asked.

"That's what his message said," Billy shrugged. "I brought

them for you." He set out the three evidence bags.

"I'll check them for fingerprints," Diane said immediately. "I'm guessing we'll find some."

"You really think he's done?" Kate looked like she hardly dared to hope it might be true.

"He says he is," Billy repeated.

Rob's phone began to trill. He answered it and moved to a corner of the room.

"If we can just match Dr. Daniels' prints to the ones we have, then all of this really will be finished." Xavier couldn't help but think that would help things with Annabelle.

"Don't speak too soon," Rob hung up the phone with a thud.

"What's wrong?" he asked.

"Bruce Daniels is MIA."

"Since when?" Kate asked.

"Since this morning," Rob rubbed tiredly at his eyes. "Called the hospital this morning to say he wasn't feeling well and was taking the day off, but when the officers went to pick him up at his house, he wasn't there."

"Was he at work yesterday?" he queried.

"No, it's his day off," Rob replied.

"So he could have taken off immediately after the Littleton murders. If he's finished what he started, then…"

"He's on the run," Kate finished.

"We might never find him," Xavier added. "He could be anywhere by now. He could have fled the country."

"Or he could still be nearby," Rob reminded them. "He's already made a second attempt on Annabelle Englewood; maybe he's sticking around to finish the job and take out the others."

Xavier's stomach churned at the prospect of the killer making another attempt on Annabelle's life. "I think he's still here," Xavier agreed. "You're right, Rob. I don't think he'd leave, he wants to see how this plays out, he wants to see if we can figure out it's him."

"All right, let's focus on finding Dr. Daniels," Rob dismissed them. "But until we get him, let's keep searching for any connections between Lachlan Thompson and the other families; we don't want to count our chickens before they're hatched."

Once he was seated at his desk, Xavier reached for the phone. Before he could do anything productive, there was a call he needed to make.

* * * * *

9:32 A.M.

Annabelle hadn't slept a wink all night.

Partly because the motel mattress was incredibly uncomfortable, partly because she was too scared of the images that would fill her dreams, and partly because she kept waiting for Xavier's call.

A call that never came.

He must be angrier with her than she had anticipated.

She hadn't meant to pry. Well, she had, but not in a bad way. She'd just wanted to understand why he might be interested in her. And she had. At least, she'd thought she had, but then her talk with Xavier's partner, Kate, had left her more confused than ever.

Annabelle wanted desperately to believe what Kate had said, that Xavier was honestly interested in her, but she couldn't. She couldn't see what Xavier might see in her, and Kate's pep talk hadn't really inspired her, though it had made her wonder. Annabelle had never thought of herself as beautiful, nor any of the other things on Kate's list, but it made her feel kind of special to think maybe Xavier had seen something in her that she herself hadn't.

Still, it didn't matter now.

She had ruined things by meddling, and Xavier was still in love with his ex-wife.

Last night it had felt weird to not have Xavier's comforting presence in the bed beside her. She had only spent three nights with him and already she was accustomed to him being there.

And she hadn't given up hope that Xavier would call.

Kate had said not to give up on Xavier, and she was clinging to that with every fiber of hope she possessed.

However, Annabelle was determined not to be an idiot about it. She'd wait for Xavier, but she wouldn't wait forever. If she didn't hear from him soon, then she was going to pack up her few belongings and head out of town. Where she would go she wasn't exactly sure yet, but she knew that she couldn't face returning to her job, and she knew she couldn't rebuild her fire ravaged house and live in it after all that had happened there.

And the fire was another thing. The man who had killed her family and yet decided to let her live, had obviously changed his mind. Now he wanted her dead, and she wasn't about to sit around and let him come and take another shot at her.

Following her argument with Xavier yesterday, Kate hadn't wanted her to leave the station without police protection, but the idea that someone would be watching her every move gave her the creeps and she had refused. Annabelle had debated going back to Xavier's and asking if she could sleep in his spare room again, but had been too timid to face him. Next, she had debated once again taking Ricky up on his offer and staying with him for a couple of days, but she hadn't been able to bring herself to do that either. So she'd returned to her motel room.

She'd been sure that Xavier would have been so worried about her that he'd come looking for her as soon as he'd calmed down a little. But the hours had ticked by and she'd sat here alone in this small, dingy room.

In the beginning she'd tried to convince herself that Xavier *was*, in fact, looking for her, but just didn't know where she was. That delusion hadn't lasted long. Twice already he had known where she would go when she was upset. That night he'd found her at her house, then again after he realized she'd seen what had been done to her parents and siblings, he had somehow known that she would seek solace at his house.

Xavier knew where she was.

He just didn't care.

Rolling out of bed, Annabelle considered walking to the café down the block and getting something for breakfast. Even though the thought of eating made her stomach churn, she thought she better eat since she needed to keep her strength up. Collecting the money Ricky had lent her, she shoved it into her jeans pocket and headed out the door.

As she walked down the block, she tried to catch hold of a thought that kept bumbling around inside her head. Something had been niggling at her brain since the fire. Something important. Something she ought to remember, because she was pretty sure— whatever it was—if she could only recall it, then she'd be able to identify the killer.

She paused at the café door, the hairs on the back of her neck were crawling and the feeling that someone was watching her was overwhelming. As subtly as she could, she turned around, surveying the street, the shops, the cars, the people, but nothing stood out.

Unable to shake the feeling, she hurried into the café, feeling safer in the throng of people. As she stood in line, Annabelle convinced herself that it was probably just a cop that Xavier had organized to keep an eye on her.

Maybe he did care after all.

* * * * *

7:31 P.M.

He hated to admit that he was nervous.

Xavier knew he shouldn't have left it so long before seeing her again.

He should have come back sooner and he hoped she wasn't too mad that he hadn't.

It had been a rough couple of days. Having his disaster of a marriage to Julia dredged back up, confronting the guilt that he tried on a daily basis to bury away in the back of his brain.

Annabelle and Kate asking him if he still loved Julia had floored him. He honestly wasn't sure what the answer to that question was. He had loved Julia, loved her deeply, despite the distance that had grown progressively deeper between them shortly following their wedding.

Throughout the trial, Julia had worked hard at pushing him away, bit by bit attempting to edge him out of her life. Then shortly after being found guilty and being sent to jail, she had him served with divorce papers. Xavier hadn't wanted to sign them; he'd wanted to fight for his wife and his marriage. He'd continued to try and convince Julia that she had been mentally unstable, suffering from post-traumatic stress and grieving the loss of a child at the time she had committed murder.

But throughout it all, Julia had remained adamant that it was over between them, so over time he'd been forced to accept it. Only Julia's decision had meant that he'd never addressed his feelings. And now he wasn't sure what they were.

He honestly and genuinely liked Annabelle, but if he was going to do something about that, then he had to be sure whether or not he was still in love with his ex-wife.

Which was exactly what he was here to find out.

"Hello, Xavier."

The voice that spoke was so familiar and yet at the same time belonged to that of a stranger.

"Rough day?"

"You could say that," he agreed, taking in the sight of her, of how much she had changed since he'd last seen her. "We need to talk."

"Yes, I assumed that was why you'd gone to the trouble of coming here. You met someone." Julia held him in a steady blue gaze.

"Let's sit," he suggested, his stomach as full of butterflies as it had been the first time he'd asked her out.

"We're divorced," Julia reminded him, her orange prison jumpsuit clashing with her blonde hair. "If you've met someone, you don't need my permission to do something about it."

"It's kind of complicated," he stammered. He may not need Julia's permission to do something about his feelings for Annabelle, but he certainly wanted it.

"Complicated how?"

"She's a victim in a case Kate and I are working," he explained. "Her whole family was murdered but the killer left her alive. At first we thought it was a murder/suicide, but then the evidence suggested Annabelle had been framed, she was pretty mad at us for accusing her of being a killer..."

"And you felt guilty about it," Julia inserted.

"Right." He was unnerved at how well Julia knew him even though they had been divorced for three years. "Then another family was killed in the same manner and then another and another. The killer left a note with the last family saying he was finished, and we think we know who he is, we're just trying to track him down..."

"So what's stopping you from being with this Annabelle?"

"Like I said, it's complicated."

"Well, it won't be soon, you and Kate will arrest this man and you'll be free to start dating her."

"It's complicated because of you."

"Because of me?" Julia repeated. "I'm in jail and our daughter is dead. It's not like I'm going to be the kind of ex-wife who's causing your new girlfriend any grief."

"Annabelle thinks that I'm just using her," he explained.

"Why would she think that?"

"Because she was…" he trailed off, not wanting to say the word around Julia.

"Because she was raped?" Julia finished for him.

"Yes." He wished for probably the millionth time that he had gone home to spend the evening with his wife that night so long ago.

"Well, why does that mean she would think you're using her?" Julia's eyes narrowed in confusion.

"Because she decided to investigate me and she found out about you."

Understanding dawned. "And now she thinks that she's a replacement for me and a chance for you to rectify the mistakes you made the first time around."

"Right."

"So tell her she's not." Julia lifted a slim shoulder dismissively.

"I did, but I kind of got mad that she went behind my back and researched me."

"Why? Didn't you do the same to her?"

Annoyed that the three women in his life had all jumped on that, he huffed out a breath. "Fine, I was an idiot about that," he acknowledged.

"But…" Julia prompted. "I know I have all the time in the world, but would you please spit out whatever it is you came all the way here to ask me?"

"Annabelle asked me if I was still in love with you," he choked the words out.

She turned as still as a statue. "And what did you tell her?"

"I told her I wasn't, but…"

"But you're not sure?"

"Why wouldn't you plead insanity?" Xavier demanded, a little more forcefully than he intended.

"Because I knew what I was doing," Julia answered plainly. "I knew I should have told you that I was raped. I knew that you would move heaven and earth to find the man who hurt me, but I chose not to. I knew I should have told you when I found out I was pregnant that the baby could have been my rapist's, and I knew when our daughter was stillborn that I should have told you it was my fault..."

"It wasn't your fault," he interrupted.

She waved him quiet. "I spent the whole pregnancy wishing the baby was dead, and then she was. Of course it was my fault."

Hating the matter-of-fact way his ex-wife said that, he began, "Julia..."

She ignored his concern. "I knew what I was doing, Xavier. I knew how devastated you were by our daughter's death. I knew how important it was to you to be a dad. When I saw that couple walking with their baby past our house, I chose to get the gun and shoot them. I chose to take that baby and I intended to keep her. I chose to do all of that, and I knew it was wrong. I wasn't insane, Xavier."

"You were in shock; you'd just been through two traumas. Temporary insanity, you could have gone to a psychiatric hospital, gotten some help, gotten better, you didn't have to end up here." He had begged her more times than he could count to do that.

"I killed two people." Teardrops formed in her dark blue eyes. "I orphaned that poor child; I deserve to be punished."

"Do you still love me?"

Tears spilled out. "I'll love you till the day I die. Do you...do you still love me, Xavier? After everything I did, do you still love me?"

* * * * *

9:41 P.M.

Annabelle had certainly made his job a lot easier today.

Other than a trip to a small café, she had remained tucked up inside her motel room.

Earlier, he'd been sure she'd known she was being watched. At the door to the café she had paused, looking around frantically, panic written all over her face. But then she had turned away, and he knew that he had remained undetected.

It would ruin everything if she saw him now.

He wanted her.

He couldn't deny it any longer.

Neither could he deny that there wasn't much time left.

The police were on to him. They were closing in on him. And it wasn't going to be long before they found him. He had to keep playing things smart. If he fell apart now, it would ruin everything he'd worked so hard to achieve, and he refused to let that happen.

He had worked so hard on this, and everything had fallen so smoothly into place. Sure, he had altered things a little as he went along. It really *had* made things more interesting with Rawlin Rankling to have him conscious, just as he'd suspected it would be after Callie Jenner had awakened at the last second. Since Rawlin had been such an enjoyment, he had decided to improvise even further and gone all out with the Littleton family.

Now *that* had been a bundle of fun.

The mix of shock and horror on Kerralyn's face when she had awakened to see him standing over her, his knife pressed to her throat. Despite that, she had put up quite the fight on the way to her sister's room.

A few whispered threats had been all it took to ensure that big sister Kaitlin was co-operative as they rounded up mom and dad.

The little rendezvous in the bathroom was positively invigorating. The pure power that had surged through him as he'd instructed Kaitlin to tie up her parents and then bind her own ankles, before releasing Kerralyn to finish the job.

The teenager had made a bolt for freedom once she had bound her sister's wrists. She hadn't gotten farther than the door.

Kerralyn had been the first to die, followed by mom and then dad, and finally Kaitlin. Much to his amusement, when he lifted the girl up, he saw she had wet her pants.

The bath had worked well to collect all the blood, and the additional stab wounds had produced a little extra—he hadn't wanted to waste a single drop of the precious liquid.

He had to admit he may have gone a little overboard—painting the Littletons in their own blood and rolling them across the floor, plus all the love hearts on the downstairs walls. But, hey, what could he say? He'd been in the moment, and all that blood was so intoxicating.

Still, what was done was done, and what still needed to be done was waiting on the other side of that door.

Climbing from his car, he was about to head for Annabelle's room when another car pulled into the parking lot. When he saw who it was, he let out a frustrated breath and returned to the safety of his car. He watched as Detective Montague stalked determinedly to Annabelle's door.

Oh well, he thought, if Xavier Montague got in the way of his plans for Annabelle Englewood, then he'd simply have to take the detective out of the picture.

* * * * *

10:13 P.M.

His heart was pounding as he knocked on Annabelle's motel room door.

Xavier knew he shouldn't have left it so long. But he'd been mad yesterday, and he hadn't wanted to face Annabelle. Now he hoped he hadn't made things worse between them.

Maybe it wasn't such a big deal that she had investigated his past. Annabelle, Kate, and Julia were right; he *had* done the same thing to her, although for very different reasons. He did kind of understand where Annabelle had been coming from.

When she didn't answer, worry began to prick at him. When he got back to his house last night and realized that Annabelle was no longer there, he'd considered calling in to get someone to watch her, but in the end decided against it. There had been no more attempts on Annabelle's life, nor any attempts on any of the other survivors' lives, perhaps Dr. Daniels really had fled town.

He hammered on the door a little harder this time, then let out his breath with a whoosh when it finally cracked open. "Annabelle." Butterflies took up residence in his stomach for the second time today. "What took you so long? I thought something had happened to you."

"I wasn't sure I wanted to talk to you," she answered in a small voice.

"Fair enough." He knew he deserved that. "Can I come in?"

She hesitated long enough that he thought she was going to refuse, but then she relented. "I guess."

He followed her inside, knowing what he wanted to convey to Annabelle but not sure how to say it. "We need to talk about what you asked me yesterday. About Julia."

"I'm kinda tired." She moved away from him. "Maybe we could do this another day."

"Annabelle, wait," he grabbed her arm to hold her in place. "Please, I really want to work things out."

"Do you still love her?" Annabelle's white eyes peered nervously at him as though they weren't positive they wanted to hear the answer.

He hesitated, then sighed—it was better to get this over and done with as quickly as possible. "Yes, I still love Julia."

Annabelle maintained a stony stare for a moment before her eyes welled up with tears and she recoiled from him. Without another word, she turned and took a step toward the motel door.

Hurting her was the last thing he wanted to do. "Belle, wait," he called. Grabbing hold of her wrist, he spun Annabelle back to face him.

Her devastated eyes refused to meet his. "I don't see what else there is to talk about, Xavier," she mumbled quietly.

"Well, I do." He counted, keeping one hand on her wrist in case she suddenly decided to flee. With his free hand he took hold of her chin and tilted her head back so she was forced to meet his eye. "Yes, I still love Julia, but that's not all I feel for her. I'm angry that she didn't trust me enough to tell me the truth in the beginning. I'm angry that she didn't trust herself enough to get the help she needed. I'm angry that she thought I cared more about being a father than I did about her. I'm angry that she thought the answer to her problems was to kill two people and steal their child. I'm sad that she didn't love me the same way I loved her. I feel guilty that I didn't protect her, that I wasn't there when she needed me, and I feel guilty because I'm mad at her and she was raped. I love her, Belle, but I'm not *in* love with her, because..." letting the sentence trail off.

"Because..." Annabelle echoed.

Seeing that she needed to hear him say it, he released his hold on her wrist and slipped his arm around her waist, drawing her close. "Because I think I'm falling in love with you," he whispered, cupping her cheek in his hand.

For the longest moment she did nothing but stare at him with her enormous white eyes, and then he saw the last of her fight, her spirit, drain from her body and he knew he had lost her. "It's not enough, is it?"

When she spoke her voice was trembling, "I've already lost everything," she murmured. "I can't start something with you if there's a chance that you're going to go back to your ex-wife."

He tightened his hold on her. "There is no chance of that."

She remained unconvinced. "You say that now, but what about when she gets out of jail? Or if you could convince a judge that she wasn't in her right mind when she did what she did and you get her moved to a psychiatric hospital? What if she needs you and you feel so guilty that you go running to her side and then you find out that your feelings were stronger than you thought? I've already lost enough; I can't lose you too." With that, she gently extricated herself from his grasp and reached up a hand to trace along his cheek.

Grabbing hold of it, he pulled it to his mouth and kissed it. "I'm falling in love with you, Belle. Your strength, your gentleness, your beauty. I think that you are amazing and I want to get to know you better. I want to see if we can have a life together."

Looking more defeated, more lost, more alone, more heartbroken than he'd ever seen her, she tugged back her hand, and with one last wistful look, she backed away from him on wobbly legs.

"Belle." He was thinking of what she had asked him yesterday. "I want you to be Belle. Please."

"Xavier, please, please just leave." Her voice was as trembly as her legs.

Reluctantly, he agreed, only because he didn't want to alienate her further. "I'll leave for now, but I'll be back. I'm not giving up on you. I'll find the man who killed your family, I'll find the man who hurt you, and then I'll convince you that you are the most amazing woman on the planet."

* * * * *

10:31 P.M.

Inside her room, tears were already streaming down her cheeks by the time the door clunked closed behind Xavier, and Annabelle worried that she had just made the biggest mistake of her life.

She made it only a couple of steps towards the bed before exhaustion took over and she crumpled to the floor.

Before she fell completely asleep, she wondered how long Xavier would stand out there watching her closed door.

* * * * *

11:37 P.M.

The man who had been impatiently watching the exchange could have told her that it was at least an hour before Detective Xavier Montague finally climbed into his car and drove off into the night.

At last he could get on with things, he was muttering to himself. He patted his pocket where a small vial of sedatives was tucked away, a little souvenir from his last visit to the hospital pharmacy.

In silence, he crept to the motel door. With his lock picking tools, he was inside in seconds. He delivered the sedative, then scooped the unconscious girl into his arms and disappeared into the night.

* * * * *

11:52 P.M.

Kate was pretty sure that Xavier would be here.

Although he hadn't said anything, she was also pretty sure that he had gone out to the prison to speak with Julia earlier today. Xavier was clearly shaken up by being confronted about his feelings for his ex-wife. Hopefully, talking with Julia had helped him sort out just where he was, because Kate didn't want to see her partner or Annabelle hurt if they started dating only for Xavier to realize later on that he was still in love with his ex.

Thinking that he'd head to Annabelle's when he'd finished at the prison she'd driven to the motel, hoping the two had already reconciled. Arriving, she'd found the room dark, Xavier's car nowhere to be seen. Assuming either things hadn't gone well with

Julia or with Annabelle, Kate had thought about where Xavier would head next.

This had been the only place she could think of.

Shining her flashlight to guide her, the last thing she wanted to do was break an ankle tripping over a gravestone. Reaching the gravesite, Kate found who she was looking for.

"I don't want to talk, Kate." Xavier's voice rumbled out of the shadows.

"Okay," she agreed. She carefully chose a patch of grass that didn't seem to have too many twigs and leaves and sat down, happy to wait until Xavier was ready.

"You don't have to hang around," Xavier said a few minutes later once it became clear she wasn't leaving.

"I know."

A couple more minutes passed before he spoke again. "I went to see Julia."

"And..." she prompted.

"And I asked her why she refused to plead insanity."

"What did she say?"

"She said that she knew what she was doing. That she chose to do it. That she deserved what she got." The disappointment and disbelief in his voice were obvious.

"I'm sorry," Kate consoled, not sure what to say.

His shadow moved in the thin light, and a moment later, she felt him sit nearby. "Maybe I was kidding myself all along. Only seeing what I wanted to see. Maybe it was always obvious that Julia knew what she was doing and I wanted so badly to believe that she wasn't capable of murder. It was a lot easier for me to believe that everything she did was because of the shock and trauma, that it wasn't really her fault, but now...now I don't know what to think."

She knew that he wanted her to reassure him, that he wanted to hear that he was right and that Julia wasn't responsible for her actions. However, Kate also knew that it didn't matter what she thought. Xavier had to come to terms with things for himself in order to move on.

After another long silence, he spoke again. "Julia said she still loves me, that she'll always love me."

Kate thought that Julia had always loved Xavier more than he had loved her. He *had* loved Julia, of that she was one hundred percent certain, but she'd always felt like their relationship was more one-sided.

"Then she asked me if I still loved her."

"What did you tell her?"

"I told her I was sorry," he answered sadly. "That I still cared about her deeply, that I still loved her, but that I wasn't *in love* with her anymore."

The beam of the flashlight caught Xavier's face as he hunched over and she could see tears gleaming in his eyes. She knew hurting Julia was the last thing he wanted to do, no matter what she had done. "Did you tell Annabelle?"

He turned away so his back was to her. "Yeah."

"It didn't go well?"

"I told her what I just told you, that I'll always love and care about Julia, but that she's not my future."

"Annabelle didn't believe you?"

"She thinks she's already lost everything, and that if she were to get involved with me she might end up losing me to Julia one day."

"What did you say to her?"

"That I wanted to be with her and that I wasn't going to give up. That I was going to find this killer and then I was going to convince her that I'm serious about her."

Kate was getting frustrated with him. "Then what are you doing here, Xavier? What's stopping you from getting what you want?"

"She is," he snarled, standing and kneeling in front of the small headstone that marked his stillborn daughter's grave.

"How is *she* stopping you?"

"Maybe Annabelle's right. Maybe we're not meant to be together. Maybe we're not meant to be with anyone. I mean, this is hardly the ideal time for her to be getting into a relationship, especially when she's made it clear that she doesn't date. She doesn't know what she wants right now, she doesn't know what she's feeling, she just lost her entire family, she was stabbed and raped. And let's face it, I wasn't very good at marriage the first time around. Not to mention the fact that I'm probably too old for her, she's twenty-three, I'm thirty-two..."

"Okay, you're reaching now, Xavier." Kate put a stop to her partner's babbling. "Bottom line is, you like her and she likes you."

"She doesn't want to get involved with me, Kate," he protested, albeit not very convincingly.

"She does, she's just scared," she contradicted. "I was speaking to her yesterday, after you left in a huff," she couldn't help adding. "I asked her why she doesn't date and she said it was because she doesn't think there's anything attractive about her. She doesn't think anyone could be interested in her, so instead of risking getting hurt, she just keeps herself isolated. She's scared that you're going to hurt her, and if you're not ready to let go of Julia, you *are* going to hurt her."

"I *have* let go of Julia." Xavier glared over his shoulder.

"Annabelle said that you still have Julia's stuff packed in boxes in your house." Kate broached the topic carefully.

"Annabelle's a blabbermouth," Xavier shot back mildly, seemingly no longer angry about Annabelle's search of his house.

"Xavier, you have to make a choice." She shifted around so she was beside her partner. "Either your focus in life is Julia or you move on and live for the future, but you have to decide what you want. You can't keep hovering in this no-man's-land."

"Do you think everything would have turned out differently if she had lived?" Xavier reached out a hand to trace the lettering on his daughter's headstone.

"You mean, would Julia have gotten better? Would the two of you still be together?"

"She'd be three years old now," he said wistfully.

"But Julia would still have been the same." She rested a hand on his shoulder. "She would still have been suffering from post-traumatic stress, and she probably still wouldn't have told you. Okay, she might not have killed two innocent people and tried to abduct their baby, but she'd still be sick, and that sickness would have come out sooner or later."

"You really think so?" he looked at her hopefully.

"Julia knew she needed help and she chose not to get it. She could have gone to you or to me or to anyone, but for whatever reason, she didn't. It's not your mistake and it's not your problem anymore. You two are divorced, and you have a really sweet young woman who likes you and needs you."

"But I love Julia and I can't just pretend I don't."

"You said yourself though, you're not *in love* with her. You need to let her go if you're going to be happy. Do you want to be happy?" Not sure that Xavier did, he thought he deserved to spend the rest of his life alone and miserable for letting down his wife.

"You know I do, Kate."

"Then do it. Be happy. Things might work out with Annabelle, they might not, but at least you'll know, and if they don't, you'll find someone else. Stop fighting it. You want to have a family, then go make one. You can have more kids—yes, you'll always miss your daughter—but it doesn't mean that you have to be afraid to try again. Come on, Xavier, I hate seeing you like this. Three years you've refused to have a life and now you have a shot at happiness and you're throwing it away for a list of stupid reasons that don't even make sense. Annabelle is good for you. Fight for her."

Xavier said nothing and as they sat in silence, Kate worked up the courage to tell her partner about her own baby. Telling Annabelle yesterday had felt wonderful. To say those words to someone, it had really made her pregnancy seem real and not just a figment of her and David's imaginations. Finally garnering enough courage to utter the words, she was just opening her mouth to speak when Xavier suddenly stood.

"Kate, I'm gonna go home. Thanks for coming and talking with me. I don't know what I'd do without you. I mean it, I really don't. You are so amazing, everything you did for me just after Julia's arrest, and now with Annabelle, you're the greatest partner a guy could wish for."

After giving her a quick kiss on the cheek, Xavier disappeared into the night. As she watched him go, Kate wondered how he was going to react when he learned he'd be getting a new partner soon. Last night she and David had sat down and talked about their future, and as much as she wanted to return to the job she loved after her maternity leave expired, she was starting to suspect that having her baby was going to change her more than she thought possible.

MAY 12TH

This time he wasn't going to take no for an answer.

This time, he was going to make things right. Set her straight.

Xavier maneuvered his car back into the parking lot at the motel where Annabelle was staying, and with perfect calm, he knocked on her door.

He was doing the right thing, of this he was positive; in fact, he should have done it from the beginning. Should have done everything within his power to convince Annabelle to give them a shot, that he was over Julia, that he wasn't going anywhere.

Once he'd convinced her of that, he was going to pack up her stuff and take her back to his house. He would set her up in the spare room, or in his room, or wherever she felt comfortable, and he would make sure that not only was she safe, but that she knew that he was there for her.

He knocked on her door again. Annabelle had looked exhausted last night and was probably still fast asleep. Xavier didn't want to disturb her, but he also didn't want her alone and unprotected for another second. Bruce Daniels may or may not have left town. He definitely should have organized protection for her. He didn't like the idea of her being alone when there was a madman out there who couldn't seem to let Annabelle go.

He knocked a third time.

Still no answer.

Now he was starting to get worried.

Peering through the grimy window, he was frustrated to find the blinds drawn. His heart was starting to really pound now. He gave the door another hammer.

"Annabelle?" he called out, hoping to rouse her in the ever increasingly unlikely event that she was just asleep. "Annabelle? It's Xavier. If you're in there, let me in; I need to talk to you."

Without even realizing what he was doing, his hand gripped the doorknob, subconsciously turning the handle. He was surprised when the door swung open. The feeling was quickly replaced by dread.

The room was empty, no sign of Annabelle.

Neither did it look like she had spent the night. The covers on the bed were smooth, the cell phone and purse her friend Ricky had gotten her were still on the dresser, and the half-eaten cup of soup he'd seen on the table when he'd been here last night was still there.

Fighting the frantic feeling that was screaming at him to completely lose it, he took a deep breath and studied the room more carefully. Maybe Annabelle had simply gone out for a walk. Sure, it was only five o'clock in the morning, but he knew that she'd been having trouble sleeping. Or maybe she'd decided to take Ricky Preston up on his offer to stay with him. Plus, she had to have known that he'd come back; maybe she just wanted to avoid another conversation with him.

After a futile search for a note that Annabelle might have left explaining where she was, Xavier started looking for signs that Annabelle had been removed from the room against her will. The door had been left unlocked, none of the windows were open, no signs of forced entry, no signs of a struggle, nothing to indicate that anyone had attacked her.

Yet Xavier couldn't think of anywhere Annabelle would have gone voluntarily. She didn't want to see him so his house wouldn't have been an option. After the fire he didn't think she'd go back to her own house, and even though she wanted support, he didn't really think she was going to turn to Ricky Preston, no matter how much the guy badgered her to lean on him.

Heading back outside, he almost ran smack into a chubby, middle-aged woman. "May I help you?" he asked distractedly, scanning the dark parking lot for any signs of Annabelle.

"No, I'm fine," the woman replied, staring at him inquisitively.

About to walk past her, Xavier stopped abruptly. "Have you seen the woman from this room?"

"Young? Pretty? Brunette?" the woman peppered at him.

"Yep, that's her."

"I've seen her on and off the last few days."

He was hopeful she knew more. "What's your name, ma'am?"

"Claudia Klump. Weren't you here earlier?"

Never in his life had Xavier been so glad to encounter a nosy busybody. "Yes, I was here late last night."

"You were arguing with her," Claudia Klump stated calmly, clearly not the least bit embarrassed about her eavesdropping. "Then you left; well, you stood outside her door for almost an hour and *then* you left. At least, I thought you'd left, so I went to get ready for bed, but on my way past the window I saw you carrying her to your car."

"You saw what?" his pulse began to pound in his ears.

"I saw you carry her to the car," she repeated.

"When was this?" he had to force the words out past the lump in his throat.

"Like I said, right after I thought you'd left..."

"Tell me exactly what you saw," he demanded, more forcefully than he'd intended.

A little taken aback, she answered, "I watched you stand at her door, then get into your car and drive off. I went to the bathroom and when I went to close the blinds, I saw you walk out of her room with her in your arms. I assumed that she'd forgiven you for whatever it was you'd done and the two of you were heading home. I didn't really give it another thought; I just went to bed. It wasn't you?"

"It wasn't me."

"Did something happen to her?"

"Did you get a look at the man?" he asked instead of answering, not wanting to quite believe yet that this madman who'd already killed thirteen people might have Annabelle.

"Not really," she shrugged. "I mostly only saw his back; he was putting her in his car."

"What color was the car?"

"Red, I think," Claudia answered. "I saw it as it went under the streetlight."

A red car.

It was him.

He had Annabelle.

"Thank you for your help," Xavier dismissed the woman and bolted back into Annabelle's room, his phone in his hand. Once again, he had placed the woman in his life in danger. Why for once couldn't he learn to put other people above himself? If he hadn't been too busy sulking about Annabelle's invasion of his privacy, he'd have made sure that someone was there to keep an eye on her.

"Hello?" Kate's sleepy voice sounded in his ear.

"Annabelle's missing."

"What?" His partner sounded a little more awake, but a lot more confused.

"I came back to the motel to talk to her, but she wasn't there. I thought maybe she'd just gone out, maybe for a walk to clear her head or something, but I ran into this lady who said she saw someone carrying Annabelle and then putting her in a car—a red car. It's him. It has to be. He has Annabelle, and who knows what he's going to do to her…"

"Xavier, Xavier," Kate kept trying to catch his attention. "Xavier!"

"What?" he snapped.

"You have to calm down a little bit," his partner sounded wide awake now.

"Last night, you knew I would go to see Julia, and you also knew that I'd go straight to Annabelle's afterwards. Did you come here last night? Before you found me at the cemetery."

"Yes."

Kate's calm voice started to rub off on him. "Did you see Annabelle? Talk to her?"

"No. When I got there her room was dark. I looked for your car and when I didn't see it I assumed that either things had gone badly with Julia and you'd gone to the cemetery or things had gone badly with Annabelle and you'd gone to the cemetery. And no, I didn't see any red cars in the parking lot, or anyone suspicious looking hanging around," Kate anticipated his next question.

"Then he must have been waiting while Annabelle and I talked, grabbed her the second I was gone." Xavier wished more than anything that he had gone with his first instinct and slept in his car outside Annabelle's room rather than visit his baby daughter's grave.

"So this lady only saw somebody carrying Annabelle?" Kate clarified.

"She thought it was me."

"Maybe it was Ricky," Kate suggested. "Maybe after she talked to you, Annabelle decided she didn't want to be alone and called her friend."

"No," he disagreed. "The woman who saw him said that after I left she went to the bathroom and on her way back was closing her blinds when she saw the man putting Annabelle in his car. No way is that enough time for Ricky Preston to make it here, plus the guy has a broken arm, so how would he be able to carry her?"

"Okay, well just try to stay calm. We'll find her, Xavier…"

He stopped listening to his partner when he spied something under the table in Annabelle's room. Dropping to his knees to reach for it, he felt what little calm he'd mustered slip quickly away.

"Xavier, you've stopped listening to me, I can tell. What happened? Did you find something?"

"Yeah, I did," he managed to croak as he carefully picked up the long, round object.

"Well, what is it?" Kate demanded.

"A syringe." His mind conjured up images of every horrible thing this man might be doing to Annabelle this very second. "He drugged her and now he has her, Kate. He has her and we have no idea where he is. He has all the time in the world to do to her whatever he pleases."

* * * * *

7:16 A.M.

Had she hit her head?

It felt like her head had been turned into a blender, filled with nails and turned up high.

Annabelle wanted to open her eyes, but it was too much effort so she let the moment slide and let her mind creep back toward sleep.

But sleep wouldn't come. She was stuck in limbo, unable to sleep and yet unable to properly wake up.

Maybe something had happened to her and she was back in the hospital.

She tried to move her arms; when she found she couldn't, her heart started to beat a little faster. Had she been arrested again? Was that why she couldn't move? Had she been arrested and handcuffed to another hospital bed?

She attempted to still her racing mind, focus it on the last thing she could remember. Xavier had come to her motel room. He'd told her that he'd been to see his ex-wife. He'd said that he was falling in love with her but then he'd said that he still loved Julia. She'd been hurt, her momentary bliss at hearing that he was falling for her washed away by the fear that he would one day leave her to go back to his wife. She had told him to leave. That she didn't want to get involved with him only to lose him. Xavier had told her that he wanted her to be Belle, that he'd be back, that he wasn't going to give up on her, but she had insisted that he leave.

After he'd gone, she had headed for the bed, intending to sleep, pretty sure she was exhausted enough to sleep soundly. Annabelle didn't think she'd ever even made it to the bed. Her last memory was of her legs giving out and the feel of the rough, scratchy carpet against her cheek.

Had Xavier come back?

Did he think that she had killed her family after all?

Maybe he thought she'd done something else, something equally as horrible.

Summoning all her strength, she managed to pry her eyelids open, a small moan of surprise escaping her lips.

She wasn't in a hospital, and neither was she in a police station.

The roof above her head looked like the bare boards of an attic; beneath her was a hard wooden surface. It didn't feel like the floor though, maybe more like a table. Tipping her head sideways confirmed this. It also confirmed the reason she couldn't lift her arms was because someone had looped rope around her wrists and tied it to the table legs. Managing to lift her head a little to look down the length of her body she found her ankles, too, had been bound.

She was trapped.

Tied to a table in some attic.

She could be anywhere, and no one even knew she was missing.

Why, oh why, had she been so stubborn with Xavier? She wasn't stubborn, she was *never* stubborn. When push came to shove Annabelle *always* backed down. The thought of anyone being mad at her was always enough to convince her to cave. And yet with Xavier she had stuck to her guns. Had even been a little proud of herself for doing so. Only now it had come back to bite her.

Now Xavier wasn't thinking about her. He was off working with his partner to try and find the man who had killed her family and so many others. When he found that man, he might come looking for her but that could take weeks or months or even years, and Annabelle was pretty sure that whoever had taken her didn't intend to leave her alive for that long.

Why had she made such a big deal out of the fact that he still loved his ex-wife? Of course he did; it made sense that he would always love Julia. But he had said that he was falling in love with her. She never thought she'd hear a man say those words to her, but when someone finally had, she'd thrown it back in his face. Told him that it didn't matter, that she couldn't deal with losing him, and sent him away. That foolish mistake could end up costing her her life.

She had to learn to stop running scared all the time. Okay, so maybe Xavier might have ended up leaving her to go back to Julia, but maybe he wouldn't have. Maybe the two of them would have been happy together. Gotten married, had children, shared their lives together.

But now that could never happen. She had thrown it all away because she'd been scared. Scared and stubborn.

Tears were welling up in her eyes, threatening to spill out if she wasn't careful. And Annabelle knew she had to be careful. Her mouth was taped shut and if she cried and got her nose all stuffed up, she'd suffocate.

She forced herself to calm down. If she was going to have any hope at all of getting out of this alive, then she needed to remain calm. Clearing her mind and forcing herself to feel nothing, no fear or terror or regret, she tried to come up with a plan. Waiting for Xavier, or anyone else, to find her was not an option. Annabelle was on her own; luckily, something she was accustomed to.

She tested the ropes that bound her, yanking and wiggling her wrists and ankles until they were ripped raw, with no results. Obviously, she wasn't going to bust herself out of here.

That really only left talking her way out, which also presented a problem. She had no idea who had taken her or why. Annabelle assumed that it had to be the man who murdered her family, and who had already made one attempt at killing her, but she didn't know who that was. Xavier and Kate had asked her questions about Dr. Daniels and Ricky, plus they'd shown her a photo of some other man. That didn't mean it was one of those men though, it could be anyone.

Annabelle couldn't believe that her kind and thoughtful friend was really a serial killer, nor could she believe that Dr. Daniels, who had been so sweet to her while she was in the hospital, was a serial killer. That still left the third man or any other man on the planet. She sighed.

Her gaze fell on a window, several feet away, she wasn't close enough to see anything more than a patch of blue sky, but help could be just outside. When the man came back to check on her, and at this point she had to believe that he would, she couldn't accept that he had tied her up here and left her to die a slow and painful death, she could scream for help the second he removed the tape from her mouth.

As hard as she tried not to, Annabelle couldn't help conjuring up possibilities as to just why this man had abducted her.

If he simply wanted her dead, then he could have killed her at the motel.

He would have had ample opportunity to do it. She was all alone there after Xavier had left, it would have been easy for whoever went to the trouble of abducting her to just stab her or shoot her or slash her throat like he had to kill her parents, brothers, and sister. But he *had* gone to the trouble of abducting her and bringing her here and tying her up. He had something in mind. He had a reason for taking her. And knowing that left Annabelle terrified.

It reassured her a little to see her clothes were still on. This man had raped her once already, something she knew she would have to deal with at some point, assuming she made it out of this alive, but for now she was locking it away and pretending it never happened.

Maybe the man had done it again while she was unconscious.

Maybe that was the reason he'd brought her here.

Xavier had said that her family was different.

Was she the reason for that?

Did the killer have something special planned for her?

Before she had a chance to ponder this further, she heard the creak of a door opening. Turning her head, she saw a man standing beside her, a child's clown mask covering his face, the blue eyes that stared intently at her chillingly familiar.

Slowly the man stepped closer, producing a small bottle and a syringe from his pocket. Panicking as she watched him prepare what she assumed was a sedative, Annabelle thrashed against her bonds, ignoring the burning in her already sore wrists and ankles. She attempted to scream through the tape that muffled any pleas for help she might make.

The man reached out a hand and began to stroke her hair. The tender way he did so made Annabelle's blood turn to ice, and she went still.

"Sleep well, pretty girl," he murmured as he rammed the needle into her thigh.

Right before unconsciousness took hold, Annabelle managed to place the voice and she wondered how she could have missed that he was this unbalanced.

* * * * *

10:35 A.M.

"You find anything?"

Starting, Xavier hadn't heard anyone approaching, not a good thing since there was a maniac on the loose. "Nothing." He shook his head in frustration. He hadn't really expected to find something here at Annabelle's house, he'd known that CSU would have found anything that the killer had left behind, but he had to do something. "The syringe? Diane get anything from it?"

"Fingerprints match the ones from the crime scenes," Kate replied.

"So he definitely has her," Xavier sighed. A part of him had been hoping that something or someone else was responsible for Annabelle's disappearance. Not that it would have really been helpful, she still would have been in harm's way. "What'd he use?"

"Ketamine."

He jumped on that. "Dr. Daniels would more than likely have access to that at the hospital, more proof that the over-attentive doctor is the killer."

"Or," Kate drawled, "Ricky Preston or Lachlan Thompson could potentially have swiped some when they were at the hospital. Both of them have been in and out recently—Ricky, with his broken arm; Lachlan with his cancer. It's conceivable that either one of them managed to somehow get their hands on some Ketamine. Or it could be any number of people. We still don't have any real proof, Xavier."

"That's why I came back here." He surveyed the badly damaged house. "Other than you, Rob, and Diane no one else knew that I was bringing Annabelle back out here and yet somehow the killer knew we were here."

"You think he was following you? Or Annabelle?" Kate plopped down in the grass and crossed her legs.

"Maybe," he dropped down beside her, fighting a yawn. "I asked Diane to check out my car and cell phone."

"For tracking devices?"

"She found nothing." Xavier rubbed at his eyes. They'd been itchy ever since the fire and the no sleep wasn't helping. "I didn't see anyone following us, and we sat out front in the car for several minutes while I told Annabelle what had happened to her."

"But he left in a car, right?" Kate's gaze moved to the tire treads on the road. "I mean, you saw him leave in a red car when you were getting the ladder to get Annabelle out."

"That's true." Xavier was so confused. They didn't have time for indecision, they needed to find definitive proof of who the killer was before he had a chance to hurt Annabelle.

"Maybe he just figured you and Annabelle would come back here eventually," Kate suggested. "Just decided he'd keep checking here and wait for you to show up and then pounce."

"Maybe." It was possible, Xavier thought, but he couldn't shake the feeling that he was missing the obvious, that there was something important staring him in the face and yet he couldn't see it.

"What're you thinking?" Kate had worked with him long enough to know when his brain was ticking something over.

"That it doesn't ring true that Annabelle's family was the only one the killer didn't call in himself."

"I thought we thought it was because he got interrupted," Kate queried.

"But how did he *know* that he'd been interrupted?" he pressed on, sure he was on the right track. "Ricky Preston didn't go into the Englewood house or alert the killer in any way. We didn't see anyone running out of the house when we got here, neither did we see anyone driving away up the street or any red cars parked outside."

"Maybe the killer looked out the window and saw Ricky the same way Ricky looked up and saw him, then realized he'd have to hurry…"

"It didn't look like he hurried." Xavier remembered the perfectly orchestrated scene in the Englewood house.

"I don't know what to tell you," Kate shrugged. "Maybe he was just finished."

"Diane said he started with Annabelle's parents," he reminded his partner. "If Ricky was standing in his yard and saw the killer standing over John and Kathy's bed with a knife and immediately phoned the police, then there is no possible way he could have killed and mutilated Paul, Julian and Katherine, then attacked Annabelle all before we got there. It's just not..." he trailed off as he realized what it was that had been bugging him.

Shooting up, he ran next door, Kate hot on his heels. "Xavier, what's going on?" she demanded as he hammered on the door.

"Ricky Preston is the killer," he explained. "Ricky? It's Detective Montague, open up."

"What are you talking about?" Kate demanded, frustration brewing in her usually calm blue eyes. "I thought we were thinking Bruce Daniels; how do you know it's Ricky Preston?"

Continuing to thump with one fist, with his free hand he gestured at the Englewood house. "You can't see John and Kathy Englewood's room from Ricky's house; it's around the other side. But you *can* see Annabelle's room."

"So he lied." Kate's blue eyes grew wide.

"He was never in his backyard; he never saw a figure with a knife standing over John and Kathy's bed; he never came running back inside to check his telescope. That's why we thought the killer didn't call it in the first time. But he *did* call it in, he just called it in as himself."

"Ricky definitely lied to us," Kate agreed cautiously. "But that doesn't mean he's the killer. Maybe he *was* using his telescope, only he was using it to spy on Annabelle. *You're* the one who's convinced he's interested in her. Maybe he's been secretly watching her and then that night he saw someone in her room. That would fit in better with the timeline. Annabelle was raped and attacked last, so if Ricky called it in when he saw the killer in her room, then by the time he'd called nine-one-one the killer

209

would have been finished and left before we got there."

"Annabelle's house was the only one that wasn't broken into," he reminded her. "As their neighbor, Ricky might have had a key, or he probably knew where they kept their spare one hidden." He jiggled the handle, expecting to find it locked but the door swung open. "He had no reason to lie if he had nothing to hide." He pushed the door the rest of the way open and stepped inside.

"Xavier, we have no probable cause." Kate stopped him.

"Ricky Preston is the killer, I'm sure of it, and that means he has Annabelle right now. I thought I just heard a call for help," he lied. "There's our probable cause." With that, he pulled out his gun and proceeded to check out the house, Kate at his side. Covering the downstairs and then the upstairs, they found nothing and he was beginning to lose hope that he'd ever find Annabelle and convince her that he at least deserved a shot at proving to her that he was serious about wanting a relationship.

"Xavier," Kate jabbed him in the ribs.

"What?" he blinked, realizing he'd gotten distracted.

"Attic door's locked," Kate whispered.

Guns ready, Kate stepped to the side, and with a well-placed foot he splintered the door with one kick. A quick survey of the small space revealed it was empty, but as his gaze was drawn to the middle of the room, he knew that someone had recently inhabited it.

In the center of the room sat a large oak table. On the ground at each of the legs was a tangle of rope. Slipping his gun away, Xavier knelt at one of the corners, something shiny capturing his attention. As he picked it up he knew he was right. Ricky Preston was the killer. Ricky Preston had Annabelle at this very second. Had held her in this very room maybe as recently as just a few hours ago.

"What'd you find?" Kate stooped beside him.

He held up the delicate gold chain with her name engraved on it so his partner could see it. "Annabelle's bracelet," he murmured, wondering if this would end up being all he had left of a woman he'd never even really had.

* * * * *

12:21 P.M.

Kate glanced over at her partner as he hung up his phone and returned it to his pocket. "And?" Kate prompted when he didn't speak.

"It's Ricky," he confirmed, rubbing tiredly at his face. "Diane matched his fingerprints to the ones CSU collected from each of the crime scenes."

"And?" she prompted again when Xavier closed his eyes and rested his head against the back of the passenger seat.

"And the blood on the ropes was Annabelle's," he finished glumly.

"Well, I guess we now know how he knew you and Annabelle were at her house," she mused. "He didn't need to follow you or use a bug; all he needed to do was sit at home and wait until you fell into his lap."

"I thought Ricky had genuine feelings for Annabelle," Xavier pried an eye open to glance at her sideways. "Why would he try to kill her in a fire?"

Pondering that, she couldn't disagree that it had seemed that Ricky Preston was truly enamored with Annabelle. "Maybe it was just a distraction."

"A distraction?" Xavier opened his other eye.

"You had taken Annabelle back to the house where she was attacked, where her family was killed. Maybe he thought she might remember something—something incriminating—so he decided to put a stop to it. The fire certainly achieved that. Who knows what else Annabelle might have remembered if you hadn't seen the smoke? She might have remembered it was Ricky and he wouldn't have been able to finish what he started."

He let his eyes slide closed again. "I should have figured it out earlier," Xavier sighed dismally.

"You were suspicious of Ricky Preston from the beginning," she consoled.

"You mean, I was jealous of Ricky Preston from the beginning," Xavier corrected. "The way he looked at Annabelle, I could tell he liked her no matter what he said. I guess he finally got fed up that Annabelle didn't reciprocate and decided to do something about it."

"It seems like kind of an overly elaborate way just to get his hands on Annabelle." Kate couldn't believe that Ricky wanting Annabelle was all that was going on. There had to be more to it.

"You think he had another reason for doing all of this?"

"If all he wanted was Annabelle, there were plenty of other ways to get her. I mean, he lived next door to her, they were friends, they spent time together—he could have snatched her anytime, there was no need to go to these lengths. I mean, killing and mutilating her family and three others, it seems like overkill if all he wanted to do was abduct her. I think taking Annabelle was just a side effect to his real plan," Kate finished thoughtfully.

"Maybe he felt like he needed to isolate and terrify her in order to get her to trust him and fall for him." Xavier rubbed tiredly at his face. "What do you think he's doing to her right now? He has her all alone. Drugged, tied up, helpless. He's already raped her once; last time she was unconscious, but if he does it again…"

"Xavier, Xavier, stop," she rested a hand on his shoulder and shook gently. "Thinking like that isn't going to help."

"I should have figured it out sooner," he said again, "but I didn't and now he has her, he *has* her. This monster has her and I don't know what he's doing to her and I don't know how to get her back…"

"Yes, you do," she contradicted firmly. "You *do* know how to get Annabelle back. We're going to get out of this car, go in there," she gestured to the shop that they were parked in front of, "and talk to Ricky's boss. We're going to find out everything we can about him, and then once we know why he did all of this, we'll know where to look for Annabelle."

"Yeah." Xavier drew a shaky breath and took a second to pull himself together before opening his eyes. "Let's do it."

Kate watched her partner carefully as they strode toward the shop. All things considered, Xavier appeared to be holding it together, but if he started to fall apart, she wouldn't hesitate to do something about it. As much as she loved and cared about Xavier and would never want to hurt him, right now finding Ricky Preston before he hurt anyone else was the priority. And she knew that Xavier wouldn't want his actions to in any way endanger Annabelle.

After a brief moment of hammering on the door, it swung open to reveal the shortest, roundest old man Kate had ever seen.

"May I help you?" he squinted up at them through glasses as round as his stomach.

"Terry McGinnely?" Xavier asked.

"Yes," he confirmed.

"I'm Detective Hannah, and this Detective Montague," she made the introductions. "We spoke on the phone earlier."

"Ah, yes." A smile broke out on Terry's bright red face. "Please come in." The large man navigated his way through the packed workshop with surprising ease, leading them down to a small room at the back. He indicated toward the table and rickety chairs that took up most of the space, "Take a seat. Does anyone want anything to drink?"

"I'm good," Xavier answered tightly, clearly wanting to get on with things.

"I'll have whatever you're having," Kate replied, as much as she, too, wanted answers, she also wanted to keep the man as comfortable and open as possible.

"Tea," Terry told her as he set on the kettle. "I'm not one for coffee, never was, never will be."

They waited in silence as Terry McGinnely made a pot of tea and joined them at the table, squeezing himself between the table and the wall to sit on a chair that creaked under the pressure of having to support his enormous frame. "I understand you wanted to talk to me about Ricky." His face was a mix of curiosity, puzzlement, and distress.

"How long has Ricky Preston worked for you?" Xavier asked.

"Uh," rolling his eyes heavenward as he thought, he answered, "four...five years."

"What kind of employee has he been?" Kate asked.

"Diligent, hard-working, skilled," Terry listed.

"Have you had any problems with him?" Kate took a mouthful of the hot tea, finding it a little strong for her taste but swilling it down regardless.

"No, he always turns up on time, and he does everything asked of him, quickly and professionally." Terry smiled uncertainly. "He's a model employee."

"He do work at people's houses or only here?" Xavier was tapping his fingers together, something he usually did when he was stressed.

"He works at people's houses sometimes," Terry replied. "It just depends on the job."

"Have you ever received any complaints about him?" Xavier continued.

"Complaints?" Terry echoed. "No. None. Ever. Ricky is great at his job, polite without being pushy. In fact, I usually get compliments from everyone he works for, some even come back, ask for him again. May I ask what this is about?" Terry watched them nervously. "Has Ricky done something wrong?"

"Ricky Preston has been identified through fingerprints as the man who's been killing families in the area and leaving one family member alive," she explained.

Terry uttered a horrified gasp, "Ricky did that?"

"Yes. I'm sorry," Xavier added sympathetically, her partner knew how Terry felt finding out someone you knew and liked was capable of such horrific things.

"*My* Ricky?" Terry was clutching at denial. "He's been going around killing people?"

"There's been no indication that he was violent?" Kate wondered how good a job Ricky Preston had done at playing the part—obviously good enough to fool both his boss and Annabelle. "He's never been physical with you or any of your customers? Never lost his temper and lashed out?"

"No, never," Terry shook his head solemnly.

"Is there any place you can think Ricky might go to hide out?" Kate asked, noting the hope that flashed through Xavier's eyes.

"Not really, we mostly had a business relationship. Talked work, sports, weather, politics but nothing much personal." Terry looked apologetic, as though it were a fault on his part that he hadn't known every detail about his employee.

"What about his mother?" she asked, thinking of the reason Ricky had given Annabelle as to why he hadn't been around to support her like he'd promised to. "I know she's been sick lately, might he be staying with her? Or maybe if she's in the hospital hiding out at her house?"

He looked confused. "That's a trick question, right?"

"Why would it be a trick question?" Xavier demanded.

"Because Ricky's mom died when he was a kid. Why would you think that she was sick?"

"Because that's what he told us." Xavier's forehead creased with annoyance.

"Why would he do that?" Terry still looked confused.

"So we wouldn't be suspicious of the fact that he wasn't around for Annabelle," she explained.

"Annabelle?"

"Does the name mean something to you?" Xavier inquired.

"Ricky rang me a few days ago to say that his girlfriend,

Annabelle, had been unwell and he was going to take her away out of town to cheer her up."

Xavier muttered under his breath and dropped his head into his hands, running his fingers through his thick brown hair.

He squeezed his meaty hands together. "Annabelle's not really his girlfriend is she?" Terry's lip quivered.

"No she's not," Kate replied solemnly. It appeared Ricky had been planning on taking Annabelle for a while.

"He's kidnapped her, hasn't he?" Terry's huge face was pained. "And he's some sort of maniac. What's he going to do to that poor girl?"

* * * * *

7:50 P.M.

Ever so slowly, she began to awaken.

Her head felt like it had been filled with cotton wool.

Annabelle tried to take a deep breath to clear her mind, but panic was threatening to overwhelm her. It terrified her knowing that she had been unconscious and at the mercy of this horrible man. Her mind began to conjure images of what he might have done to her, the visions playing out on her eyelids as clearly as though she were watching a movie.

Why couldn't he just keep her drugged and unconscious? At least then she would remain blissfully unaware of all his awful deeds. She didn't want to be awake if he raped her again. Last time he had drugged her, and even though she didn't remember it, it still made her feel sick to her stomach. But if he did it again, and she was aware of every disgusting second, then she was sure she would never survive it.

And then what would he do to her?

Would he torture her before he killed her? The pictures she had seen of her mom and dad and sister and brothers' mutilated bodies were flashing vividly in her mind. What if he did that to her? What if she was alive when he did it? What if he did something worse to her?

How was he planning on killing her?

Was he going to stab her, shoot her, strangle her, drown her, smother her, drug her, leave her alone to die from starvation and dehydration?

Was he planning on keeping her hostage for a while before he killed her?

What if he was planning on keeping her for weeks or months or even years? Keeping her locked away. Scared and alone. No one to talk to. How would she survive that?

Horror was welling up inside of her. Starting in the pit of her stomach and reaching its tentacles out to every single molecule of her being until it was almost choking her. At last she could stand it no longer and forced her sticky eyes open.

She gasped when she caught sight of her surroundings.

Annabelle couldn't believe where he had brought her.

The room where he had left her was not the same one she had first awakened in. No longer was she in that attic. Now she was in a basement.

A very familiar basement.

In fact, it was her own basement. He'd brought her back to her own house and locked her up in the basement. Probably the only part of the house not destroyed by the fire. Still, it was damp down here. The water had seeped down, leaving several puddles on the floor, including the one she was sitting in.

Why had he brought her here?

Why would Ricky be so stupid as to keep her here at her own home? Surely the police were bound to come back here eventually.

Annabelle's heart dropped as she remembered seeing her best friend's—really her only friend—face, hovering above her in the seconds before the drugs knocked her out. Now that she knew

Ricky Preston was the killer, the face from that night that had once been fuzzy was now crystal clear, the voice whispering an apology had also become recognizable.

Ricky's betrayal was like a knife through her heart. One that almost took away the fear. When she thought of all the times she had sat in his house, comfortable and at ease, talking more about herself and her life than she would dare to disclose to anyone else, she felt chilled to the bone. She didn't have many friends—acquaintances and colleagues—but not many friends that she would go shopping with or out to lunch with. Annabelle never felt at ease with people; she always felt like she had to act a certain way. But things were different with Ricky. He had made her feel safe and she had confided in him.

While she had been sitting in Ricky's den baring her soul, he had been sitting there pretending to listen and care, all the while planning how best to destroy her life.

Now she knew the truth.

Ricky Preston was a lunatic.

A lunatic who had kidnapped her and tied her up and left her in her basement.

Annabelle's only hope now rested on Xavier figuring things out.

Her already cut and bloody wrists were bound behind her back, at an angle that kept sending arrows of pain down her injured shoulder. The end of the rope had been fastened to the hook supporting her brother Julian's punching bag. If she moved even a little, the pressure from the rope almost popped her shoulders out of joint.

Annabelle knew that once again she wasn't going to be able to brute force her way out of this. Since Ricky had been avoiding her while she was conscious, it was also highly unlikely that she was going to get an opportunity to attempt to talk her way to freedom.

That only left Xavier.

She was sure that he would figure it out eventually.

Xavier had been suspicious of Ricky from the first time they'd met. She was pretty sure that had more to do with the fact that Xavier was jealous of her relationship with Ricky, but that didn't matter. All that mattered was that Xavier think to check Ricky's house. If he searched the house, he was bound to find the bracelet she'd left behind in the attic. With the use of only one hand, it had taken her ages to work the thin chain loose and caused her middle finger to dislocate. In the end, her perseverance had paid off and the bracelet, a gift from her parents on her twenty-first birthday, had fallen to the floor where Xavier was sure to find it.

Annabelle prayed that Xavier hadn't given up on her just yet.

He'd promised her that he wouldn't. He had also promised her that he was going to find the killer. Surely he'd put the pieces together sooner or later.

As footsteps clunked on the steps behind her, Annabelle prayed that Xavier would figure it out sooner rather than later or by the time he got here it might be too late.

MAY 13TH

10:19 A.M.

"Ricky Preston never broke his arm."

He looked up as his partner entered the room. "How do you know that?" Xavier asked. The fact that he hadn't slept in forty-eight hours was beginning to catch up to him and he was starting to struggle to keep his mind focused. Kate had insisted that he go home last night, and he had. He had even been good and gone straight to bed after eating some dinner and taking a shower, but he hadn't been able to get even a wink of sleep. Every time he closed his eyes he'd been haunted by pictures of Annabelle. Memories of holding her as she slept beside him in his bed contrasted violently with images of what Ricky might be doing to her as he lay there. Or what he might have already done to her. The possibility that Ricky had already killed Annabelle left him so terrified it almost rendered him frozen.

"Xavier, you haven't listened to a word I've been saying," Kate's voice pierced his skull. "Are you okay?"

"Yes," he answered shortly. He didn't want Kate distracted by worrying about him; if they were going to find Annabelle and Ricky before it was too late, they both needed to remain focused.

"Did you sleep last night?"

"Sure," he nodded emphatically. "What were you saying about Ricky's arm?"

Raising a suspicious eyebrow to indicate that she didn't believe him, Kate plopped down into a chair to repeat what she'd just said. "There are no medical records for Ricky's broken arm."

"He faked it?"

"Terry McGinnely said he never saw an x-ray or anything," Kate elaborated. "Ricky just turned up a month ago with his arm in a cast and a letter from a doctor saying that he'd fallen and broken his arm and would need the next two months off work."

Xavier could believe that. Terry McGinnely seemed like a very trusting individual and, based on past experience, he had no reason to think that Ricky Preston was being anything other than truthful. "The letter from the doctor, let me guess: it was a fake."

"No such doctor exists," Kate nodded. "Ricky wrote it himself."

"Well, I think I found out not only how his mother died but also the reason he's been doing all of this," Xavier couldn't quite keep a grin from taking over his face. Finally, he felt like he was making progress, and the closer he got to understanding Ricky Preston and his motivations, the closer he got to finding Annabelle. Carefully, he pushed away the wave of fear that lapped at his toes as he thought of Annabelle, scared and alone and helpless at the hands of a maniac. Fear wasn't going to help him right now; it was only going to slow him down. Plus, he already knew that Kate was watching him like a hawk, ready to have him removed from the case if she thought he couldn't handle things.

"How did his mother die?" Kate asked.

"House fire."

"Interesting," Kate arched a brow. "So I guess not a coincidence that he tried to burn you and Annabelle alive."

"This year is the thirtieth anniversary of Lisbeth Preston's death," he continued. "Ricky was sixteen when his mother died. No siblings, absent father, young Ricky and his mother were very close. The fire happened one day while he was out with some friends, his mother was home alone, fire was caused by some candles setting the curtains alight."

"How does that tell us why he's doing this?" Kate looked confused.

His grin grew bigger. "Because Ricky Preston didn't believe his mother died because of some candles."

"What did he believe happened?"

"He believed that his mother died because no one ran inside the burning building to rescue her. Apparently, Lisbeth Preston was trapped upstairs when the fire broke out downstairs. She couldn't get out. Witnesses saw and heard her screaming for help through a window, but the fire was too fierce and they couldn't get inside. When the fire was finally put out and they got inside, Lisbeth's body was found in the attic. The fire hadn't gotten to her, she died of smoke inhalation. Her hands were all cut and bloody from trying to break through the glass windows to escape…"

"That's why he cuts off their hands," Kate inserted.

"And I'm guessing he cuts out their eyes and tongues because he thinks people watched his mother begging for help and didn't do anything about it. I suppose in his twisted mind it's symbolic for him. Cutting out the tongues is his way of punishing them so they can't call for help and the eyes because they looked and did nothing."

"So Ricky thought his mother, his only family, died needlessly, that if only someone had gone inside and rescued her, then his mother would have lived and his life would have been fine."

"More specifically," he added, "Ricky Preston thought his *neighbors* should have gone inside the house to save his mom. That's what he told the reporters, said his mom was murdered."

Her dark blue eyes grew wide. "You think he's hunting down all his old neighbors?" Kate asked.

"At the time of his mother's death, he only had one neighbor; they lived on a new housing estate and most of the other houses weren't occupied yet. I think he's hunting down all the neighbors he's ever had," he clarified. "He started with the Englewoods, his current neighbors, and I'm going to guess that at some point in his life he also lived next door to the Jenners, the Ranklings, and the Littletons."

"With the Littletons he left that message, that he was finished. Do you think that they were the family he was living next to when his mother died?"

"Unconfirmed at the moment," he replied. "We're waiting for the police reports to be faxed over, but right now, I'm hoping that the house where Ricky's mother died is where he's currently holed up with Annabelle." Xavier also hoped that whatever Ricky had in mind for Annabelle, he hadn't yet had a chance to act out.

* * * * *

12:03 P.M.

Why didn't Xavier come?

He should have figured it out by now, she *needed* him to figure it out.

Annabelle couldn't stand spending another second tied up in her basement, she needed to get out of here now.

She was going crazy.

Her shoulder was aching horribly, the stitches had been ripped out and blood had been oozing out for hours. Her arms were numb from so many hours in the same awkward position. Earlier, she had managed to work herself into a standing position. It had taken her a long time. Weak from the drugs Ricky kept giving her, her legs had refused to cooperate, her knees buckling each time she got halfway up, sending her dropping back down. Each time she slipped, her shoulder was jerked painfully, and she began to wonder whether Ricky had positioned her that way on purpose. She had eventually made it to her feet, and the relief to her arms and shoulders was immediate. Unfortunately, she hadn't managed to remain standing for long. With little energy, she had soon collapsed, once again sending pain shooting up her shoulder, as she thumped down onto her knees.

Strength sapped, Annabelle attempted to curl up in the most

comfortable position she could manage and waited.

For what, she wasn't quite sure.

Waiting for Xavier to come and find her?

Waiting for Ricky to come back?

Waiting to die?

As she attempted to rest her head against her good shoulder, she caught sight of the scars that crisscrossed her chest and arms, she couldn't see them but she knew they marred her back too.

Annabelle didn't know how she had gotten them.

Well she knew, but she didn't know. Something had happened to her when she four. Something bad. But she only remembered bits and pieces. A dark room, a man with a scary face, and screaming. Lots of screaming.

But she had been rescued.

Returned home to her family.

Only her family hadn't been the same anymore.

After that, her parents had been different. They had been distant with her. Closed off. No longer the loving parents she remembered. As she looked at the scars, she understood why— they couldn't love her anymore after what had happened to her. And that was the real reason she didn't date. If even her own parents couldn't love her, then how could she expect anyone else to?

Before she had a chance to dwell, Annabelle heard the unmistakable sound of the basement door opening, and moments later Ricky appeared.

"Afternoon, Annabelle," he smiled at her cheerfully, just as he had so many times before when she would come and visit him in his home. The knowledge that she had shared more of herself with this man, this horrible murdering man, than any other person on the planet, left her feeling nauseous.

"Please let me down, Ricky," she begged. "My arms are numb."

"Sure thing," he said agreeably.

That had been too easy. He was up to something. "Why are you doing this, Ricky?" she asked as he used a knife to cut through the rope binding her. This had been her first opportunity to actually talk to him, and attempt to talk her way out. Every other time, Ricky just came in and drugged her. She had to take advantage of this opportunity while it lasted.

"Revenge," he answered simply.

"Revenge?" she repeated, confused. "On me?" Grunting as the rope broke and she tumbled forward, caught off guard, her head banging painfully into the concrete floor.

"On you?" Ricky laughed like she'd just said the funniest thing he'd ever heard.

"Well, on who then? I have a right to know since you involved me in all of this," Annabelle challenged. Pain was shooting up and down her numb arms like an arrow as circulation slowly resumed, but she did her best to ignore it.

"You have no rights," Ricky growled, lunging at her and flinging her onto her back, his hands clamping around her neck, squeezing tightly.

Hands still tied behind her back, Annabelle was helpless to fight him off. Still, she squirmed desperately as Ricky's hands tightened. Her vision began to fade, and Xavier's face popped into her mind. She wished desperately that she had been able to believe him when he'd told her that he was falling in love with her. If she hadn't been so stupidly and uncharacteristically stubborn, then instead of lying on a cold basement floor with a maniac's hands wrapped around her throat, she could be in Xavier's living room, safely tucked up in his arms, right this second.

Just when she'd thought she was about to die, Ricky suddenly released her. Annabelle struggled to suck in breath after breath of precious air. As he knelt beside her, Ricky's breathing was almost as ragged as her own. Taking advantage of his distraction, Annabelle attempted to half crawl, half drag herself across the floor, wanting to be as far away from her psychotic neighbor as she could be.

"Not so fast," Ricky's hand grabbed her injured shoulder, shaking her and making her cry out in pain.

Tears brimming, she fought them back, she didn't want him to see her cry. "Please, Ricky, just tell me what you want, whatever it is I'll give it to you, just please let me go," she whimpered.

"You'll give me whatever I want, will you?" Ricky snarled.

"Yes," she whispered, sure she wasn't going to like where he was headed. Before she knew it, he was pressing his lips against hers, kissing her roughly. The feel of his lips on hers was nothing like the feel of Xavier's. Relieved when he finally pulled away, she couldn't suppress a shudder.

"Not quite the same as when your new *boyfriend* does it?" Ricky sneered.

"He's not my boyfriend," Annabelle whispered, still trying to get her breathing to return to normal.

"That's right," his sneer changing to a malevolent grin. "Poor little Annabelle is too scared to date."

Unfortunately, she couldn't come up with a retort to that. She *was* too scared to date, and Ricky knew it. She'd told him so on numerous occasions.

He was laughing cheerfully now. "You didn't tell me about the scars."

The scars were about the only thing she hadn't told him.

He laughed again. "Little, weak Annabelle, too scared to get out in the real world and live her life, so she hides in her house all the time."

"I have a life," she protested, even though she knew it wasn't true.

"You have a job and a family and your only friend is a serial killer." He laughed again. "You forget I know all about you. I've spent hours and hours listening to you drone on and on about how scared you are to live your life, to let anyone get close to you because you don't think anyone could love you. So tell me about these scars, how did you get them?"

She flinched as he reached out a finger and traced it along the scars on her chest. Usually, Annabelle made sure to dress in a way that kept her scars completely hidden, she didn't want anyone catching sight of them, but Ricky had removed her clothing, leaving her only in her underwear. Those scars and how she had got them were the only piece of herself she hadn't shared with him, and she wasn't about to let him take it now. "You killed so many people, Ricky," she said instead, hoping to distract him. "Why?"

"I told you. Revenge. For my mother's death," he added.

"I thought your mom died in a car accident?" That was what Ricky had told her anyway, but as she thought about it, she realized that the two of them had talked a lot more about her than they had about him.

"She died in a fire." His eyes grew distant. "It was just the two of us, but I was out. She was upstairs and didn't know that she'd left some candles burning. They set the curtains on fire, then the whole place was burning. She was trapped upstairs." His eyes were cold now. "She screamed for help, but they ignored her. Listened to her begging for someone to help her, but they did nothing. They'd said the fire was too fierce and they couldn't get inside. She died and now they will too."

"Who will?" Annabelle asked softly, positive that Ricky's mother's screams had not been ignored, but that whoever had been there had truly been unable to reach her through the flames.

"Our neighbors."

Catching on, she asked, "Your neighbors didn't save your mom, so you're hunting them all down and killing them?"

"They watched and did nothing, so I made sure they couldn't do that again. They heard her screams and did nothing, so I made sure they couldn't scream. My mother's hands were all cut up from trying to escape on her own because nobody would help her, so I made sure they lost their hands."

Quaking as she remembered the photos of her family's mutilation, Ricky had done that to them, and who knew why he hadn't to her. "Ricky, your mom's death was just a horrible accident, those neighbors..." She broke off as Ricky's fist connected with her face, sending her sprawling.

"My mother was murdered," he roared, looming over her.

"Okay, Ricky," Annabelle nodded, her cheek ached and she could feel blood dripping down her face; she didn't want to make him angry again. "Xavier said that you raped me." She had to force the words out her mouth. "Why did you do that? That doesn't have anything to do with getting revenge for your mom's death. Xavier thinks you like me. Do you?"

Ricky burst into peals of near-hysterical laughter. "That is the funniest thing I have ever heard." He wiped at the tears streaming down his cheeks. "You are nothing more than a distraction, something to keep the police occupied so I can finish what I started. And I'd say you did just that. You had Detective Montague so well occupied he didn't know what he was doing."

"So you were just using me? All this time that I thought we were friends, you were just using me?" That thought hurt her more than anything else. She had allowed herself to open up to this man because she thought he was a true friend, and the whole time he had just been plotting how best to manipulate her to get what he wanted.

"There was one thing I always wanted from you." The glint in his eyes changed.

Remembering what he had said to her that night, that he'd been waiting a long time for her. "Please don't," she whispered desperately.

"Every time you sat in my living room wallowing over what a weak, pathetic person you were, I thought about it, played out fantasies in my head. I couldn't wait to sleep with you and take that pole out of your snooty little behind. Last time was good, but, unfortunately, you don't remember it; this time you will though."

* * * * *

2:02 P.M.

"She has to be here somewhere." Xavier thumped an angry fist into the nearest wall.

Kate watched her partner closely. He was hanging on by a thread. She knew he hadn't slept last night and panicked concern for Annabelle was written all over his face. Xavier had pinned all his hopes on finding Annabelle here at the house where Ricky Preston's mother had died. However, they'd already been here for a good thirty minutes and so far there was no sign of either Annabelle or Ricky.

When they got back to the station she was going to talk to Rob about removing Xavier from this case. She didn't want to hurt her partner's feelings, and she hoped he understood, but with Annabelle missing, Xavier could barely function, much less do his job. She knew he'd never forgive himself if anything happened to Annabelle because he couldn't focus.

"Let's go through the house again," Xavier snapped.

"We've already searched it thoroughly," Kate reminded him patiently. The house Ricky's mother had died in had been completely destroyed in the fire, and the plot of land had sat vacant for many years. Since being rebuilt, the house had changed hands numerous times; now it stood empty. When they'd arrived, they'd searched it from bottom to top. Every room. Every cupboard. Every closet. The basement and the attic. And they'd found nothing. Not even a sign that Ricky had stashed Annabelle here at some point.

"Then we'll search it again," Xavier said tightly.

Reluctantly, Kate followed him back down to the basement, and patiently helped him to recheck the nooks and crannies they'd already searched.

"Maybe there's some sort of secret room down here," Xavier suggested.

Kate needed to put a stop to this. "She's not here, Xavier. We checked the whole house. You need to face facts. Wherever Ricky took her, it wasn't to the house where his mom died. But that doesn't mean we won't find her," she said firmly.

"There's no guarantee we'll ever find her," her partner said, voice stark.

"Xavier . . ." He was right, but still—she wanted to offer some platitudes to make him feel better.

"No, Kate, we both know that we may never find her. Or we might not find her until it's too late." Xavier's hazel eyes were bottomless pits of fear and pain and guilt.

"It's not your fault he got her," she said softly. Kate was truly worried about how Xavier would cope if anything happened to Annabelle. He was already a mess of guilt over what Julia had done and the part he believed he played in it. It didn't matter how many times she told him that Julia could have told him what happened to her and ask him for help. She knew he knew it in his head, but she also knew he didn't believe it in his heart. If they didn't find Annabelle alive, she was concerned the guilt would eat him alive.

"I left her alone and unprotected," Xavier's voice was raw with self-recrimination. "I knew that the killer wanted her taken out, and yet I left her all by herself because I was angry that she invaded my privacy and found out about Julia. What was I thinking?" He dropped his head to his hands. "I should have just told her about Julia like you told me to. What was so bad about her looking it up, anyway? She had every right to know about my history with Julia because..."

"Because you went through every aspect of her life with a fine-tooth comb?" she asked when he trailed off into silence.

He shook his head. "No. She had every right to know

everything about my past because she was falling in love with me."

"We need a profile," she announced suddenly. Xavier needed a distraction. "We need to know if he took Annabelle as a distraction or because he's obsessed with her."

"He looks at her like he's obsessed," Xavier muttered.

Unfortunately, that was Xavier's jealous side talking, not his cop side. "Hold on," her phone began to buzz in her pocket. "Detective Hannah." She was listening intently. "Okay, thanks."

"Who was that?" Xavier asked with a raised eyebrow, he seemed to have regained his composure.

"Rob. He said that the Littletons were indeed the neighbors that lived next door to Ricky and his mom when she died; at least Ken Littleton and his parents were. Ken was only seven years old at the time he witnessed the fire."

"So then he *was* already finished." Xavier's face paled so dramatically that Kate was worried he was going to pass out. "And he took Annabelle anyway."

"Xavier…" she began.

"I don't know what's worse," he muttered tonelessly. "That he took her as a distraction so he could get away or that he took her because he's obsessed."

She bit the bullet. "Xavier, I'm going to tell Rob to take you off this case." She waited anxiously for his response. Kate considered her partner one of her closest friends, and intended to ask him to be the godfather of her baby. Which reminded her she still needed to *tell* him about the baby. She didn't want to mess with their friendship, but she was too concerned about him right now to sit back and do nothing. No matter what the consequences.

"Maybe that's for the best," he murmured tiredly. "I can barely think, Kate. I'm no good to Annabelle right now."

She let out a relieved breath. "Okay, then. She's not here, we'll drive back to the city, I'll drop you off at home, and then I'll go talk to Rob. We'll find her, Xavier. You have to believe that. And

I'll keep you up to date. I'll let you know the second that we find anything."

"Okay," Xavier nodded distractedly.

Taking his elbow, she guided him up the stairs, and out through the house. She paused at the car and held out her hand. "Keys?"

He stared at her vacantly as if she'd spoken in another language.

"I need your car keys," she reminded him.

Xavier pulled the keys from his pocket and handed them over, then flopped into the passenger seat.

Kate slid into the driver's seat of Xavier's car, turned on the engine, then paused. She was just going to tell him. "Xavier, I'm pregnant."

His eyes grew wide in shock. "How far along are you?"

"Sixteen weeks."

"Why didn't you tell me before now?" he looked crestfallen.

"Because you've been so distracted lately, and then everything with Annabelle, and..." and I was a coward, she finished silently. "I'm sorry, Xavier. I was scared because I...I don't know if I'm going to come back after my maternity leave. I didn't know how to tell you. I wanted you to be happy..."

"But you weren't sure I would be because of Julia and the baby we lost," he finished for her. "Kate, we've been friends for a long time, and you were there for me through the whole Julia thing. I'm happy for you." The smile he shot her was genuine. "Congratulations, Kate, you're going to be a great mom, and David is going to be a fantastic dad."

She let out another relieved breath. Now she couldn't even remember why she'd been afraid to tell Xavier. He was her friend; of course he'd be happy for her. "We want you to be the godfather," she could feel tears shining in her eyes.

"I'm honored," his smile was serious, but in his eyes she saw joy.

"Then let's go find Annabelle, and maybe one day I'll get to be a godmother."

* * * * *

4:26 P.M.

Annabelle lay there dazed.

In shock, she supposed.

Her shoulder ached badly, but at least it had stopped bleeding. The cut on her face where Ricky had hit her earlier had also stopped bleeding, but it, too, ached and Annabelle thought Ricky had probably broken her cheekbone.

It was sticky between her legs. Ricky hadn't used a condom when he'd...

No, she told herself firmly. She wasn't going to think about that right now. Wasn't going to think about him on top of her. Wasn't going to think about whether he was going to come back and do it again.

But it was too late, of course. She was already thinking about it. And tears were streaming down her cheeks again.

Curling herself into a ball as best she could with her injuries and her wrists still bound behind her back, she let herself cry.

Obviously Xavier wasn't going to find her.

Maybe he wasn't even looking.

No, she reminded herself. The last time she had seen Xavier he had promised that he was going to find the killer. She had to hold on to that belief or else she was going to lose it.

Already she was only hanging on to sanity by a thread.

And only because of Xavier.

She wasn't sure how someone she had only known for a few days could have made such a big impact on her. He was her knight in shining armor. And she could see herself falling in love with him. Maybe she already was.

She allowed herself to daydream about a happy future with Xavier. Of a wedding, and a family, and all the wonderful things she had been sure she'd never have. If she made it out of this alive, she was going to tell Xavier how she felt. She was going to let herself believe him when he promised her that his ex-wife was his past and she was his future.

Her panic was just starting to ebb a little when she heard Ricky at the door.

He was back.

Her breath caught in her throat as he loomed over her. She tried to meet his eye bravely but couldn't force herself to do it. "What do you want, Ricky?" she asked quietly, hoping desperately he wasn't planning on raping her again; she didn't think she could go through that again.

"I'm here to put you to good use," he grinned.

"What?" she asked, confused.

"Well, my dear, you are my little distraction tool. I'm going to make sure that your boyfriend and his partner are too busy rescuing you, so I can finish what I started."

"You have another family to kill," Annabelle said flatly. Another family who was innocently going about their lives, completely unaware that a killer was waiting to destroy them. Another person who was about to lose their whole family in an incomprehensibly horrific manner.

"Last one," he nodded agreeably. "Only the police think I'm all finished. Didn't want them getting in the way of this one; it's the most important." His face grew dark. "So I'm going to tuck you away someplace where you can be helpful, and then saving you will be all that boyfriend of yours can think of. I'll be able to kill the last family and get away."

"What are you going to do with me?"

Bending over, he hoisted her over his shoulder, making her groan in pain, and carried her to the corner of the basement where her father had built a wine cellar a few years back. Balancing her with one arm, he swung open the door and deposited her on the floor inside the small room.

"You're going to leave me in here?" fear laced her voice.

"Yep."

"It's a wine cellar. An airtight wine cellar," she told him, even though she knew he already knew this.

"Yep."

"You're leaving me here to die." Even though she'd known that Ricky probably planned on killing her, hearing just how he intended to do it still terrified her.

He shrugged. "I don't really care if you die or if your boyfriend finds you first. I just need you to keep him occupied."

"You can't do that," she protested, panicked.

"Of course I can." He was already closing the door. "Thanks for your help, Annabelle." He winked at her, then slammed the door, locking it behind him.

Wiggling herself to the door, she positioned herself so she could kick at it with her feet. She knew this was not going to get her out and yet she couldn't seem to stop herself. After a couple of minutes her energy was all used up and she slumped back against the cold, hard floor, gasping for breath.

Forcing herself to calm down, Annabelle did the math. The room was approximately five feet by five feet by five feet, which at best gave her maybe eight or nine hours before the carbon dioxide levels became toxic.

But that was a best case scenario.

Her body was already weakened from the injury to her shoulder and the associated blood loss. Plus, she was panicked and her respiratory rate was increasing as fear about her impending death took control of her mind. The faster she breathed, the faster she would produce carbon dioxide, and the faster death would come.

Once again, she attempted to calm herself down. Xavier was looking for her. He had to be. Which meant that she had to do her part. She had to keep herself as calm as possible so she would still be alive when Xavier found her.

Ricky had said that he didn't care if she died or if Xavier found her first. Which had to mean that he thought it was a genuine possibility that Xavier would find her here. Reminding herself that she meant nothing to Ricky, that he was just using her, he wanted Xavier to find her, wanted him either in a blind panic about her death or a blind panic rushing her to the hospital.

She was trying desperately to keep herself controlled. Imagining Xavier breaking down the door, scooping her up into his arms, cradling her gently, telling her he loved her.

But it did no good. Annabelle knew what was coming. Over the next couple of hours, she'd start experiencing headaches, dizziness, fatigue, her vision and hearing would begin to be affected, her blood pressure would increase, she'd lose control of her limbs, then unconsciousness and death.

It was too late, all attempts at calm were gone. Annabelle began to sob hysterically.

* * * * *

10:53 P.M.

Xavier felt closer to Annabelle here.

Maybe he should feel closer to her at his house since she'd spent several nights there with him, but he'd been drawn here, back to Annabelle's house, to the place where he felt like he had first managed to connect with her.

After Kate had dropped him off at his place, he had moped around for several hours, but couldn't settle himself to anything. He'd tried cooking dinner but all he could think of was Annabelle sitting in his kitchen watching him cook. He'd tried watching some TV but all he could think of was Annabelle sitting beside him watching movies. He'd tried taking a shower to relax but all he could think of was washing Annabelle's hair. He'd even tried getting some sleep but all he could think of was Annabelle curled up beside him.

So instead, he'd been drawn back here.

He remembered the night he had found her here. When he'd held her in his arms as she'd cried. If he concentrated he could still feel her breath against his neck, her hair tickling his nose, her arms encircling his waist as she clung to him, the way she'd gone still when he'd called her Belle. Because in her dreams that was what the man who would love her called her. She'd called him out on switching between calling her Annabelle and calling her Belle. He hadn't realized he'd done it, but she'd been right.

Sighing, she'd been right about a lot of things.

Climbing from his car, Xavier wandered through the Englewoods' front yard, recalling the last time he'd seen her. Her white eyes had been full of devastation when she heard he still loved Julia. Devastation changing to raw fear when she'd told him she couldn't cope with losing him if she let him get close and then he left her for Julia.

Leaning wearily against a tree he slid to the ground, completely worn out from the stress and emotions of the last few days. Xavier knew he shouldn't have left her alone that night. He should have stayed and convinced her that there was zero chance of him ever going back to Julia. He should have stayed and held her in his arms until he'd wiped that defeated, lost, heartbroken look from her eyes.

He should have convinced her that he wanted her to be Belle.

At the very least, he should have sat in his car outside her motel room to make sure she was safe.

One thing he was determined not to do though was play the what if game. He'd already been playing it for three years. What if he'd been home the night of Julia's assault? What if he'd paid more attention? What if he'd noticed that she wasn't excited about the upcoming birth of their baby? What if he'd been able to stop her from killing that couple and orphaning their child? What if he'd been able to get her to plead insanity and go to a psychiatric facility? So many what ifs and none of them changed the facts.

He wasn't going to make the same mistakes with Annabelle that he'd made with Julia.

He wasn't going to waste time on what if. He should have kept Annabelle safe but he hadn't; now he needed to focus on getting her back and then helping her deal with all of this.

He was going to get his life back. Three wasted years was enough.

Glancing at his cell phone, Xavier wanted to call Kate and see if there had been any progress made in finding Ricky and Annabelle, but he didn't want to distract her. Initially he'd been shocked and furious when Kate had told him that she was going to have him removed from the case, but almost immediately he had realized she was right. He was too emotionally involved to be able to do his job. And Annabelle's life depended on clear headedness, not panicked turmoil.

Xavier knew he was lucky to have a friend like Kate. A friend who was prepared to do what was tough because she knew it was also what was best for him. It made him sad that she hadn't told him about her pregnancy because she wasn't sure he'd be completely happy for her. It was also something he intended to rectify. He was thrilled to pieces to be a godfather to Kate and David's baby.

Kate was right. Her pregnancy did make him think of his daughter. He would always love and miss the little girl he had never gotten a chance to know, but he was also ready to move forward.

He dialed Kate's number when he became aware of a presence nearby. Without looking up, he reached a hand slowly to his gun. Keeping his cool, he asked, "Where's Annabelle?"

"Waiting for you," came the reply.

"She's still alive?" He held his breath as he waited for the answer.

"She was last time I saw her," Ricky answered.

"You know I'm going to arrest you." He wondered what Ricky was hoping to achieve by turning up at Annabelle's house.

"We'll see," came the bemused reply.

"Why did you do it, Ricky? You have to know that your mother's death was just an accident."

"No one helped her, they watched her die and didn't do anything. That's murder." If Ricky was surprised that they'd figured out what he was doing, he didn't show it.

"But the Englewoods, Jenners and Ranklings weren't there; they had nothing to do with the fire and your mom's death." He tried to keep Ricky occupied while he surreptitiously dialed Kate's number.

"Drop the phone, or I won't tell you where Annabelle is." Ricky was suddenly beside him.

Xavier complied. "Where is she, Ricky?" Xavier asked desperately.

"I told you, she's waiting for you to come and save her," the smile Ricky gave him was bone-chilling.

"I'm going to get my handcuffs and take you to the station, Ricky. Then you can tell me where Annabelle is and I'll go get her. It's over," he said softly, already reaching for his handcuffs.

"I think I better tell you where Annabelle is before you arrest me, in case you change your mind," Ricky was grinning smugly.

"Why?" Xavier was getting a sinking feeling that he'd just played right into Ricky Preston's hand.

"Because you can't have both."

"Can't have both of what?"

"You can either arrest me or you can save Annabelle's life. You can't do both."

He clawed at denial. "I can arrest you and then find out where you've hidden her."

"But not in time to find her alive," came the singsong reply.

"You were using her all along." Xavier's fear was replaced by rage.

"Yep," Ricky nodded agreeably. "And she's doing her job just perfectly."

"Did you hurt her?" his hands curling into fists.

"So what's your decision?" Ricky asked instead. "Me or Annabelle?"

"How do I know that she's really still alive?"

"You don't."

Wavering, Ricky was a danger to anyone and everyone he came into contact with and yet this was Annabelle they were talking about. It was one thing to let Ricky go if it saved Annabelle's life, but if he let Ricky go only to find Annabelle was already dead...

"Ticktock, ticktock. By my calculations, Annabelle doesn't have long left. So what do you choose? Are you going to arrest me and let the woman you love die, or are you going to be her knight in shining armor and save her life?"

He battled his indecision. His heart was telling him to pick Annabelle, his head wasn't all that far behind. But Annabelle was Ricky Preston's ticket to freedom. As soon as he gave up her location, he knew Xavier would go running to her rescue and he would use that time to flee. Flee the country if he was smart. They had enough to convict him. Fingerprints, DNA, not to mention Annabelle's statement.

"Last time I ask. Are you going to let me go or do you want Annabelle's blood on your hands? Me or Annabelle?"

"Annabelle."

* * * * *

11:21 P.M.

She was unable to move now.

Annabelle was too weak.

She was panting, struggling for breath. Her head spun every time she moved it. A headache pounded viciously at her temples.

241

Her eyes were clenched shut. If she opened them, she saw sparks and stars, the sensation adding to the dizziness.

It didn't look like Xavier was going to find her.

At least not in time.

It had been hours since Ricky locked her away in here. He had probably killed the last family and was ready to leave the country by now.

Annabelle wished that she could have a chance to live her life the way she always should have. Ricky had said that she was weak and scared, and she had been. Her whole life.

Twenty-three years wasted.

Because she was too scared that no one could ever love her, and too weak to put herself out there and try.

Too bad she'd learned her lesson too late.

If she had any energy left, she'd cry.

But she didn't have any energy left.

Already she was gasping desperately, the oxygen levels in the room had dropped dangerously low. Annabelle knew she had maybe minutes left before unconsciousness came. Death would follow soon after.

The pain in her head prevented her from forming any more logical thoughts.

She couldn't catch her breath.

She was choking.

And then everything faded away.

* * * * *

11:30 P.M.

"Kate, I need paramedics and officers at Annabelle's house now," Xavier yelled into his phone as he headed for the Englewoods' basement.

"What?" came his partner's confused reply.

"I was at Annabelle's house thinking about her, Ricky showed up, he has Annabelle locked away in her father's airtight wine cellar." Clattering down the basement stairs, "I have to go now, I have to get her out, Ricky said she didn't have long left. Hurry up and get here."

Not bothering to listen to Kate's response, he hit end, and shoved his phone into his pants pocket.

"Annabelle?"

Hammering on the cellar door. It was locked.

"Annabelle, just hold on, I'm coming."

Searching desperately for a key, he was hesitant to kick down the door because he didn't know if Annabelle was too close on the other side, or what condition she was in.

He was about to give in and risk breaking down the door when he saw a keychain hanging on the wall by the bottom of the stairs. There were three keys on the chain, and Xavier struggled to insert the first key into the lock because his hands were shaking so badly.

Thankfully the key turned, and with a soft clunk the wine cellar door swung open, revealing Annabelle's body lying in front of him. Blood streaked her face from a gash on her cheekbone, blood also streaked her arm and chest from the wound to her shoulder. Her arms were pulled behind her back, and she rested awkwardly on her side, head lolling limply.

Xavier dropped to his knees beside her. "Annabelle?"

She was barely breathing, and when he pressed his fingertips to her neck, he could hardly detect a pulse.

He needed to get her out of here. Scooping her gently into his arms, ignoring for the moment the rope that bound her wrists, he ran with her up the stairs and out into the night. He carefully set her down on the soft grass. "Annabelle?"

No answer.

Her whole body was shaking violently. Leaning over her, he covered her mouth with his and forced oxygen into her starving lungs.

"Come on, Annabelle," he urged, brushing the hair from her face.

Still nothing. Covering her mouth again, he breathed into her.

"Annabelle, please, wake up," he begged. Surely he couldn't lose Annabelle now, not when he'd just found her, not while she didn't believe that he loved her.

Ever so slowly, Annabelle's eyelids began to flutter.

"Come on, honey," he encouraged, taking her face in his hands.

Her eyelids fluttered a little more and then he was looking down into her stunning white eyes.

"Hey, welcome back." Relief flooded through him at the sight of her conscious.

She was groggy, her gaze disoriented, she moved her lips but no sound came out.

"Don't try to talk," he cautioned gently. "Don't try to do anything, I've got you, just concentrate on breathing." She was still gasping, each breath shallow and harsh. Hopefully the ambulance would be here soon, she needed oxygen, and she needed it quickly. Drinking in the sight of her, his fingers tracing her face, running through her hair.

"Xavier," her voice so faint he could hardly hear it. "You came."

"Of course I came," he admonished softly. He didn't like the way Annabelle was so overly grateful over every little thing people did for her, like she didn't deserve it. When she was stronger they were going to discuss that.

"My head hurts." Her eyes fell closed again. "And I feel sick."

"I know, honey, you need oxygen, an ambulance will be here soon," he assured her. "Here, let me untie you." Carefully, he sat her up, propping her against his shoulder as he reached for his knife and sawed through the rope binding her, trying to hide his wince at the sight of her badly damaged wrists. The ropes had ripped all the skin off, leaving them bloody and raw, fibers from the rope left behind in the wounds.

Annabelle noticed his wince. "How bad are they?"

"Pretty bad," he answered grimly. "What happened to your face?"

It was her turn to wince. "Ricky hit me. I think it's broken."

She was probably right, her cheek was swollen and already turning black. Anger rippled through him at the thought of Ricky hurting Annabelle. Now that he had Annabelle safe, he was going to hunt down Ricky Preston before he had a chance to get away.

"My shoulder," her gasping voice continued, "I think all the stitches pulled out while I was trying to stand up."

He wasn't sure what she meant by that, but he didn't need the details right now. Annabelle needed to remain calm, not relive every detail of her abduction. "They'll re-stitch it at the hospital," he soothed. "Try not to worry about that right now. Just try to relax." He settled her against his chest.

"Xavier?"

"What is it, honey?"

"Ricky raped me," her voice quivered.

He tightened his grip on her. "I'm sorry, sweetheart." Xavier pressed a kiss to the top of her head.

"No, I'm sorry." Annabelle tried to lift her head from his shoulder, but he pressed it back down. "I should have believed you, when you said you wouldn't go back to Julia, but I believe you now. I do, I really do," she implored.

"Shh," he whispered in her ear, wanting to keep her as calm as possible until help arrived. "I believe you. And I'm the one who should be sorry. I left you alone and unprotected and Ricky got you. I'm sorry, Annabelle; I'm so sorry."

"Not your fault," she murmured, sounding sleepy now.

He eased her back so he could see her face. "Stay with me, Annabelle," he commanded. "Paramedics will be here soon, but you stay with me, okay?"

Energy levels depleted, she was quickly fading back towards unconsciousness.

"Hey," he gave her a firm shake. "I want you to be Belle. Do you hear me? I want you to always be Belle."

Offering him a weak smile as her eyes fluttered close, and her breathing eased a little as she passed out.

"Belle?"

"Xavier?" Kate suddenly appeared beside him. "Is she okay?"

"No, she's not. Where are the paramedics?"

"They should be here any moment," Kate assured him. "Where's Ricky Preston?"

"I had to let him go." He was rearranging Annabelle in his arms; if the paramedics didn't arrive shortly, he was going to drive her to the hospital himself.

"What?"

"He used her," stroking Annabelle's hair. "That's why he took her. He wanted to get away while I was distracted. He made me choose: him or Annabelle. He had her locked away, said he wouldn't tell me where she was unless I let him go. I'm sorry, Kate, but I had to choose Belle."

"It looks like you made the right choice, she wouldn't have lasted much longer," Kate reassured him. "Why wouldn't he have just run? Why the ruse with Annabelle?"

"Xavier," Annabelle's faint voice spoke beneath him.

"Everything's okay, Belle, just rest."

"No, Xavier," she continued, agitated. "Ricky said he wasn't finished."

He exchanged glances with Kate above Annabelle's head. Her brain had been deprived of oxygen for a long time, she was groggy and confused, he wasn't sure she knew what she was saying. "Okay, honey," rubbing her back to calm her.

"I'm serious," came the weak reply. "He said he had another family left to kill. That's why he took me. So you'd be preoccupied with me." She wearily lifted her head from his shoulder to meet his eyes. "And you wouldn't figure out he wasn't done until it was too late."

"Are you sure?"

"Mmm hmmm," she nodded.

A glance at Kate confirmed that she, too, believed Annabelle.

Moaning, Annabelle pressed her fingers to her temples; tears squeezed out the corners of her eyes as she scrunched them shut. "My head," she whimpered pitifully.

Unable to wait any longer, Xavier stood, lifting Annabelle into his arms. "I'm going to take you to the hospital," he assured her. "Just hold on a little while longer."

Before he'd made it even a step towards his car, sirens sounded in the distance, growing quickly closer. As the ambulance pulled to a stop in front of Annabelle's house, the paramedics climbing out, Xavier let out the first easy breath he'd taken since Annabelle had been abducted.

Gently, he laid her down on the gurney the paramedics produced. He relaxed bit by bit as he watched them put an oxygen mask on her, check her vitals, apply dressings to her shoulder and face, and begin an IV. Annabelle was going to be okay, and once she was stronger, they'd sort out their feelings and potential relationship.

Now he was going to track down Ricky Preston and stop him before anyone else got hurt.

MAY 14TH

1:32 A.M.

Everything was going perfectly.

Ricky couldn't be happier.

If Annabelle had already been dead when Detective Montague found her then he was probably a basket case right about now. He'd be blaming himself. If only he'd said or done this or that, then Annabelle would still be alive.

Ricky had done a little research on Xavier Montague when it seemed that the Detective had become enamored with Annabelle. He'd read all about his ex-wife, Julia. Apparently the woman had been sexually assaulted and then suffered a complete breakdown, culminating in her killing two innocent people and taking their infant. It seemed Detective Montague blamed himself for his wife's actions, and Ricky was counting on that same guilt over Annabelle to keep the man distracted long enough for him to finish.

The beauty of his plan was that if on the other hand Annabelle had been found still clinging to life, then Detective Montague would be hovering at the hospital by her side right about now. Ricky wasn't sure Annabelle could have survived much longer in the wine cellar. Last he'd checked on her, she'd been barely conscious. It was possible though that she'd still be alive, but if she was, she'd be in need of immediate medical attention, which again should be enough to keep the detective distracted long enough for him to finish.

Thankfully, he'd timed things perfectly.

It had been a risk abducting Annabelle. A calculated rick. He'd

249

known that Detective Montague was on to him. That it was only a matter of time before he had enough proof to come and arrest him. So he'd devised the plan with Annabelle. She'd been his insurance policy. Ricky had known that Xavier would eventually be drawn back to Annabelle's house.

He was a little concerned, though, that perhaps he shouldn't have disclosed to Annabelle that he had one more family left to kill. Ricky was pretty sure that Annabelle would already have been unconscious by the time Detective Montague found her, if she was even alive. If he had gotten to her in time, it would be unlikely she'd regain consciousness for at least a couple of hours. Even if she did, she should be confused and disoriented, and unable to recall what he'd told her.

Still, Ricky was on edge.

This final kill was the most important.

It was time to punish the person who was most directly responsible for his mother's death.

Annabelle and Detective Montague were wrong; his mother's death was not an accident. It was murder.

Ricky had been three when his father left them. Things had been rough, but his mother had always worked hard to provide a safe home for him. She had always made sure that he had a roof over his head, clothes to wear, and food on the table. Sometimes working three or four jobs just to ensure that they had the basics. Still, no matter how busy or tired she was, his mother always made time for him. She helped him with his homework, baked him homemade cookies, planned his birthday parties.

His mother had been a saint.

And she had been taken from him too soon.

It wasn't fair.

Life after his mother's death had not been the same.

Only sixteen, he had entered the foster care system. The family he had been sent to live with weren't bad, but it wasn't the same as living at home with his mother.

Ricky still remembered that horrible day perfectly.

He'd been out with a friend, trolling the shopping mall for girls. Young Ricky had been obsessed with girls. He was never without a girlfriend. Still, he tried to find a balance between his girls, his friends, and his mother. Despite the fact that he was a teenager, and most teenagers found their parents to be a huge embarrassment, Ricky had always enjoyed hanging out at home with his mom. In fact, that day he had intended to hang out with her, but his mom had insisted that he go out with his friends. *He was a teenager*, she'd said, *he should be out there enjoying his youth*. And so he had reluctantly agreed.

Dread had begun to pool in his stomach as they neared his house. Smoke was thick in the air. Fire trucks and police cars lined the streets. People milled about, anxious to be part of all the excitement. Only it wasn't excitement to him. When they'd finally reached his house, it had been burned beyond recognition. Half the walls were collapsed, only one bit of the roof remained, his home destroyed.

A police officer had approached him slowly.

A look of horrified empathy on the woman's face.

He'd known immediately.

Still, he'd clung to denial as the police officer had sat him down and gently explained that his mother had been inside the house when the fire started. That she'd been unable to escape the blazing inferno.

As he'd stared at her in shocked silence, he had noticed the neighbors. They were standing around. Doing nothing. The Littletons. The husband worked from home, the wife didn't have a job, the little boy was always playing in the front yard. They must have seen the fire. They must have seen his mother trapped inside. And yet, they hadn't saved her. They had let her die.

It was at that moment that Ricky knew they had to pay.

They had watched his mother and not helped.

They had listened to her screams and not helped.

They would suffer a horrible death just as his mother had.

Identifying his mother's body in the morgue had been the worst. The flames hadn't touched her. She had died from smoke inhalation. When he'd seen her, she'd looked like she was simply asleep. There wasn't a mark on her. Except her hands. His mother had tried to escape through the glass windows in the attic. Her hands were ripped and bloody. The sight of them had fueled his already burning rage.

And there was one more family left who still had to pay for their actions on that fateful day.

If it hadn't been for Barney Adams and his parents, then Ricky would have been home that day.

Barney Adams was the friend he'd been out with that day. In fact, going out had been Barney's idea. He'd been most insistent about it. Barney was jealous that Ricky did better with girls than he did and had wanted Ricky to teach him how to score.

When Ricky had declined, saying he already had plans, Barney had gotten his parents to call Ricky's mom and ask if he could spend the day with him instead.

If Barney and his parents had simply left him alone, then he would have been at home that day.

He would have made sure the candles had been put out before his exhausted mother had gone upstairs to take a nap.

He would have made sure that, even if the fire had started, his mother had gotten safely out.

But Barney Adams had prevented him.

And now it was time for Barney Adams to pay.

Climbing from his car, he headed towards the Adams' backyard.

* * * * *

2:12 A.M.

252

ONE

Vanessa was sitting in her room staring out the window, waiting.

Waiting for Vince to come and get her.

She was going to run away from home. Well, that made her sound too childish. She was leaving home to marry Vince. She wasn't going to let her parents tell her who she could and couldn't date, and she wasn't going to let them tear her and Vince apart by sending her to boarding school. So she and Vince were going to hide out until her eighteenth birthday, then they'd get married.

A shadow moved through her backyard.

Vince was here.

With her stomach all aquiver with anxious anticipation, Vanessa grabbed her bag and slipped silently out her bedroom door, listening carefully to make sure the house was quiet. When she heard no one stirring, she continued on down the stairs, through the kitchen, and at the back door she paused again.

She briefly wondered if she should write a quick note telling her parents good-bye. She decided against it since she hadn't spoken to them in the five days since they'd told her they intended to ruin her life by sending her away. If they loved her, they would at least try to understand where she was coming from. She owed them nothing. Not even a good-bye.

Giving the kitchen a last look over, Vanessa stepped out into the night and gasped.

A hand clamped across her chest, pinning her arms. Stunned into silence, Vanessa couldn't move, couldn't scream, couldn't do anything. Senses returning, Vanessa was about to open her mouth and yell for help when something cold and sharp pressed against her neck.

"Make a sound and I slit your throat," a voice rumbled in her ear.

Panicked, Vanessa didn't know what she should do. Should she risk trying to make an escape? Should she do as he told her? Should she scream to warn her family? And what about Vince?

Where was he? Had this man killed him?

Tears trickled down her cheeks. "Please, don't hurt me. What do you want?"

He chuckled, "You."

"My...my boyfriend...he'll be here any minute..." Vanessa stammered desperately.

"Actually, he's a little tied up at the moment." The man laughed at his own joke.

"Did you hurt him?" A wave of anger rolled over her at the thought of this man hurting the love of her life.

"As much as I'd love to stand here and chitchat with you, I'm on a timeline," the man sobered. "Let's go."

She was surprised when instead of dragging her away from the house, he pulled her toward it, opening the door she'd just come through and stepping them both indoors.

"Vanessa?" a voice demanded from somewhere inside the house.

The man quickly moved them into the farthest, darkest corner of the kitchen.

"Is that you, young lady?" her father demanded. "You better not be sneaking out again."

Involuntarily, Vanessa tried to move toward her father. He was her dad, and he'd be able to make everything better. The man tightened his grip, pressing his knife against her neck, and she let out a whimper.

"Vanessa?" her dad sounded confused now, and a moment later the light flickered on. Her father's eyes scanned the kitchen, and Vanessa could tell the exact second that he saw her because his eyes grew wide and panicked. "Vanessa," he took a step in her direction.

"Uh, uh, uh," the man holding her clucked. "That's close enough."

His eyes grew wider still, shocked and baffled. "Ricky?" her father asked.

"Long time no see, Barney," Ricky's voice was quietly menacing.

"Is this some kind of joke?" Her father's brow furrowed in bewilderment.

"No joke," Ricky replied, tone conversational now. "I'm here for my revenge."

"Revenge?" her father looked puzzled. "I haven't seen you in thirty years, since we were teenagers, since the day of your mother's..." her father trailed off, horrified, understanding dawning on his face. "Ricky, your mother's death was an accident. A tragedy, but an accident."

"My mother died because of you," Ricky spat out viciously, his arm across her chest squeezed so painfully Vanessa couldn't help but cry out. "If it hadn't been for you, I would have been home that day."

Barney kept his gaze on Ricky's face. "Let my daughter go, Ricky. If you're angry with me about your mom, then this is between us, just let Vanessa go."

"Unfortunately, that's not going to happen," Ricky regained his calm. "You cost me my only family, now you're going to lose yours. Now, let's go gather the rest of the family."

"Ricky, no." Her father took another step toward them. "Don't hurt my family. Please," he begged.

With lightning speed, Ricky moved the knife from her neck to her cheek, pressing the tip into her flesh and dragging it down a couple of inches. Vanessa cried out at the pain, and tried to pull herself free, but Ricky repositioned the knife back at her throat and she froze.

"Next time, I slice her carotid artery." Ricky's voice was terrifyingly calm and controlled. "She'll be dead in less than a minute. Now, let's go get the rest of your family," he repeated, enunciating each word.

She squeezed her eyes shut as her father released a defeated sigh. If her father had given up, what hope did she have? When

Ricky began to drag her through the house, Vanessa tried to fight the panic that was quickly welling up inside her. She was being held hostage, a knife at her neck, by a madman who wanted revenge on her father for the death of his mother.

Vanessa had never heard her father mention a man named Ricky. Her father had said that he hadn't seen this Ricky in thirty years. Had Ricky been planning his revenge all that time? If he had, just what did he plan to do to them? Her father had said that Ricky's mother's death was an accident, but the man obviously disagreed. Vanessa wondered how his mother had died, and if that was how he intended to kill her and her family.

"Hurry up, Barney, go grab your other kid, your parents, and that pretty wife of yours," Ricky was instructing her father. "I'll be waiting here with your daughter. In case you even think about doing anything stupid, just know that I'll make sure she suffers horrendously before I kill her."

Vanessa shuddered violently at the threat, and Ricky chuckled.

With a last desperate look at her, her father headed up the stairs, and Vanessa couldn't hold back her tears any longer. She wished more than anything she could take back everything she had said and done the last couple of weeks. She wished that she hadn't fought with her parents, that she hadn't said she hated them.

She didn't.

She didn't hate them.

She loved them so much she was physically aching at the thought that they were all about to be murdered and she'd never have a chance to make things right. Now Vanessa couldn't even remember what was so bad about them not wanting her to sleep with Vince. They were her parents. Of course they didn't want to think of her having sex. What she should have done was let them get to know Vince and see for themselves what a great guy he was.

"Too bad we don't have more time," Ricky whispered in her

ear. The hand he had on her shoulder moved to her breast and squeezed tightly. Vanessa fought revulsion. "I would have loved to have a little more fun with you before I kill you."

Whimpering, Vanessa wanted desperately to get away from this horrible man, but before she could dwell on his words and his hands and his hot breath on her neck, footsteps sounded on the stairs. Her father re-entered the room. Trailing behind him were her grandparents, her mom, and her brother, Justin. Her grandparents' arms were entwined around each other, both their faces wet with tears. Her mother tightly clutched Justin, but her eyes glared defiantly at Ricky.

"Mom," Vanessa couldn't help crying out, her mother's eyes met hers, the glare fading away into horrified panic.

"Long time, no see," Ricky singsonged at her grandparents. "As much as I'd love to take our time and really make the most of tonight, I'm unfortunately a little pushed for time, so you'll have to forgive me for rushing."

A pop sounded over her shoulder, and Vanessa found herself surprised to see a bright red spot appear on her grandfather's head. He seemed to fall to the floor in slow motion, a puddle of blood growing wider and wider around his head. Vanessa could see the mouths of her family moving, and she assumed they were screaming, but all she could hear was Ricky's heated breath panting in her ear.

Another pop and her grandmother dropped.

Ricky's breathing quickened further. The sound reminded her of Vince, and how he had sounded just before they had made love for the first time.

As the third pop sounded, Vanessa slipped into a shocked haze where nothing could touch her.

* * * * *

3:01 A.M.

257

"I hope I'm right about this, Kate," Xavier murmured as he and Kate silently made their way through the Adams' backyard.

He'd ridden in the ambulance with Annabelle to the hospital and hovered by her side as she was treated in the ER. Once they had her settled in a room, Xavier had sat beside her bed and begun to think. Annabelle had said that Ricky told her he had one more family left to kill. They'd tracked down all the houses where Ricky had lived and established that he had already killed all his neighbors. So there was obviously one more person that Ricky Preston blamed for his mother's death.

It had hit him all of a sudden.

Ricky had been out the day his mother died. Out with a friend. Ricky was clearly unbalanced, and he seemed to be blaming anyone who was even vaguely associated with the fire. It didn't seem like much of a leap to think he'd blame the people he was out with the day his mother had died.

He'd called Kate immediately, asked her to find out what friend Ricky had been hanging out with the day of the fire and track him down. His partner had managed to find out that Ricky's friend was a Barney Adams, now married to Hilda, with two children, thirteen-year-old Justin and seventeen-year-old Vanessa. The family currently lived with Barney's parents. Very convenient for Ricky Preston.

Annabelle was stable. She hadn't regained consciousness yet, but she was responding well to oxygen therapy, and she was safe in the hospital. As much as he wanted to stay by her side, Xavier also wanted to make sure she remained safe. The only way to do that was to take out Ricky. So Kate had come to collect him, and they had just arrived at the Adams' house.

Before Kate had a chance to comment on whether or not he had read Ricky Preston correctly, a shot rang out.

Quickening their pace, they reached the backdoor and slipped quietly inside. The commotion seemed to be coming from the living room, so they moved closer, pausing in the kitchen door to survey the scene before them. Four bodies lay on the floor, each with a bullet hole in their head. The puddle of blood from each wound was quickly melding together forming one giant pond around the bodies. Barney Adams sat in this pond, clutching his young son in one arm, his wife in the other.

Off to the side stood Ricky Preston. In one hand he held a gun, which was currently pointed at Barney's head; with his other hand, he held a knife at a teenage girl's throat.

Vanessa Adams was standing completely still. Her face a blank mask of shock. Her brown eyes stared unseeingly at the bloody scenes before her.

Ricky, on the other hand was staring, mesmerized at all the blood. He was panting, aroused, an eerie smile on his face. Xavier remembered the blood covered rooms at the other crime scenes; they'd been right about Ricky's attraction to blood.

With a slight nod to Kate, Xavier took a step into the room. "Ricky, put the gun down and let Vanessa go. It's over."

Barney's head snapped in their direction. Ricky's turned much slower, as though he were unable to rip his gaze from the blood. Vanessa didn't move at all.

"Ah, Detective Montague." Ricky's eyes cleared. "I was hoping not to see you again. I guess that little pest Annabelle managed to wake up and tell you I wasn't quite finished."

He refused to be baited into losing his temper, Barney and Vanessa Adams' lives depended on him keeping his cool. "Ricky, let the girl go; she doesn't have anything to do with this."

Ricky held Vanessa in front of him to prevent Xavier and Kate from getting a clean shot. Ricky smiled, "No offense intended, but I'd rather not hang around and chat with you, Detective Montague. Tell Annabelle I say hi."

With that, Ricky fired off a shot at Barney Adams and one at Kate, both dropped to the ground. Then, still using her as a human shield, Ricky dragged Vanessa after him as he darted off through the house.

Xavier dashed to his partner's side. "Kate?" Pressing his fingertips to her neck, he was relieved to feel her pulse beating strongly. Thankfully, the bullet had hit her vest. Turning his attention to Barney, the man had been shot in the shoulder; he didn't appear to be bleeding too badly and his eyes were open.

"Vanessa?" Barney whispered.

"Go after them," Kate's weak voice insisted as she drew a harsh breath. "Go, Xavier," she repeated when she saw him hesitate. "I'm okay, back up will be here any minute, I'll call for medics."

"Stay still," he instructed Kate. "You're hurt, stay where you are till I get back or medics get here."

Gun drawn, he headed off in the direction Ricky had gone. Assuming Ricky had gone back outside to flee, he made straight for the backdoor. He was right. As soon as he exited the house, he caught sight of Ricky at the end of the yard, attempting to drag Vanessa over the fence.

"Ricky," he yelled, moving slowly towards him. "Stop, or I'll shoot."

"You won't risk the girl," Ricky mocked. Even in the thin moonlight, Xavier could make out his smirk. "Just like you wouldn't risk Annabelle."

"You used Annabelle like she was nothing." Xavier was seething with hate towards this man.

"She is nothing," Ricky shot back snidely.

"Then why did you listen to her bare her soul?"

"It amused me," Ricky shrugged, disinterestedly.

"You took what she told you and used it against her," Xavier snapped.

He shrugged again. "It amused me. Annabelle thought she was better than everyone else, she deserved to be taken down a peg or two."

"So you raped her?"

A wicked grin spread across his face, reminding Xavier of the Grinch from Dr. Seuss' *How the Grinch Stole Christmas*. "I'll be a first she'll never forget."

"You know after what you did to Annabelle nothing would make me happier than to kill you, so let the girl go and turn yourself in." Xavier was struggling not to just start firing his gun at Ricky regardless of the consequences. Nothing *would* make him happier than killing Ricky Preston, but he wouldn't unless it was his only option.

"You know, you are more of a pain in the neck than Annabelle ever was," Ricky sighed. "Here's another choice for you." With that, Ricky sliced his knife across Vanessa Adams' neck and threw the girl to the ground, then jumped at the fence.

Muttering a curse, Xavier dropped to his knees beside the teenager. The cut on her neck was gushing blood. Ripping off his shirt, he pressed it against the wound, hoping to stem the flow of blood enough to buy the girl time until the paramedics arrived.

Once again, Ricky Preston had outplayed him.

* * * * *

5:43 P.M.

Consciousness came back slowly.

Her mind was fuzzy.

Annabelle wasn't sure where she was.

Was she still in her basement? Or maybe the wine cellar?

Where was Ricky?

She tried to move but her limbs were heavy.

Was she still tied up?

Her head ached and she moaned a little.

Then someone was looming over her. Her eyes were still closed but she could sense the presence. Hands gripped her shoulders and she let out a terrified shriek. Ricky must be back.

She didn't want him to touch her again.

"Belle, it's okay," a voice soothed. "You're in the hospital, you're safe now. Shh, it's all right. I'm here."

"Xavier?" She was barely able to believe what her ears were hearing.

"I'm right here," he said again, gently brushing his fingertips across her forehead. "I'm not going anywhere."

A sob caught in her throat. Xavier had come looking for her, and he'd found her. Saved her.

"Hey, it's okay," Xavier began to stroke her hair. "Open your eyes for me, Belle."

She wanted to do as he asked, but she was scared. Scared that perhaps this was all just a hallucination, that when she opened her eyes she'd be back in her basement with Ricky Preston.

"Come on, Belle, open your eyes," Xavier urged.

Tentatively, she obeyed, forcing her eyes open to find Xavier smiling down at her. She let out a relieved breath. She really *was* in the hospital. And it was really *Xavier* hovering at her bedside.

"There you go," Xavier grinned, relief flittering through his eyes.

"You're really here," she murmured.

"I'm really here," he agreed. "And you're really safe now. Do you remember what happened?"

She concentrated. "I remember Ricky locking me in my father's wine cellar. I think I remember you finding me. You told me to rest, to concentrate on breathing." She looked at him for confirmation, and he nodded. "You said you were sorry for leaving me alone, and then you told me to stay with you, but I was so tired." She was tired now, too, and her eyes fluttered closed as sleep lapped at the corners of her mind.

"Okay, that's enough for now, you need to rest," Xavier said softly.

But something tugged at her mind. Something important. Forcing her eyes back open. "There was another family Ricky was going to kill. Did I tell you that?"

"Shh," Xavier resumed stroking her hair. "You told me. Kate and I found them."

Something flashed through Xavier's eyes, but Annabelle was too tired to figure out what it was. "How long have I been here?"

"Almost eighteen hours. The doctors said you were lucky to be alive, another few minutes in that cellar and you might not have been."

Another flash in his eyes, this time Annabelle could see it was fear. Before she could say more, a knock sounded at the door. It swung softly open to reveal Xavier's partner.

"Hey, Annabelle, you're awake," Kate smiled. "How're you feeling?"

Considering this, her head was pounding, her face felt tight, she assumed from stitches on her cheek, but otherwise her pain was like a distant hum. "Tired, but not in too much pain."

"Morphine's good for that." Kate cast a glance at Xavier.

"Belle was just telling me what she remembers after I found her," Xavier answered Kate's unasked question. "But I think she's had enough for now," he added firmly.

"Something's wrong." Looking from Xavier to Kate and back again, she may be tired but she wasn't so worn out that she couldn't see that they were hiding something from her.

"We need you to tell us everything you remember about your time with Ricky," Kate told her.

"Xavier?"

"It's important, Belle," but he looked conflicted as he took her hand and squeezed it.

"I don't remember Ricky taking me," she began, she'd tell them what they wanted then she'd get the answers she needed. "After you left I didn't even make it to the bed, I was so tired, I just collapsed on the carpet. The next thing I remember is waking up tied to a table in an attic. I didn't know if you'd be looking for me." She caught Xavier's pained look. "But I hoped you would be, so I worked at getting my bracelet off, so if you found that attic you'd know I'd been there."

"We found the bracelet," Xavier smiled encouragingly.

"Ricky came back and drugged me, and the next thing I remember we were in my basement. He'd tied my hands behind my back and then tied a rope to my brother's punching bag. It made my shoulder ache so badly." Her voice faltered a little as she remembered the pain. "When Ricky came back I tried to talk to him, tried to find out why he was doing it, and if I could talk my way out. But I made him angry, and he tried to strangle me." Again, she trailed off as she recalled Ricky's hands wrapped around her neck, squeezing so tightly.

Xavier let out a muted growl, his eyes furious; he looked like he wanted to throw something. Kate placed a calming hand on his shoulder.

"I'm okay, Xavier," Annabelle squeezed the hand that still held hers. "Ricky told me about his mom, and then I accidentally made him angry again and he hit me. Then he…he…" Unable to hold back her tears any longer, she blinked and they spilled out, trickling down her cheeks. "He raped me," she forced the words out. Xavier attempted to embrace her but she pushed him away, wanting to finish. "He left me alone for a while then when he came back he told me that he had one more family to kill, and that I was his distraction. Then he locked me in the cellar," she finished determinedly. When Xavier reached for her again, this time she let him wrap her up in his arms. Burying her head against his chest, she twisted her hands into his shirt and clung to him as she wept. When she'd calmed a little she asked, "Did you find the other family?"

He hesitated before answering, "Yes."

"But?"

"We weren't in time to save them all," Xavier replied reluctantly.

"Oh." Tears were brimming in her eyes again. She had hoped

Xavier and Kate had been able to save the other family. Ricky had been right, Xavier had been too preoccupied with her and people had died because of it.

"I'm going to go and get your doctor to give you something to help you sleep," Xavier murmured softly, settling her back against the pillows.

"Xavier, she needs to know," Kate stopped him with a hand on his arm as he moved to stand.

"Later, Kate," he protested. "She's weak, she needs to rest now."

"What do I need to know?"

"When you're stronger," Xavier answered firmly.

"Tell me," she didn't want any more secrets.

"Belle," Xavier's voice held a warning note.

"Please," she begged.

He sighed. "Ricky Preston got away," he told her.

She was sure she must have heard wrong. "Wh-what?" she stammered.

"I'm sorry, honey—Ricky Preston got away. He's still out there," Xavier repeated, his eyes filled to the brim with anger and fear.

"Do you remember Ricky talking about any place he may go, any person he trusted?" Kate asked.

"No." The world was beginning to spin. Ricky was still out there. That meant he could come back. Any time. He could come back and take her again. Hurt her, rape her—whatever he wanted. Maybe next time he'd kill her.

"I won't let him hurt you again, Belle," Xavier perched on the side of her bed and gripped her shoulders so tightly she couldn't help but cringe. "I promise, Belle. He will *never* hurt you again."

"It's my fault," she whispered, recalling her conversation with Ricky in the basement before he'd raped her. He'd told her she was weak and scared—and she was. That's why he had used her. He'd known she'd never be able to get away on her own. That someone else would have to come and save her. And while Xavier had been wasting time on her, Ricky had been free to destroy another family.

"It is not your fault," Xavier shook her gently.

She nodded her head. "Yes, it is. Ricky said I was weak…"

"You're not weak, Belle," Xavier told her.

Ignoring him, she continued, "…that I was too scared to have a life. He was right. He said I just hide in the house all the time, that I don't have a life. He was right again. I am weak and pathetic and useless." Annabelle caught the hysterical note in her voice, but she was beyond caring. "You should have let me die, saved the other family, made sure Ricky didn't get away. You should have let me die."

"No, Belle," Xavier said fiercely. "No to all of that."

The aching in her head grew so severe that it sent everything else shimmering to the background. She vaguely heard Xavier tell Kate to go and get a doctor. He needn't have bothered; she didn't need sedatives to help her sleep. Her vision began to fade in and out, the going backwards and forwards making her nauseous, so she let her eyes fall closed. Then when a wave of blackness washed over her, she let it knock her down and pull her back out with it.

* * * * *

8:57 P.M.

Xavier needed to sleep. He knew that, yet he couldn't take his eyes off Annabelle.

She hadn't regained consciousness again since she'd passed out following her hysterical outburst. He'd known she wasn't strong enough yet to hear that Ricky Preston was still out there somewhere. It worried him that she blamed herself. That she thought she was weak. It made him angry that Ricky had obviously used things that she'd told him against her.

When she woke up next they needed to talk.

About a lot of things.

He needed to understand why she didn't date, why she hadn't felt loved throughout her childhood, why she was so afraid, and why she believed that she was weak. He needed to understand so he could help her.

There were things she needed to understand about him, too.

First of all, he needed to properly explain the Julia situation. Despite her declarations that she believed that he was falling in love with her and that he wasn't going to leave her for Julia, he wasn't quite sure that she really believed it. He thought maybe she had needed to convince herself that he wasn't going to leave her in order to survive her abduction. He wanted her to know that it was okay if she couldn't believe it right now, that he would prove it to her if she was willing to put her faith and trust in him.

For the moment at least, he was just going to be happy that he had her back alive and that she was recovering. He leaned over the bed, tracing his fingertips over her face, trying to convince himself that she was really here. That he really had a chance to begin a relationship with her.

A whoosh behind him announced the arrival of his partner. He sighed. "You should be home resting, Kate, you're injured."

"Just a bruise."

"And cracked ribs, and you're pregnant," he reminded her reproachfully. "Go home, take some painkillers, and get some rest."

"I will. How's she doing?" Kate asked softly.

"She hasn't woken up again, but she's stable."

"And how're you doing?"

"I'm okay."

She raised a skeptical eyebrow. "I meant, how are you doing really?"

He sighed. "I'm tired. I'm grateful Belle's alive, but guilty that I had to let Ricky Preston go to get her back. I'm angry that he's got her thinking that she's weak and to blame for him still being on the loose. And I'm terrified that he might come back and finish what he started. I'm scared that I'm going to mess things up with her before we've even started, or that she's going to walk away as soon as she's through the worst of this… I guess that about sums it up."

"Well, as much as I'd love to fix all those things for you, I can't. I do, however, have something that may at least help you sort out one of your problems. I dropped by your place to grab you some clean clothes." She set a bag down on the floor beside him, trying to hide her wince and failing terribly. "And to feed your rabbits. I picked up your mail, I didn't mean to look but I couldn't help noticing this one," she held out an envelope.

He took it tentatively; it was from Julia.

"I hope it gives you some closure. I'm going to go home now, get some sleep. Call me if there's any change in Annabelle's condition, or if you need to talk." She paused at the door. "Once you've read the letter, try to get some sleep. You need it, and Annabelle needs you."

Once he was alone, Xavier tore open the envelope and slid out a single piece of paper. Turning on the light beside Annabelle's bed and pulling his chair closer, he slowly unfolded the letter.

Dear Xavier,

I'm writing to say good-bye. I don't want you to come and visit me again. It's time for you to let me go. You're holding on to me for all the wrong reasons. You're doing it out of guilt and responsibility, not out of love. I know you love me, but I also know that I love you more than you ever loved me. Now that I look back, I've always known it. I don't want to cause you any more pain, but as long as you hold on to me, I am. I did horrible things, and yet you never turned on me. You've stood by me when most men would have walked away. I'll always love you, Xavier, but I've accepted the fact that you no longer love me, and I love you enough to want you to be happy. So please move on. I'm your past. I'm not your future. I want you to let me go and let yourself be happy. That's the way you can honor our daughter, by having a life. I hope that you'll always remember me as not a completely unpleasant part of your past. You know where your future lies, so go get it. Be happy with this Annabelle. Be happy enough for both of us.

Love,

Julia

He stared at the letter for a full minute before folding it and returning it to its envelope.

He considered Julia's words.

That she had loved him more than he had loved her. He supposed that was true. He'd been bewitched by Julia's beauty, fallen hard for her, but they had never had much in common. That didn't mean he didn't love Julia. He did. And it hurt to know that Julia thought he'd only stuck by her because of guilt and a sense of responsibility. Hurt mostly because if he was honest, she was probably right.

He switched off the light and stood beside the bed, watching as Annabelle's chest rose and fell evenly as she slept. She whimpered quietly, her face creasing in fear. Xavier reached out a hand to smooth the lines in her forehead.

He remembered the nights he'd come home late from work or hanging out with friends when he used to lie in bed and watch Julia sleep. Then he'd pull her close and fall asleep with her tangled in his arms. He'd missed that. The intimacy of having someone special in his life. He wanted it again. With Annabelle.

Gently, he moved Annabelle over a little, carefully so as not to mess with the wires and tubes still attached to her, so he could stretch out on the bed beside her.

"Xavier?" her faint voice mumbled sleepily.

"I'm here," he assured her.

"Don't leave me," she begged, turning into him and burrowing her head against his neck.

"Never." He pulled her closer, pressed a kiss to the top of her head. "Wild horses couldn't drag me away from you."

MAY 15TH

10:29 A.M.

"How're you doing?" Xavier asked as he pushed her wheelchair toward the hospital's cafeteria.

"My head's a little fuzzy," Annabelle replied. This was the first time she'd properly sat up since Ricky had cut the ropes binding her to the punching bag nearly forty-eight hours ago, and her head was protesting a little. Still, she was tired of being cooped up, and when Xavier had offered to take her to the cafeteria, she had readily agreed.

"You want me to take you back to your room?" he asked.

"No." She wanted to at least pretend she was on the road back to being a normal person.

"Good," he smiled down at her. "What do you want to eat?"

Her stomach churned at the very thought of food. "I'm not really hungry."

"You need to eat; you need to keep your strength up so you can get better. What about some fruit salad?"

"I guess," she reluctantly complied.

"All right, I'll be right back." He pushed her wheelchair up to a table, kissed the top of her head, and then went to the counter to order.

Annabelle's chest tightened a little in panic as she watched him walk away. She couldn't seem to cope with being alone anymore. More specifically, she couldn't seem to cope without Xavier by her side. He'd stayed with her all night, slept in the bed beside her, only leaving briefly this morning to attend a meeting at work.

"Hey, I'm back," Xavier appeared before her.

271

She let out a relieved breath.

"Try to eat as much as you can." He set a cup of fruit salad in front of her.

Her stomach lurched, but Xavier was watching her intently, so Annabelle picked up the fork and forced herself to swallow a few pieces of fruit.

Nodding approvingly, Xavier sat beside her. "We need to talk," he announced.

"About what?" She could hear the panic in her voice. Xavier was going to tell her that he wasn't interested in her after all. That he had just wanted to keep her safe. That he was still in love with Julia.

"Relax," Xavier soothed, taking her hands. "There are just some things we need to discuss so that we can make our relationship successful. I want this to work, Belle." His hazel eyes were serious.

Nervous anticipation fluttered in her stomach. She still wasn't sure if she was ready for a relationship, but at the same time, she wanted this to work, too.

"I need to know what you're so scared of. I need to know why you don't date, why you keep getting surprised every time I do something I said I'd do, like you don't think you deserve it."

She chewed on her lip. She wasn't sure she could face telling someone her secrets again after Ricky. She considered telling Xavier that she was tired and wanted to go back to bed. It wasn't a lie, she was still exhausted—the doctors had said she could expect to feel drained and tired for the next several days at least.

Sensing her reluctance, Xavier cupped her face with his hand. "Belle, you can trust me. Tell me why you think you're weak. I want to know what's going on inside your head so I can help you."

"The scars," she whispered quickly, before she could talk herself out of it.

"How did you get them?" he asked gently.

Her eyes grew wide as she realized something. "You already knew I had them. Before you found me in the cellar. In the shower, after I found out what Ricky did to my family, you would have seen them then. But you never mentioned them, never asked me about them. Why?"

"Because I knew you'd tell me when you were ready." He gave her an encouraging smile. "How old were you when you got them?"

"I was four."

"Your parents?" he asked tightly. She could see the fury crackling in his eyes.

"No." It warmed her to see how outraged he was over what had happened to her.

"What happened?"

"I don't really know; I don't remember it properly."

"What do you remember?" he pressed.

"A man with a scary face and lots of screaming, and we were in a dark room. But that's it, then I remember police officers coming, and then I was back home." Annabelle had spent the last twenty years debating whether or not she wanted to know exactly what had happened.

"What happened after? When you were back home?"

"Everything changed," she replied softly.

Reaching over, Xavier lifted her out of the wheelchair and settled her on his lap. "Changed how?"

"They didn't love me anymore," her voice wobbled.

He wrapped his arms tighter around her. "How do you know that?"

Resting her head on his strong shoulder, she said, "They were cold and distant. They didn't love me anymore. How could they?"

"That's why you don't date? Because you think if your parents couldn't love you, no one else could?" He pulled her back so he could see her face. "Belle, listen to me, I'm sure your parents still loved you. Maybe they blamed themselves and that's why they couldn't be affectionate with you anymore. I don't know. But I do know that I don't want you to feel like you're unloved ever again, because *I* love you."

Annabelle wanted to believe that. She *really* wanted to believe that. When she'd been tied up in her basement, she had convinced herself that she believed it. But now that she was safe, she wasn't sure if she really did.

"It's okay, Belle." Xavier was smiling at her. "If you can't believe it just yet, you will. If you just trust me, then you'll believe it one day. Now, about Julia…"

"You don't have to explain, Xavier," she cut him off. "I understand. I'm not sure I believe quite yet that you'll never leave me for her, but I will," she finished firmly. She had been given a second chance at life, and this time she wasn't going to waste it by being weak and scared.

"There's something else we need to talk about," he announced.

"What?" She rested her head again against his shoulder. It was beginning to ache, and she was starting to feel sleepy.

"You need counseling," he said gently. "You haven't even had time to process losing your family, then Ricky abducting you, assaulting you. You need to get help. I don't want it to destroy you."

Annabelle understood that given what had happened with his ex-wife, Xavier needed her not only to get help but also to not shut him out like Julia had.

"It's not just for you; I need counseling, too. Kate said to me just after we met you that I was in no place to be helping anyone deal with trauma. She was right. I haven't dealt with what happened with Julia, but I'm going to. If you're willing, I'd like us to do it together."

Catching the nervousness in his voice, Annabelle realized that he was as anxious about starting a relationship as she was, and that knowledge was comforting. "I'd like that, too," she murmured, fighting to keep her eyes open now.

"Time to go back to your room, I think." Xavier gently set her back in the wheelchair.

They were halfway to her room when a thought occurred to her. "Xavier, where am I going to go when I get released from here? I can't go back to my house. I can sell it and buy another, but that will take time. I don't want to go back to the motel where Ricky abducted me. Obviously I can't go and stay with him, and I don't have any other friends..." She was rambling but unable to stop.

"Shh," Xavier knelt in front of her. "You know I want you to stay with me, but I don't want you to feel pressured. If you want, we can find another hotel. Or maybe you could stay with Kate and her husband; I'm sure she wouldn't mind. Whatever makes you feel safe and comfortable."

She hesitated. "I want to stay with you, but..."

"But what, honey?" he asked, when she didn't continue.

"I'm scared. I don't want to hurt you. I think that I'm...I'm falling in love with you. But what if I'm just scared? What if I just don't want to be alone, and I'm just deluding myself into believing that I love you because I need someone with me?" Annabelle thought that she was truly falling for Xavier, but she couldn't deny the possibility that he had been her rock through all this, and maybe that was all he'd ever be.

He rested his elbows on the arms of the wheelchair so his face hovered just inches from hers. "I've already thought of that."

"Then why are you still here?" For the life of her, Annabelle couldn't understand what it was Xavier thought he saw in her that was so attractive.

"I've already told you, I'm falling in love with you," he answered simply.

"Why?"

"There is no why." He brought his face closer. "We fall for whomever we fall for, and I've fallen for you. I'm going to take some time off work."

"Because of me?" Annabelle couldn't deny that knowing Xavier could be by her side every day was comforting, but she didn't want to disrupt his life any more than she already had.

"Yes and no."

"You don't have to do that." She wasn't used to people wanting to help her.

"It's not just for you; it's for me, too. We both need some time to sort things out. So I don't want you to worry about being alone. I'm not going anywhere." His voice dropped to a whisper and he brushed his lips softly against hers. "All right, back to bed for you, you're wiped out."

He pushed her back to her room, then lifted her into his arms. Xavier paused for a moment and she felt his contented sigh. When he placed her on the bed, he arranged the blankets around her.

Half asleep now, she grabbed his hand. "Hold me. Please."

"Gladly."

Just as he had last night, he stretched out beside her, spooning her against him. Tucking her hand under her cheek, Annabelle froze as she felt a piece of paper under her pillow. Thinking that seemed odd she picked it up. "Xavier?"

"What is it, Belle?"

"This was under my pillow." She passed him the folded piece of paper.

He took it, read it, and his body tensed.

Immediately on edge, she asked, "What is it?"

"Go to sleep now, Belle," Xavier commanded quietly.

"What is it?" she repeated, wearily pushing herself up so she could see him properly.

"Go to sleep," Xavier was sitting now, reaching for his phone.

"Xavier?" Annabelle couldn't quite keep the whimper from her voice as panic was rapidly welling up inside her.

Sighing, he paused, his hazel eyes met hers. "It's a note from Ricky."

Trembling, she asked, "What does it say?"

"It says, 'Annabelle, thanks for the good times, until we meet again'," he answered reluctantly, watching her closely.

"Oh," was all she could utter. It was bad enough knowing Ricky was still out there somewhere, but to know he intended to come back was beyond terrifying.

He crushed her fiercely against his chest. "I'll find him, Belle."

Xavier kept hold of her with one arm, with his other he dialed Kate and explained about the note.

Tuning out his voice, Annabelle tried to let his warmth soothe her, his beating heart comfort her, his promises reassure her. She tried to believe that somehow there could one day be a light at the end of the dark tunnel she was trapped in.

* * * * *

12:00 P.M.

Ricky felt pleased with how things had turned out.

Barney Adams was still alive, but he'd lost his parents, his wife, and his son. All he had left was his troublesome teenage daughter. Perhaps that was enough to make him suffer just as Ricky himself had suffered all these years. And, if he changed his mind, he could always come back and kill them both.

He'd come back for Annabelle, too.

Knew he wouldn't be able to resist.

There was something about that girl that intrigued him. She was weak and scared and pathetic, and yet at the same time strong and resilient. He knew he would enjoy finally taking her out. In the meantime, he could revel in the knowledge that she was tormented knowing he was out there somewhere waiting to come back and get her.

He tingled delightedly as he thought of all the fun he could still have. He was free. Free to kill over and over again. Nothing could make him stop. He was addicted. When he'd started on this journey, Ricky had simply been after revenge for his mother's murder. He'd never realized he would enjoy killing so much. But enjoy it he did. And the bloodier, the better.

Relaxed and happier than he'd ever been, Ricky breathed in the spring sunshine. With a last look at the hospital, he smiled. "Until we meet again, Annabelle," he murmured as he climbed into the cab.

Jane has loved reading and writing since she can remember. She writes dark and disturbing crime/mystery/suspense with some romance thrown in because, well, who doesn't love romance?! She has several series including the complete Detective Parker Bell series, the Count to Ten series, the Christmas Romantic Suspense series, and the Flashes of Fate series of novelettes.

When she's not writing Jane loves to read, bake, go to the beach, ski, horse ride, and watch Disney movies. She has a black belt in Taekwondo, a 200+ collection of teddy bears, and her favorite color is pink. She has the world's two most sweet and pretty Dalmatians, Ivory and Pearl. Oh, and she also enjoys spending time with family and friends!

To connect and keep up to date please visit any of the following

Amazon – http://www.amazon.com/author/janeblythe
BookBub – https://www.bookbub.com/authors/jane-blythe
Email – mailto:janeblytheauthor@gmail.com
Facebook – http://www.facebook.com/janeblytheauthor
Goodreads – http://www.goodreads.com/author/show/6574160.Jane_Blythe
Instagram – http://www.instagram.com/jane_blythe_author
Reader Group – http://www.facebook.com/groups/janeskillersweethearts
Twitter – http://www.twitter.com/jblytheauthor
Website – http://www.janeblythe.com.au

sic enim dilexit Deus mundum ut Filium suum unigenitum daret ut omnis qui credit in eum habeat vitam aeternam

www.ingramcontent.com/pod-product-compliance
Lightning Source LLC
Chambersburg PA
CBHW020735250626
47155CB00003B/765